# Soul Sprints

By
John Gibson

© 2019 by John Gibson. All rights reserved.

Words Matter Publishing
P.O. Box 531
Salem, Il 62881
www.wordsmatterpublishing.com



ISBN 13: 978-1-949809-30-5
ISBN 10: 1-949809-30-7


Library of Congress Catalog Card Number: 2019944479

# PROLOGUE

L ake Barrow is a small, central Florida town of just over 7,000 people, whose primary livelihood is farming, though you wouldn't know it by the two wealthiest families that live here.

Neither the Gills nor the Danforths ever had any significant background in farming. I suppose this is strange, given that our small town of Lake Barrow, is largely known for agricultural activity. Still, in all, it is a bit out of the ordinary that the two wealthiest families never raised a cow or harvested a crop.

James Harrison (Jim) Gill, III owns the largest car dealership in the region. Jim Gill Automotive is a third-generation-owned enterprise as well as the oldest business in the region. Had Jamie Gill, my high school teammate and close friend, not been killed in 2002, Jim would have made his eldest son the next heir.

The Danforths are a different story. They came to the area back in the 1940s, long after the Gills had established themselves in Sims County. Rupert Danforth, their patriarch, was a successful businessman and inventor who built his fortune step-by-step with hard work, frugality, and shrewdness. His fortune, as well as his business skills and ego, were passed on to his eldest son, Martin. After Rupert's death in the early 1980s, "Marty," as he was known, received a sizable inheritance and founded what would soon become the largest and most successful real estate development firm in the region, not to mention one of the most prosperous in the state.

Danforth Properties today has several locations throughout our county and is the second-largest employer in the area, next to Jim Gill Automotive.

It was the summer of 1990 when things began to take a turn for the worse between the two families.

Margery Gill Hanceford, Jim's sister, who was also my twelfth-grade English teacher, lived in a small house near the center of Lake Barrow, which had been in her husband's family for decades. As fate would have it, the house sat on a piece of land adjacent to a new shopping center owned by Danforth Properties. Marty was looking to expand his operation and had a contract drawn up to purchase the land.

Jim, who up to that point had always had an amicable relationship with Marty Danforth, tried to persuade him not to buy the house. He wanted his sister and brother-in-law to be spared the pain of moving and having to give up a piece of their family history, so he pleaded with Marty to instead expand in a different direction from the house, and even tried to bribe him with cash under the table in order to get his way.

Marty, however, was steadfast, and Danforth Properties proceeded with the expansion.

A vicious legal battle ensued, the result of which was probably inevitable. In the end, a judge ruled in favor of Marty and his company. The Gills were furious, and none more so than Jim, who moved his sister and brother-in-law onto his own expansive property, on the shore of Barrow Lake, and built them a house.

Margery Hanceford and her husband would be taken care of. Jim would see to it. Nevertheless, a bitter seed had been planted.

As I look back, the court ruling that was issued on that day in the Gill-Danforth land dispute changed more lives than anyone could have imagined…mine included.

# CHAPTER ONE
# Summer 2002

I had become a decent public speaker during my days as a college athlete, thanks to press conferences and other speaking engagements.

Yet as I glanced at my notes from the pulpit of First Baptist Church of Lake Barrow, staring out at the throng of family, friends, and others with whom I had grown up, I felt as though any oratory skills that I had developed were flying out of the very sanctuary where I had once cut up with my best friend during countless services.

Even though I was just over six feet tall and around two hundred pounds, the pulpit seemed imposing to me as I stood behind it and tried to regroup and proceed.

The words on the paper were clear enough: Lance Corporal James Harrison Gill IV; killed in action after only a short time in Afghanistan; one of the first Marines on the ground in that country with whom we were now at war; beloved son, brother, and friend. I remembered having sat in my mother's kitchen early that morning, poring over my notes, rehearsing them again and again, and trying to determine whether or not I should add an anecdote here, or funny story there about Jamie.

*Focus,* I whispered inwardly, struggling to employ the calming techniques that I had utilized just before taking the field during big games.

Why was I locking up now? Nerves? Grief? A combination? Whatever the cause, I felt as though I was about to let down my best friend's family, who had asked me to speak at his memorial service that summer day in 2002. Maybe that was my problem; fear of failure, something I had rarely ever let hold me back from anything I'd tried to do in life.

"I was Jamie's high school teammate and friend," I began.

I paused and cleared my throat. The bright lights hitting the stage at that moment seemed to radiate more heat than the central Florida sun which had been baking our little neck of the woods all summer.

"I always knew Jamie to be a guy you could count on," I continued,

"on and off the field. He was the kind of guy you could confide in for just about anything."

Miraculously, the words then began to flow freely. I relaxed and felt more comfortable as I delivered my very first eulogy. Looking back, maybe it was just getting started that allowed things to come out easier. Speaking on behalf of a friend was a bittersweet experience, but there was no doubt that the bitterness far outweighed the sweetness.

Jamie's parents, along with Principal Andrew Starr, and Ted Skipper, our high school's current head coach, had organized the memorial service separate from the actual funeral which was to take place the next day. All of them sat in the front row. Jacqui Gill, Jamie's mom, sat grim-faced, wearing a black dress that matched her long, dark hair, and dabbed her eyes as I spoke. Her youngest son, Jordan, a rising eleventh-grader, sat next to her and seemed to be fighting back tears. He was taller than me and weighed close to two hundred and twenty pounds. His short, sandy blond hair was almost identical to how his late older brother had worn his. He sat stoically, his strapping frame in an upright position.

Then there was Jim Gill, the family patriarch, who sat and stared straight ahead as if the numbness he appeared to feel was the only fortification between him and the grief he was experiencing. It clung to him like the black suit that hugged his stout frame. As I watched him, my heart ached for him in the singular way that a son's heart aches for his father.

Next to Jim was Andrew Starr, who had been our principal and athletic director for over ten years. He was a tall, lanky man with thinning gray hair, a pale, lean face, and caring eyes which had been red-rimmed since before the service had begun.

Coach Ted Skipper appeared to be the most impassive of the bunch as he sat on the other side of Starr. His stout, muscled frame was situated upright in the pew, and his brown hair was neatly combed for the occasion. His expression never changed, except for when he was chewing players out—a side of him I experienced regularly during my days as a high school player, back when he was still our offensive coordinator.

First Baptist Church of Lake Barrow is by far the largest church in our little region and is usually packed each Sunday. But I remember thinking that the memorial service for Lance Corporal Jamie Gill had to have set an unofficial attendance record for First Baptist Lake Barrow on that sweltering day.

I finished my speech and went back to my seat directly behind the Gills. Jacqui was now wiping her face instead of the occasional dabs that I had witnessed throughout the service, and I had come close to losing control myself.

My emotions were running wild as I sat, fighting back tears, and as I watched Deke Hudson, our old teammate and close friend, take the stage. His hulking figure, which strained at the silk threads of his designer suit, dwarfed the medium-sized dais made of stained oak which I had just spoken from.

Deke began speaking in a deep, grave tone about our

fallen friend and teammate. All eyes were fixed on him as he paid tribute to Jamie, and it was unclear if his voice was really that captivating or if his status as the only professional football player ever to hail from our town was drawing the rapt attention.

Deke told several stories about Jamie, many of which drew laughter, and I was amazed at his grace under pressure. He was hurting like the rest of us, but his sense of humor was on display for the entire town to see.

When he finished, it was Coach Skipper's turn. He, too, gave a heartfelt tribute to Jamie, and I remembered thinking how uncommon it seemed that someone as gruff as Skipper could still have the capacity for feelings so profound.

Following him was Lane Faraday, our venerable old retired football coach whom Skipper had replaced in the previous year. Coach Faraday had coached generations of Lake Barrow men at Sims County High School, including Jamie and me, and had just retired. No matter how many successful coaches our small-town high school attracted in the future, Lane Faraday would forever be a legend in Lake Barrow.

His deep southern brogue resonated throughout the giant worship hall as he talked about "the little ol' rascal who cut up on and off the field, but grew up to be a man and a Marine."

"Nothing makes a coach prouder," Faraday intoned, "than seeing his boys grow up to be the men God made 'em to be."

Jacqui was sobbing now, and Jim's composure was waning as tears rolled down his cheeks. Jordan leaned forward and put his forehead into his hands.

Once Coach Faraday had finished, he came back to his seat and gave me a somber smile as he sat. Then the church's music minister came forward and led the throng of people in a closing hymn.

Everyone dispersed after the final stanza of "Amazing

Grace" while the organ continued playing.

I had arrived in town late the previous evening and had only been home for less than a full day. As I made my way out of the sanctuary, there were plenty of people waiting to see me, hug my neck, and shake hands.

The fact that it was a funeral didn't fully register with several of the smaller children in attendance, who scampered up to Deke Hudson afterward and begged for autographs. Being his usual gracious self, Deke obliged and was scribbling away as I greeted old neighbors and community members.

Unlike Deke, I didn't get any requests for autographs, but there was still no doubt that I was something of a hometown hero just the same, having starred for the mighty Sims County Spartans and gone on to play college football after graduation.

Jim and Jacqui Gill approached me, accompanied by Jordan and several of their extended family. I hugged each of them and felt tears coming as our embrace continued.

The summer heat, along with the exhaustion from speaking at my friend's memorial service, had drained me, and all I really wanted was to go home and rest.

My mother, who was sitting near the back, was still drying her eyes as I approached her and gave her a hug. I began helping her to her feet, being careful not to pull her up too quickly. Though her physical therapy was going well, she was still moving gingerly.

"You feeling okay?" I asked her.

"Fine," she said, bracing herself against her walker, which I had already unfolded. "You know me. Once I finally get going, it's all a breeze from there."

I smiled and told her to take her time.

I felt a tap on my shoulder, followed by a thick female

southern accent that I recognized. "Jayce?"

I turned, and sure enough, Mrs. Margery Gill Hanceford, my twelfth-grade English teacher and Jamie's aunt, was standing with a grateful smile and red-rimmed eyes.

"Thank you so much, Jayce," she beamed, hugging me tightly. She was a big-boned woman with a large frame and an even larger personality. With a few notable exceptions, almost everyone who had ever been taught by her loved her.

"You're welcome," I said simply. "I just told the truth."

"I know you did. You always have," she said, looking me in the eye with a look that conveyed sincerity and gratitude.

I nodded, as a memory stirred.

"You feeling okay?" I asked.

"About as good as can be expected," Mrs. Hanceford said, glancing at Mom again. "Your mother has been such a blessing; spending time with my brother and helping to get arrangements made. Bless her heart, she's done more than any of the rest of us."

My mom, who worked for Jim Gill Automotive as Jim's administrative assistant, smiled and thanked her.

Mrs. Hanceford smiled at me. "We love you so much, Jayce. You know that, right?"

"Yes, ma'am. I love you too," I said.

"Will we see you tomorrow?"

"Of course," I assured her.

She touched my arm gently as she left. I turned back to Mom.

"You ready to go?" I asked her.

Mom nodded and began moving slowly. "I would suggest inviting Deke to come over," she said, "but it looks like he's pretty much booked for the rest of the afternoon."

I looked over and, sure enough, Deke was still occupying a pew on the far side of the church, surrounded by adoring locals. I couldn't help but chuckle.

After Deke Hudson had broken every rushing record

there was to break for the Sims County Spartans and earned first-team All-America Honors, he had pretty much had his pick of top-flight colleges. After signing with the University of Florida, he wasted little time in nearly duplicating his high school effort by breaking Florida's single-season rushing record as a sophomore. After a junior season in which he was a Heisman Trophy finalist, something that was almost unheard of for a running back at Florida during that time, Deke had entered the NFL draft and was drafted by the Tampa Bay Buccaneers in the first round.

"I'll see him later," I told Mom. "You need to rest."

She nodded sleepily, fatigue starting to hit her, "I do need to be in early tomorrow. Jim's going to be preoccupied with a dozen other things, and I need to be ready to cover."

I just nodded and looked at my mother as she walked with the aid of her walker. Though she seemed tired at times, I knew that I could rest easy knowing that she was at least taken care of financially.

Truth was, the fact that she was still alive, to begin with, was reason enough for gratitude.

# Chapter Two

My mother and my biological father divorced when I was three. When I was five, Mom began working as a waitress at a small restaurant in Miami, which is where she met Rex Leonard. He was in the city working as a contractor but was originally from a small map dot in north central Florida called Lake Barrow, a place we had never heard of. He and my mother hit it off, began dating, and were married after just over a year of knowing each other.

Shortly after the wedding, Rex moved us back to Lake Barrow and adopted me not long after that.

After living in Miami for as long as we had, life in a small town took some adjustment. But we soon grew to love my stepfather's hometown and were involved in its vibrant little life in no time. I fell in love with sports, mainly baseball and football. Though Rex was working, he often found time to coach, or at least help out with, my teams whenever time permitted. Mom was usually pretty active in everything I had going on, too, when she wasn't working part-time at the Barrow Foods grocery store.

Things were going great, which is why I don't think anything could have prepared us for how our lives would be turned upside down again in the summer of 1988.

My mother had the day off from work and was taking advantage by getting caught up on some yard chores. I was out of school and helping out wherever I could.

The phone rang.

I watched Mom amble onto our porch from the small flower bed by the house which we'd been tending together, and pick up the portable receiver. I remember not hearing anything for several moments as I focused on pulling the weeds which had sprouted out of the thick soil.

Suddenly, there was a loud *clack* of the phone hitting the wooden deck as Mom dropped it. My head snapped up, and I glanced at her as she began to collapse to the ground; her back facing me, shoulders hunched, while her hands flew to her face.

She then let out the most awful wail I had ever heard.

Rex had been working just south of us in Orlando, putting a new roof on a multi-story condominium complex. He was under deadline and had been in a hurry to finish quickly. My mother always chided him about his tendency to be absent-minded, especially when he was zeroed in on a task of any kind.

That must have been the case that day as he worked high above the ground. He was finishing up the last few shingles and had become completely unaware of how close his foot was to the edge of the roof until it was too late.

My step-father fell fifty feet from that roof and was dead before a passer-by could get him to the ER.

Life was a whirlwind in the days that followed. As Mom and I both battled grief, our house was filled with homemade dishes, flowers, offers to help out around the house, and other gestures that are too numerous to recall. Additionally, my mom's boss gave her all the time off that she needed. When she came back to work, he promoted her to manager, giving her more hours and more pay. It took a while, but things slowly began to stabilize for us financially after Rex died. Between Mom's promotion and Rex's life insurance payout, we would be okay going forward.

Emotionally, we were struggling. I've heard it said that losing someone is like losing your house to a fire. Only gradually do you really begin to appreciate the magnitude of what you've lost once the initial shock wears off. In a fire, you lose furniture, appliances, and other large-scale items, sure. But you also lose mementos; objects and other specific parts of the home that hold memories that you know can never be replaced.

For me, losing Rex manifested itself over time, and mostly in the small things that make up a life spent together. Neither Rex nor I were any good at math, but he was always there to help with homework whenever I needed it. After he died, I can remember one time in particular when I was struggling. I called out for him, only to remember that he was no longer there. Right at that moment was when it hit me that he wasn't coming back.

During baseball season, I would always turn to look at the stands when it was my turn to bat. For years, the image of Mom clapping for and encouraging me with Rex beside her giving me a thumbs-up was ingrained in my psyche. After his death, Mom still clapped as I stood in the batter's box, but there was always either an empty seat next to her or someone I didn't recognize sitting in it.

Lonely as I felt, I don't believe anything could compare to the anguish that Mom was feeling. At night, she would always send me off to bed with a kiss and the same smile that always brightened her thin face, which I knew I would always remember her by. And yet, on one night in particular when I decided to sleep with my door open, I could hear faint sobs coming from her room as she went in and closed the door not long after I had told her good-night. I wanted to go in and comfort her on those nights, but something stopped me. The more I turned it over in my mind, the more I considered her smile, and the more I realized that she needed for me to think that she was okay, even though she wasn't. For her, not doing that would somehow rob me of my childhood, and she knew it. Looking back, I know I'll always love her for that.

The tearful nights intensified for a period, and then they began to lessen. Gradually, Mom and I both got to a point where we still missed Rex deeply, but were able to think and even talk about him without experiencing the sharp pangs of desperation and deep sadness that had been there during those early dark days and months.

We were getting through, slowly but surely.

Then things took another downturn during my twelfth-grade year.

Mom was working her regular day shift at Barrow Foods, which is located on one of the busier thoroughfares in town. She had gone out to check the mail that day at the box which was located right by the curb.

Out of nowhere, a car began speeding toward her, its driver either inebriated or simply not paying attention. Mom still has no recollection of the exact events, but she had to have been preoccupied with something. It's the only rational explanation, given how cautious she's always been when it comes to busy streets.

The car's driver lost control and swerved onto the shoulder where my mother was about to walk back into the store. Before Mom could react, its front bumper slammed into her at full speed, catapulting her like a rag doll into a nearby drainage ditch. The driver of the car didn't slow down, much less stop, and sped away never to be seen by us again, much less apprehended and held to account for what they had done to Cheryl Leonard.

The collision left my mother with a concussion, a gash

in her forehead, a broken arm, and, worst of all, a shattered right hip.

Miraculously, there was no internal organ damage, and the broken arm was not as severe as it could have been. The damage to her hip, however, would likely result in her never again walking like she once had.

After a lengthy hospital stay, we went home, and Mom began her physical therapy. Her body was responding well to it, and her physical condition, though pain-stricken, was progressing according to the doctors.

And yet, in the back of our minds, another large problem was looming.

While our medical insurance covered some of her expenses, it did not cover the care she would need going forward. We were suddenly faced with the choice of having to end the treatment and care that Mom was getting, and confine her to a wheelchair for the rest of her pain-filled life, or go into massive debt in order to pay for all of her care going forward. The new reality was that money was going to be an issue for us, especially since we could not penalize the driver of the car who had never been caught.

Adding insult to injury, I was about to graduate and had just verbally committed to play football for Yearwood State University, located in Yearwood, Kentucky. The prospect of having to back out of my full ride became real, and I would likely now have to stay home, get a job, and support the same woman who had bent over backward to ensure that I had the best upbringing, even with the terrible misfortune we had endured.

Mom was having none of it. In her mind, I was going to college, come hell or high water, even if it did mean a life of physical pain and limited mobility for her. I, on the other hand, was having none of *that*. How could I turn my back on her? How could I watch her grimace and grunt in her struggle just to get from her wheelchair to the recliner in the living room? How could I continue to cover my ears as her agony-filled yelps echoed from the bathroom as she wrestled with activities that been no problem for her since she was three years old? How could I let this happen to the same woman who had worked her ass off just to make sure I was taken care of; and who had, at times following Rex's death, foregone purchasing make-up because I needed a new pair of cleats or new uniforms or money for camp?

My mind was made up. I was calling Yearwood State and backing out, so help me, Jesus.

Or so I thought.

When people think of Florida, images of beaches and palm trees usually spring right to mind, and with good reason. Whether you find yourself on the sugary white sands of the Gulf Coast or the drab brown which meets the Atlantic, our beaches are second to none.

Little do most people realize, though, that Lake Barrow is a little over sixty miles from the nearest beach, and more closely resembles a town you might find in Alabama or Georgia. As the old adage goes when referring to small southern towns, there's "a church on every corner and a swimmin' hole through every thicket of trees." Change here isn't usually welcomed with open arms if it's even welcomed at all.

Still, there's no better place on earth to live, especially if you've fallen on hard times. Our family misfortunes proved that.

Many people stepped forward in the aftermath of my mother's accident to help us, but no one more so than Jim Gill.

# Chapter Three

On a warm spring Saturday in 1998, First Baptist Church had planned a picnic in honor of the graduating seniors from Sims County High School. I didn't want to go, but Mom did. Therefore, we were going.

We arrived at James Harrison Gill, Jr. Memorial Park, named for my friend Jamie's grandfather, shortly after things had kicked off. Mom was still in a wheelchair, and as I pushed her up to the main pavilion, the scent of sizzling beef and chicken was hanging heavy in the thick humid air.

But I had no appetite.

Earlier that week, I had decided to call Jeff Swicegood, the offensive coordinator who had recruited me, and back out of the commitment I had made earlier that year to play for the Mustangs of Yearwood State.

My future as a college football quarterback had been stolen from me by a spineless, careless person behind the wheel of a car, and there was nothing I or anyone could do about it.

I drifted through most of the afternoon, oblivious to much of what was happening around me. There was plenty of food to be eaten, but I ignored it.

"Hey, faggot," a deep voice called out.

I turned and smiled as Jamie strode toward me. He wore

khaki shorts with a belt and loafers with no socks. His muscles strained against the polo shirt which he wore tucked into his waistband, his trademark smug grin plastered over his ruddy face.

"Who are you calling 'faggot,' pansy?" I asked with a wry grin, taking a sip from a Mountain Dew can.

"You," he answered. "At least you've been pouting like a faggot all afternoon. What's wrong with you?"

I just shook my head and stared off into space. Jamie gave a faint nod and seemed to get the hint. For as long as we knew each other, I can only think of one or two times where Jamie and I talked about anything even remotely dealing with feelings or emotion. Most of our conversations revolved around girls, video games, and sports; sometimes in that order, sometimes not.

And yet, there was no need to talk about deep stuff whenever we hung out. He knew me well enough to know when things were going south; whether it was missing Rex, or problems I'd been having with Mom, or grades, girls, whatever. It was an unspoken signal, virtually indecipherable to anyone but us, and whenever one of us gave it off, that meant the topic was closed.

"You call Yearwood yet?" Jamie asked.

"No."

"Good," he said, causing me to look his way again. There was an unfamiliar twinkle in his eye. "Because my dad wants to talk to you and your mom," he had said, pointing to a table where my mother was now sitting in her chair. Jim Gill sat next to her, and they seemed to be discussing something important. Mom appeared to be crying, which alarmed me. I glanced at Jamie who now had a knowing grin on his face and walked over.

"What's wrong?" I asked Mom as I approached.

She looked up, and it didn't take long for me to realize that the tears were not the same sort that I had seen her cry when Rex died, or when she was upset about something important. Joy, not sorrow, was behind the red rims.

"Have a seat, Jayce," Jim said in a husky voice, motioning for me to sit across from him, his thick face and neck framing a grin that barely hoisted the corners of his mouth.

He was a large man with an even larger personality, a round face, and thick gray hair which was always well-groomed. He always carried himself with a confident air and fatherly demeanor that drew others to him immediately.

As I took my seat at the table, my eyes darted back and forth between the two of them.

"What's going on?" I asked.

"Been talking to your mom here, Jayce," Jim began. "And I'm curious about something. Have you called Yearwood State yet?"

"No sir."

"Good. Because unless your mother turns down the offer I just made her, and I don't believe that she will, your future as a Yearwood State Mustang should still be intact."

Mom dabbed her eyes with a tissue and wiped her nose.

"Offer?" I asked.

"Gill Automotive is expanding," Jim continued, "and I need a new executive assistant. Turns out, everything I've heard from Lonny Brock over at Barrow Foods leads me to believe that your mother would be ideally suited for the position, which I can assure you will pay substantially more than what she was making as a grocery store manager."

I sat there stunned as the pieces began to fall into place.

"It's a desk job," Jim answered before I could even think to ask about her hip. "No heavy-lifting, nothing but computer work and some filing."

I looked at Mom, and then at her wheelchair.

"Flexible hours, too," Jim added, reading my mind. "Her therapy schedule and doctors' appointments should continue with no problems. And speaking of which, full benefits—

medical and dental."

I was speechless.

"It's okay to smile, Jayce," Jim said with a chuckle. "You're going to be a Yearwood State Mustang after all."

I fought back tears as Mom clutched my hand and patted it with her free one. "I don't know how to thank you," she told him.

A jowly grin spread out across Jim's face. "You show up to work on Monday," he told Mom. Then looking at me, he added, "And you, young man, go show those hillbillies up in Kentucky how football's supposed to be played."

"Yes sir," I almost giggled, unable to conceal my joy any longer.

Given my friendship with Jamie, it was safe to say that Jim had almost been like a second father to me ever since Rex had passed away. After that day, however, I was certain that there would no longer be anything "almost" about it.

I was going to college after all, thanks to the efforts and kindness of our lifelong family friend.

## Chapter Four
# Summer 2002

The mid-summer Florida heat, in a strange way, seemed to intensify the somber mood during the funeral service of Jamie Gill on that hot summer day in 2002. I was a pall-bearer, along with with Deke Hudson, Ahmad Floyd (another one of our closest friends), and a few other of our high school teammates.

As I helped transport the casket to the burial site, I glanced at Deke and Ahmad and began to reflect again.

In the early going, it had been a lonely time when I first moved to Lake Barrow with Mom and Rex. My stepfather had several friends with whom he kept in touch, but most of them had kids that were older than me by several years. Thus, those initial days in our new hometown were spent lounging around and watching countless hours of television.

Finally, Mom had enough and banished me from the house.

"Ride your bike!" she had admonished in a harried tone. "Just get on it and start pedaling. Who cares where it takes you, as long as it gets you away from here!"

I did as I was told, and made my way down the street at a

sluggish pace; the chain connecting my bicycle's gears making a faint metallic sound as I pedaled at a lethargic pace.

I didn't pay much attention to what was going on around me; only enough to keep me from getting hurt somehow. Soon, I found myself near a park and scarcely noticed three boys—one white and two black— tossing a football. I ignored them and kept up the meandering tempo of my bike's pedaling.

In the distance, I heard a loud *thok*, the sound of the ball being kicked. Seconds later, I felt the violent, jarring sensation of my bike's metal frame being hit with something as I lost control and fell over.

I landed with a thud on the sidewalk and sat up immediately. The first thing I noticed was a brown football rolling and bouncing nearby. I assessed the damage and determined that both my bike and I were okay. I then looked toward the large field inside the park and saw that the three boys were now running toward me.

"You okay?" the white boy asked, as he ambled near. He was slightly taller than me and had blond hair, a stocky build, and freckles. He wore a red and white 49ers jersey with the number 16 on the front and, I would notice later, the name "Montana" on the back. He also wore long, baggy athletic shorts which came down below his knees and large hi-top sneakers. There was an arrogant smirk on his face, even as he was checking on me.

I slowly got up, righted my bike, and nodded.

"It was an accident," said the shorter and skinnier of the two black boys. This one had a fade hairstyle and wasn't wearing a shirt, which displayed his gangly limbs and thin shoulders. He, too, wore the same style of baggy shorts that his white friend had on.

"It's okay," I told him.

"Toss the ball back, man," said the larger black boy, who looked to be the same age as the rest of us, but whose hair was cut short, and whose muscles were already showing signs of developing underneath a gray tank top. He wore sweatpants and a pair of cleats.

I picked up the ball and, without even thinking, launched it back toward the group. It sailed over their heads, and I remember impressing even myself with that throw. Rex had told me on several occasions, as we tossed baseballs back and forth in the yard, that my arm strength was above average. But I had never played organized sports and therefore had no way to actually measure what talent I had against other boys my age.

"Whoa," said the white boy as the ball whizzed past them.

"Damn," said the larger black boy.

The smaller black boy just chuckled and glanced back at me, as I got on my bike and began pedaling away. As I reached the far corner of the park, I turned my head and noticed that all three boys were running after me in my direction.

"Hey!" the white boy called out. "You want to play with us?"

I stopped pedaling. "Me?" I asked.

"Yeah you," said the smaller black boy. "You got a cannon, man."

"Dude, I ain't never seen a kid your size throw a ball like that," said the larger boy.

"Seriously," the smaller boy said. "You come play with us, we can run two-on-two drills."

I thought about this a moment.

"You're not a pussy, or a fag are you?" asked the white boy, sneering at me.

"No," I said in defiance.

"Then what's the hold-up?" said Tank-Top. "Bring your bike inside the fence, and let's go."

I reluctantly complied. After I had entered the park and set my bike on the ground, I walked up to the group.

"I'm Jamie," said the white boy. "Jamie Gill. My daddy

owns Jim Gill Automotive."

"Man, why you always gotta tell everyone that," said the smaller boy.

Jamie glared at him.

"Deke Hudson," said the larger boy.

"Jayce," I returned. "Jayce Leonard."

"What kind of name is 'Jayce Leonard?'" asked the smaller boy.

"What the hell kind of name is Ahmad Floyd," Jamie challenged him.

"Your momma named me that," Ahmad said.

"Ahmad, that doesn't even make no sense, man," Deke chided.

"We gonna play, or keep running our mouths?" Jamie said to the group.

From there, the four of us had been inseparable throughout childhood. In the fall, Jamie, Ahmad, Deke, and I played on the same Pop Warner and high school football teams; winter found us shooting hoops at various locations around town; and when spring and summer rolled around, we must have hit a thousand baseballs on the expansive property belonging to the Gill family. Even more importantly, those three guys had been there for me during both the aftermath of Rex's death and during Mom's recovery following the accident. Throwing the football, shooting hoops, playing video games, or just hanging out; very little was said, and it rarely mattered what sort of activity it was. All that mattered to me then was that I wasn't alone.

At Jamie's gravesite, I stood there as Dr. Rich Blake, First Baptist's pastor, delivered the eulogy. I could not focus on it. Instead, my eyes and mind were transfixed on the portraits of Jamie that had been erected on easels near his closed casket.

There was one taken of him in his Marine dress blues, looking grim-faced, with the American flag in the background. In another one, he was dressed in his high school football uniform; Spartan colors, green and white; wearing number forty-four, like he always had. The look on his face was that same familiar mixture of cockiness and toughness that he'd always worn, and that I had always admired and resented at the same time; mainly because I had seen it each time he had beaten me at Madden NFL or sacked me during practice from his middle linebacker position.

Next to the football portrait was a third enlarged photo that I was certain would always represent how I remembered my best friend. It had been taken during the summer following graduation, not long before I had left for Yearwood State. Jamie had thrown a party on the dock of the Gills' lakeshore home; one last hurrah before everyone went their separate ways. Per usual, there were plenty of girls and plenty of beer, which Jamie had managed to artfully smuggle down to the dock without either of his parents knowing about it.

In the picture, he is sitting back on the wooden bench near the edge of the dock, holding an aluminum can in such a way that no one could see what he was drinking (though most people probably knew). On his face, which was partially concealed by sunglasses and a straw farmer's hat, was that same smirk.

It was vintage Jamie; the same guy whom I had grown up with; the football stud who had busted heads on the football field as a Sims County Spartan; the same guy who had gone to college for a semester before dropping out (much to the chagrin of his father) and enlisting in the Marine Corps; the same guy who had always lived life on his terms…right down to the end.

While tears had been falling all throughout the morning and afternoon, it wasn't until Jenna Blake, our pastor's daughter and Jamie's girlfriend, got up and flawlessly sang "I Will

Remember You," by Sarah McLachlan that no dry eye could be found in the crowd. After high school graduation, she and Jamie had stayed together, despite him going into the Marine Corps and her going to Julliard on a vocal performance scholarship.

Pastor Rich kissed his daughter and consoled her one last time before standing to deliver the closing prayer.

When it was over, people stopped by to pay their final respects to Jamie and offer condolences to the Gills. I watched Jordan who, as an eleventh-grader, would soon be competing for the same middle linebacker spot at which his brother had starred during high school.

Slowly, the crowds dispersed. Once the Gills left, the only people remaining under the canopy near Jamie's grave site were Deke, Ahmad, and myself. Slowly, the three of us made our way to the casket one final time. Soon it would be lowered into the ground, and for a moment, none of us said anything, instead opting to let the whippoorwills and robins serenade us as we paid our final respects.

Finally, Deke broke the silence, as he placed his hand on the casket.

"Tested and tried," he said.

"Spartan pride," Ahmad and I said, almost in unison, as we gently caressed the smooth mahogany.

Later that afternoon, Mom and I rode in my ancient Mazda hatchback toward the large compound belonging to the Gills that had been in their family for decades. It was located on the outskirts of town and backed up to the northeast shore of the large body of water that bore our town's namesake.

Like many of the inland communities of central Florida, ours had become largely known throughout the region for citrus production, cattle ranching, and other forms of commercial agriculture. Lake Barrow is the county seat and the primary hub of political and commercial activity in Sims County.

As I've said already, change is not usually welcome here, and even when it is, it's only allowed to happen slowly. Downtown Lake Barrow is the perfect illustration of this.

Interstate 75, which takes you south to Miami, doesn't run through our town. Instead, you have to get off and drive about 20 miles east through forest and swampland before you begin to see the first farm. From there, other signs of civilization begin to materialize; a few cattle ranches here, more farms there, several orange groves. Only then does Lake Barrow come into view.

Our small town is about equidistant between Gainesville, where Deke played college ball at the University of Florida, and Orlando, where millions of people from all over the world flock to visit Mickey Mouse each year. The only way anyone could find us without intending to is by taking the wrong exit off the 75, and refusing to turn around after realizing their mistake.

Coming into town is a gradual process, kind of like change, I suppose. After the farms, you begin to pass smaller yards and properties, most of which are home to older houses built in the sixties, seventies, and early eighties. Very few fancy subdivisions, like the ones you're apt to see in the suburbs of larger and mid-size towns. You come to a stop light, and at that point, you have three options: you can drive straight and leave Lake Barrow almost as quickly as you came in; you can turn left and head back out into the rural communities of Sims County, or you can turn right and visit Town Square.

The best way I can describe our small town's square is to have you imagine going back in time to the 1950s. It sounds clichéd, but it's true all the same. Government buildings line the streets, interspersed with what few privately-owned small businesses still exist in that area; an old drugstore, and an aging floral boutique, just to name two.

At the far end of the Square, sitting side-by-side like two stern overseers ready to mete out justice or maybe squash an unwelcome new development on their beloved town, are the Lake Barrow Town Hall and the Sims County Courthouse. Many an argument has been settled in both of these two buildings, as well as many a grudge born, many a law passed, and even a few backroom deals solidified in the musty corridors and inner chambers.

It was in this very courthouse that the Gills and the Danforths first established their long-running feud.

Outside the Town Square lies another world, slow but sure in its movement out of the time-honored snares of Lake Barrow's past. Positioned just beyond the stern glares of the courthouse and town hall lie the modern shopping centers, small in stature and providing a home to a few of the more popular retail chains. Fast-food restaurants locally franchised by life-long residents are interspersed within the sprawl as well, and Lake Barrow even took the modern leap several years back of building its own small indoor shopping mall on the main drag leading out of town.

At the far end of this paved road into modernity lies Jim Gill Automotive, which is ironic since the Gills, more than most families, have generally been on the front lines when it came to the preservation of "how Lake Barrow's always been." As you continue heading southbound lies the great Barrow Lake, and the Gill property.

Our town's lake is unique in that its imperfect round shape is characterized by a few small peninsulas jutting inward toward the center, so that if you look at it from the viewpoint of a helicopter or airplane, you would see a neck of land poking in from the north, one from the southwest, and another from the east.

On that northernmost tip, and on the twenty acres lo-cated immediately inland from there, is where the Gill family has called home for decades.

Mom and I pulled onto the Gills' property, and I smiled as the memories of pick-up games and hunting trips flooded over me.

While a few meager attempts at farming had been made by various Gills over the years, the land was now mainly used for hunting when it was in season. Jim charged a reasonable fee for permission to hunt on his land, and consequently his place had become the location of choice for harvesting deer and other wild game when the weather began to turn cooler.

I entered the land by way of a long, winding dirt road which also took me past the Hanceford residence, where Margery (my old teacher) and her husband had lived since Marty Danforth had "robbed them of their home," as the Gills characterized it.

As I drove down the dirt road, my small car gyrated in response to the holes and other variations in the unstable clay terrain of the main path, and I found myself praying that she could make it. My car was the first one that I had saved up just enough money to purchase during my sophomore year of college. At that time, the mileage on it was already in the six-digits, but I was happy to call it my own, nonetheless and proud of the fact that I had bought it with my own money.

On that day, I was also thankful that Lake Barrow had been going through a dry spell, much to the chagrin of the local farmers. While it meant less water for crops, I also knew that the likelihood of my small car sliding and getting stuck in the mud was lower, as well.

I rounded a bend and was soon able to see the house through a canopy of solid oak trees lining the drive. Even through the thick, hanging Spanish moss, the painted white antebellum was still majestic-looking. Anyone who saw it would swear that it had not been touched since the late 1800s. They would soon know better once they saw the inside, which was stocked with modern appliances and up-to-date furnishings.

There were two wrap-around porches, one each for the lower and upper stories, and both of which were adorned with stately-looking rockers and several potted ferns that hung from various locations. Around the perimeter of the house was an assortment of flower bushes and other shrubs; mostly azaleas, with a few roses and geraniums which added color.

I parked, got out, and came around to the passenger side to help Mom, mopping the sweat off of my brow with the sleeve of my white, button-down dress shirt as I circled the car. Given the large number of people that had shown up to bring food, I had to park further away than I had hoped, which forced Mom to have to walk farther. We took our time, though, and Mom remarked several times at how lovely the Gills' place was and how much she had always enjoyed visiting and walking around.

Once we reached the front porch, a few men that were standing around pitched in to carry Mom's walker and help her up the steps. I thanked them all and endured the slaps on the back and barrage of questions about college life and football. We entered the front door and were soon surrounded once more by people wearing black, several of whom offered to help Mom and asked about how I, the hometown football hero, was doing.

I fixed a plate but didn't eat much. Soon I found myself uncomfortable with the large crowd and decided to head outside for some fresh air. Mom seemed okay sitting with a group of ladies in the Gills' living room as I walked through the front door. The sky had become overcast, lessening the heat, but also making the mood seem that much more down-cast and somber. On top of that, the humidity lingered, and I felt my shirt sticking to my back, though I was glad to get away from the crowds, if only for a moment.

"Jayce?" a female voice called out from behind me.

I turned, and my heart skipped a beat.

*Meredith.*

"I thought I saw you come in."

My pulse quickened as my old high school girlfriend neared me. Meredith Lee and I had dated off and on through-out high school and had not seen each other since our break-up right before graduation. Very little about her had changed; at least physically. Her shoulder-length blonde hair was as wavy as I had remembered it, and her blue, penetrating eyes were still the same bright and mischievous-looking ones that had originally attracted me to her in the first place.

My own eyes gradually went from her face downward, and I quietly marveled at how shapely she had remained since we had said our good-byes years earlier. The black dress she wore hugged her lithe figure tightly, showing off the same perfect hourglass cheerleader curves that my hands and eyes had caressed on more than one occasion.

"It's good to see you," she said as she walked up and gave me a hug, causing me to sweat even more profusely.

"You too," I managed, thankful that my voice wasn't go-ing hoarse. "How have you been?"

"Good," she said in that chirpy southern accent that I was sure still drove guys crazy. "You?"

"Doing well," I answered. "Sad day."

"I know," she said. "I always loved Jamie."

For a brief moment, neither of us said anything.

"How long are you in town?" she finally asked.

"End of the week," I said. "Then back to Yearwood."

"Didn't you graduate already?"

"Yeah, back in December," I said. "But I'm a grad assistant now."

"That's great," she said. "My dad followed you online, and would sometimes give me updates about how you were doing up there."

I smiled. "I didn't know I was that big of a star."

She grinned, showing off a set of perfect white teeth. "You, Deke, and Ahmad…Coach Faraday's last three college signees."

"I guess so," I said. "How about you? Are you still in the area?"

"Yeah," she said, looking down. "Went a semester to UCF after high school didn't go back, but stayed in Orlando. Met a guy, got married too quickly, and just finalized the divorce."

"I'm sorry," I frowned, trying to convince myself that I really was sorry, and not elated that she was single again.

"I'm not," she said, looking off toward the lake. Then, turning back to me and fixing me with the blues, said, "How about you? Girlfriend? Fiancée?" She pushed a wisp of blonde hair from her face.

"Had a girlfriend," I said. "Broke up right before my senior season began."

"I'm sorry."

I shrugged.

"How's your mom doing?"

"Best she can," I answered. "Physical therapy's helped a lot."

"She was always sweet."

I nodded and smiled, remembering how Mom had never liked Meredith. "Do you keep up with anybody?" I asked, changing the subject.

"Just a few folks," she said. "Everyone kind of scattered after graduation."

"No surprise there."

For a moment, neither of us spoke. Of course, our relationship had never been marked by a lot of conversation to begin with. We were the "quarterback-cheerleader" combo that virtually everyone had expected us to be, and had stayed together largely for that reason.

"Well, we should hang out while you're home," she finally said. Then before I could answer, she added, "Are you free tomorrow night?"

"Yeah," I said, trying to conceal a grin.

"Want to meet at Guadalajara at 6 pm?"

In college, I'd had a semi-serious girlfriend with whom I had broken up almost a year prior. And while I knew it was for the best, I'd been hurting for some female companionship over the past year. What did I have to lose? It was just dinner, anyway.

"Sounds good," I said.

"Great," she said. "I'd better get going. But I'll see you tomorrow night."

"Looking forward to it."

She gave me another hug and turned to walk away. I watched her as she left, and found myself hoping that tomorrow night would progress into something more than just dinner.

# Chapter Five

Maybe it was seeing Meredith again, or maybe it was the summer heat. Whatever it was, something had caused my mouth to run dry, and I needed a cold drink.

I went back in the house and found a cooler filled with ice and an assortment of beverages. Opening a Gatorade Fruit Punch, I downed nearly a fourth of the bottle and stood there, letting the air conditioner and the cold drink recalibrate my body temperature.

I've always been a wanderer. It used to drive Mom crazy when she would take me into a department store and lose sight of me within minutes. The idea of sitting still for too long bothers me, and I eventually need to get up and move around.

I suppose that's one reason why I found myself meandering through the Gills' house that afternoon as I stood finishing off the Gatorade. I'm sure it also had to do with the memories I was reliving on the day of my best friend's funeral, as I soon found myself going up the stairs to the second level of the Gills' house. As I reached the landing, my eyes instinctively glanced to my right where Jamie's old room was. My head began to spin, and my heart ached. How many hours we had spent playing Madden NFL and Mortal

Kombat in that room was anyone's guess.

I walked through the small corridor leading to the rear porch and glanced through the screen door as I approached. Jim was leaning against the white-painted railing and appeared to be gazing across his massive backyard and toward the lake. The sun had reemerged from behind the clouds, and the reflection of its rays shimmered as they struck the tiny ripples on the water's surface.

As I studied Jim Gill, it occurred to me just how rarely I had ever witnessed him standing by himself. Normally, he was surrounded by people and was often the jovial center of attention in whichever group he happened to be part of. At that moment, however, he looked completely alone.

I opened the porch screen, causing him to snap out of his reverie and turn toward me. His downcast eyes did not appear red-rimmed, and I remembered how differently many people had grieved when Rex died. *Some people hurt so bad they can't even cry,* Mom had told me during that time.

"Hey, Jayce," he greeted me, trying to force a smile.

I nodded and slowly approached. Standing next to Jim, I leaned against the railing and cast my eyes out toward the lake; toward the Gills' dock, which Jamie and I had jumped from thousands of times during our childhood summers. Almost every object and place in my line of sight had a memory. Truthfully, just about every place I had seen during my visit home held a memory of some kind; most of which were now bittersweet, since Jamie was gone.

"Beautiful service," I said to Jim, not entirely sure if it was the right thing to say.

Jim nodded. "It was."

"Jenna's always had a beautiful voice."

"Always."

"I can leave if you want to be alone," I said to him.

"No," he shook his head. "I'd like you to stay."

I nodded and continued looking out toward the water,

where a ski boat raced near the shoreline pulling an inflatable raft full of squealing kids. Moments passed.

"When do you go back?" Jim finally asked, looking at me.

"Friday," I answered.

"Ready for the season?"

"I think so," I said, glad that the silence was now broken, and the subject changed.

"Think your players are ready?" Jim asked, a faint smile creasing his lips.

I chuckled. "They're not really my players," I said. "But yeah, they'll be good to go."

"You're a coach, aren't you?" Jim pressed.

"I put together game film and spreadsheets on opposing teams," I told him. "Doesn't exactly make me Steve Spurrier or Bobby Bowden."

"You gotta start somewhere," Jim said good-naturedly. "You'll be a great coach someday, Jayce. You've always had the tools, you just need to learn how to use them."

"I've learned from some good ones already."

Jim nodded. "I wouldn't mind seeing you come back down here to coach someday," he said.

I looked at him. "At Sims County?"

"Where else?"

I grinned. "Skipper's replaced a legend, and if I had to guess, I'd say whoever replaces Skipper someday will probably have some big shoes to fill, too. He's going to do great things."

Jim took a sip from a water bottle he had in his hand and shook his head. "I don't know about that," he said.

Puzzled, I studied Jim for a moment, waiting for him to go on. "What do you mean?" I finally asked.

"I'm not impressed with Ted Skipper at all…as a coach or as a person."

I was taken aback. "Why?"

"He plays favorites, Jayce," Jim answered, standing up

straight. "Faraday was a crusty old hard-nose, but at least he gave everyone a fair shake. You of all people should know that."

I finished off the Gatorade and was silent.

"Heck," Jim said, his face a picture of contempt, "if you had played under Skipper instead of Faraday, there'd have been no way you would have started at quarterback your senior year, no matter how many interceptions Matt Danforth threw. Skipper would have continued playing him week after week, simply because of the fact that Marty Danforth was his daddy."

I was silent, unsure of what to say next.

Jim continued. "Jordan's probably not going to start at linebacker this year," he said, his voice bitter. "Skipper's too hell-bent on showing the blacks in this town that he's not just about creating an all-white starting roster. That's why Isaiah Waters gets more reps in practice and is probably going to be the starter."

"Skipper always treated us fairly," I said, feeling the need to defend our former offensive coordinator.

"That's because Faraday was always there to kick him in the ass if he didn't," Jim replied, looking at me with bile in his expression. "Believe me, Jayce, there was a lot that went on behind the scenes you and Jamie never saw. Faraday hired Skipper because he was one of the brightest young offensive minds in the state. What Faraday didn't realize, though, was that he was getting a whole lot of extra baggage that he wasn't equipped to handle."

"Baggage?"

"Not only does Ted play favorites," Jim continued, "he also doesn't come to Quarterback Club meetings, doesn't engage with the parents the way Faraday did and sends out his assistants to do it instead. The man's got poor people skills, and seems more concerned with making himself and the program look good than about fielding a solid team and doing what's right."

I said nothing.

"He's not a good fit for the school or the community," Jim said. "For all the good Lane Faraday did for Lake Barrow and the boys that played for him, he was often a poor judge of character, and it was never more evident than when he brought in Ted Skipper."

I was shocked at what I was hearing. For one thing, I had a difficult time believing any of it. And on top of that, I had only rarely heard Jim speak ill of anyone, least of all one of his sons' coaches. He had always brought up Jamie and Jordan to respect authority, no matter how much they disagreed with the decisions made. Now, he seemed to be going against his own advice. Part of me wondered how much of it was just the grief over losing Jamie that was doing the talking.

I looked at Jim, as he seemed to go deep into his own thoughts once more. Suddenly, almost without warning, he began to cry.

I didn't know what to do. After a moment of standing there, I reached over and placed my hand on his shoulder.

"I'm sorry," I said.

"I hate to cry in front of you, Jayce," Jim sobbed.

"You don't need to apologize."

Moments passed as Jim wiped his eyes with the back of his hand. Gradually, he regained control of his emotions, wiped again, and took a deep breath.

"Just hits me at random times," he said. "Jacqui, too."

I nodded, understanding completely and remembering the days after Rex passed.

"Thank you for being here," Jim said. "It means more to us than you know."

"Of course."

Jim wiped his nose with the tissue. "Getting back to what we were discussing, I need to ask you a question."

I looked at him.

"If you were offered a job coaching down here would you take it?"

I started to speak, but couldn't. Coaching football had been a dream of mine since before I graduated from high school. At Yearwood State, I had dual-majored in sports management and education, and could usually be found in the film room when I wasn't in class or on the practice field. Dissecting our opponents' defenses and learning the tendencies of all eleven players trying to stop us had become a hobby of mine, the way beer pong and scoring chicks was with many of my classmates. Off-seasons would find me with my receivers on the practice field, sometimes in triple-digit temperatures and sometimes with snow on the ground; all for the sake of getting in those additional practice sessions. I had learned diligently at the feet of every coach I had played for, in high school and college, and was now serving as a graduate assistant coach, hoping to transition into a head coaching role of my own someday.

At the same time, it had never crossed my mind that I might end up back in Lake Barrow as a coach for the Spartans.

"I would definitely think about it," I answered Jim.

"I'll talk to some folks, then," Jim said, "Skipper included, and see if there isn't some way we can get you on the staff down here…not this season, of course, but maybe next season."

I was too surprised to speak.

"This town needs more folks like you, Jayce," Jim said. "Good people who have grown up here and know this town."

"You'd do that?"

"Of course I would."

I shook my head. "You've already done more for my mother and me than just about any other living person in this town, Jim."

Jim looked at me seriously with his tear-stained eyes and

smiled. "It's the least I could do, given what you did for Margery during your senior year."

## CHAPTER SIX
# Fall 1997 – Jayce's Senior Year

*Mrs. Margery Hanceford was passing out graded book reports that had been assigned to us after reading Hawthorne's "The Scarlet Letter" over the summer.*

*Literature, English, and writing have always been my best subjects, and I was elated when Mrs. Hanceford handed my paper back to me with an "A-" on it. I immediately began reading over it and was glad to note that the only thing that had kept me from getting an "A" were some minor punctuation errors.*

*Mrs. Hanceford smiled at me as she continued handing out reports, and I remember thinking how my senior year was getting off to a pretty amazing start. Having Mrs. Hanceford for 12th grade English would certainly help, especially since I had known her for almost as long as I had known Jamie.*

*Matt Danforth, who sat behind me, had not been so lucky with his grade. For that matter, his start to our senior year had been going south pretty quickly. Earlier that week, he had lost the starting quarterback job to me and would not get it back, especially once the coaches started letting me throw the ball more as the season progressed.*

*"A D-minus'?!" he exclaimed loudly, once he saw his graded paper.*

*"Well, Mr. Danforth," Mrs. Hanceford said, without looking up as she continued distributing papers, "if you're that anxious to broadcast your grade to the class, by all means, do so."*

*A few people laughed as Matt flounced back into his seat with petulant anger, and glared at his teacher. Throughout the previous three years, Mrs. Hanceford and Matt had managed to avoid each other, as the fiasco between his father and her brother had continued to loom large over Lake Barrow. Now that our senior year had begun, both of them were having to tolerate one another, like it or not.*

*"That's just wrong," he mumbled, fuming as he studied his paper.*

*"Or maybe it's your study habits that are wrong and need improvement," she said, without missing a beat.*

*Matt was slouching in his chair as he held his graded report with both hands. His eyes looked up in narrow slits as they zeroed in on our teacher, glowering with hatred.*

*"Maybe it's your whole family that needs improvement," he snarled.*

*A sudden tension came over the room, as Mrs. Hanceford turned and fixed Matt with a glare. Her eyes, usually ebullient and warm were now focused with razor-sharp intensity on the teenaged boy who had fired the latest salvo in an ongoing feud that extended beyond the walls of our classroom.*

*The entire class was frozen in fear and rigid anticipation.*

*Mrs. Hanceford held Matt with a death-like gaze, as he returned the stare and refused to avert his eyes for even a moment. Both combatants were breathing heavily, their heartbeats seemingly choked with the fury that seemed desperate to be let loose.*

*Finally, Mrs. Hanceford broke the silence.*

*"Don't…you…ever…say that to me again." she snarled at Matt through clenched teeth, seemingly measuring each syllable as if to ensure that each was tinged with just the right amount of wrath.*

*Matt said nothing but gave a slight shrug as he held her gaze for several more minutes.*

*The classroom remained still with a tense silence for what felt like another hour when in reality it was more like thirty seconds. None of us* dared to move as the two of them were frozen, refusing to budge.

"Open your textbooks," Mrs. Hanceford finally said, her words putting an end to the standoff and lifting the tension.

I glanced over at Matt, who had neither taken his eyes off of Mrs. Hanceford nor changed his facial expression from the glare he had worn since receiving his graded paper.

The next morning, I had a one-on-one meeting with Coach Skipper before classes began. As offensive coordinator, he took a very meticulous approach to the play of his quarterbacks. And since I was the new starter, who had just taken over earlier that week, he wanted to ensure that I was ready for the next game. That meant extra film sessions whenever we could get them in, which usually ended up being before school began.

I met him in our field house at 0600, and we sat for almost an hour before the first bell rang. We watched film, dissected coverage schemes, and went over checks at the line before I headed to class.

The bell still had not yet rung as I made my way to Mrs. Hanceford's classroom, and I figured the chances were good that I'd be the first arrival. With a little luck, maybe I could even get a few extra winks of sleep before class began.

I was wrong. As I reached the doorway, I saw that there were three people already in the classroom; Mrs. Hanceford, Matt Danforth, and another student named Dixie Johnson, whom I noticed was sobbing as she sat at her desk.

Mrs. Hanceford sat next to her and consoled her. Matt sat across the room from both of them.

I stood in the doorway and watched what was happening for a moment, before realizing that Mrs. Hanceford was actually praying for Dixie out loud.

Initially, none of the three noticed me as I stood there. I glanced at Matt, whose face was contorted in a disdainful glower as he kept his eyes on Mrs. Hanceford and Dixie. I noticed that he looked every bit as livid and hate-filled as he had the day before during the standoff with

*Mrs. Hanceford.*

*Dixie looked up from her desk and saw me before bowing her head again.*

*I decided to move away from the door while waiting for the bell to ring. Standing there, I studied Dixie, whom I had known for a while, and I began to feel sorry for her.*

*She had been another one of the first people I had met when I moved to Lake Barrow. We had become friends after being seated next to each other in first grade, which was unusual, given the natural aversion boys and girls generally have to each other at that age. Somehow, though, the two of us had hit it off, especially during recess.*

*She was always a bit of a tomboy, which I suppose is part of why I got along so well with her in the first place. While other girls were sitting in circles, talking and looking on the boys with disgust, Dixie was apt to follow me up, down, over or under any piece of jungle gym equipment I could climb. We'd hang out after school, while waiting for our moms to pick us up in front of the building, talking about anything from how much we hated our teacher, to who could jump the highest, to what we were going to be when we grew up.*

*Whenever I told her she couldn't be a baseball player, because only boys could do that, she would stick her tongue out at me, and level me with her deep green eyes. Even at that young age, I remember thinking of how pretty they looked, even when she was angry.*

*Years passed, and Dixie and I gradually grew apart and saw less of each other. I excelled in sports and consequently rose to the top of the social pecking order that exists in American schools everywhere. Cheerleaders became my priority, and Dixie had never been one, nor would she ever be. She was short, plump, and had stringy blonde hair, along with a generous smattering of pimples that lined her face. It seemed that the older we got, the fewer friends she had, which occasionally made me feel bad, but not enough to do anything about it. Looking back, how I ignored Dixie during those early years of middle and high school is one of my biggest regrets.*

*Occasionally, we would pass each other in the hallway, and I would smile and wave, especially when I was certain no one else was looking.*

*During these times, I often wished that we could arrange to meet some-place so that we could chat some more and catch up.*

*But I didn't. She was at one end of the social stratosphere, and I was at the other. I never admitted it during those days, but it hurt me to ignore my friend that way.*

*The next week, after I had seen Mrs. Hanceford, Dixie, and Matt in the classroom together, Mom and I went out for ice cream after clearing the dinner table.*

*Coming back, we pulled onto our street, and I noticed an unfamiliar shadowy figure sitting on our front steps. The porch light was silhouetting whoever it was, making it hard to determine their identity.*

*As we got out, the stranger rose and made their way toward me before I could even call out to them. Once out of the shadows, the beam from our outdoor floodlight revealed who was there, and I was surprised.*

*"Dixie," I said, surprised. "What are you doing here?"*

*"I need to talk to you," she said in a soft, feeble voice; almost as if she thought I might throw her out on the street. I studied her more closely and saw that she had been crying again. Those deep green eyes that I had always loved throughout childhood were puffy and red-rimmed.*

*"What's going on?" I asked her.*

*"Well…" she began, and then put her hands to her face, and began bawling once more.*

*For a moment, we stood there, and I was unsure of what to do.*

*Finally, Mom spoke up. "Why don't we go inside. I'll fix us some tea."*

*She marched ahead and opened the front door. I stood aside to let Dixie through first. The light from our porch bulb shone on her face, and at that moment I saw evidence of not only crying but also signs of having lived a difficult life. It could have simply been the way the light hit her, but right then it looked as though Dixie, at age seventeen, was already developing worry lines across her forehead.*

*She certainly had plenty of good reasons to worry. To know Dixie*

*Johnson was to know what was easily one of the sadder stories in Lake Barrow.*

*She had been born out of wedlock to parents who had never married and lived with her mother, as well as the loser her mother had taken up with several years before. His primary contribution to the family consisted of working odd jobs when he wasn't drinking and pissing away most of what little income the family had when he was. Dixie's mom worked as a custodian for Danforth Properties, and as such, was barely able to make ends meet as the primary breadwinner.*

*On the morning that I had stood in the classroom doorway and seen Mrs. Hanceford praying over her, Dixie had just arrived after witnessing yet another ugly alcohol-related episode at home that morning. And she had broken down after sitting at her desk.*

*Terrible as that incident had been, it paled in comparison to the reason why she had come over to my house that night in the first place.*

*"Are you sure about this?" I asked Dixie.*

*She nodded, as her hands clasped the small teacup that Mom had prepared for her. The three of us sat at our kitchen table.*

*"You were the only one who saw what was happening," Dixie told me. "That's why you're the only one who can help."*

*I glanced over at Mom across the table. Her soft eyes were firm as they looked back at me, letting me know that she agreed with Dixie.*

*"I don't know if I should get involved with this," I said, causing Dixie to look down at her teacup. "There's the team, and my future, and..."*

*"You're already involved, son," Mom said softly. "You didn't intend to be, but you are."*

*I glanced back at Dixie, whose green eyes were filled with tears again, then back at Mom who still had not averted her gaze.*

*"Where do I need to be and when?" I asked Dixie, wondering if I was making a mistake in getting deeper involved than I already was.*

*"Principal's conference room," Dixie said, her voice almost a whis-*

*per. "Tomorrow morning, before the first bell."*

*The morning after Dixie's visit, I sat outside the principal's office and waited.*

*Inside the conference room, everyone was already seated and had been introduced. On one side of the rectangular conference table, there was Dixie, who was flanked by her mother and Judith Rothstein, a legal representative from the Religious Equality Foundation (REF).*

*On the other side sat Marjorie Hanceford, who sat stoic and upright, despite the fact that a bombshell had just been dropped on her moments earlier.*

*Principal Starr sat at the head of the table, where he had a good vantage point of everyone present. Behind him, an assistant principal sat in a wooden chair.*

*"Good morning," Principal Starr said solemnly to the group, knowing full well that it was anything but. He didn't want to be there but knew he had to be, just the same. In his twenty-six years of being an educator, he had never seen a set of circumstances like this one; let alone faced the possibility of a lawsuit like the one he was now faced with.*

*"Let's get going with this," he instructed.*

*Taking her cue, Judith Rothstein spoke first. "As you are aware, Mr. Starr," she said in a raspy voice, "we have here in front of us an unofficial statement from Dixie Johnson, stating that on the morning of September 2, 1997, she was sitting in her first-period classroom with Mrs. Marjorie Hanceford. During this time, Ms. Johnson became distraught and began crying. At the time, Mrs. Hanceford and Ms. Johnson were in Mrs. Hanceford's classroom along with another male student, a Mr. Matthew Danforth. According to Ms. Johnson and Mr. Danforth, Mrs. Hanceford approached Ms. Johnson and began offering prayers as well as quoting Scripture from the Bible in a way that was unsolicited, as well as intrusive and discomforting. So brazen and so forceful was the imposition of these unsolicited gestures from Mrs. Hanceford, that the student and her mother now claim that she was emotionally traumatized as a result."*

*"I was only praying for her," Mrs. Hanceford blurted out, no longer able to control the tears that were starting to come down her face, as she studied her student in disbelief. "Why are you doing this, Dixie?"*

*Principal Starr held up his hand in front of her. "You'll get your chance to speak, Mrs. Hanceford," he said firmly but gently. Turning back to Rothstein, he said, "Please continue."*

*Picking up where she left off, Rothstein went on, "It is our recommendation, given the flagrantly unlawful and unconstitutional nature of the actions behind these accusations, that Mrs. Hanceford's employment be terminated forthwith. If her employment is not terminated, it is our intention to move forward with a lawsuit against the Sims County school district once an official confirmation on the part of the accuser is submitted."*

*With that, she put the paper down, and gave a faint nod to Principal Starr, indicating that she was finished.*

*Principal Starr then turned his attention to Dixie, who was now beginning to fall apart herself.*

*"Is this true?" he asked her.*

*Dixie hesitated, simultaneously gathering her emotions and seeming to waver between two possible answers. A long silence ensued. When Dixie still did not answer after several moments, Rothstein looked at Principal Starr, who narrowed his eyes at Dixie once more.*

*"Dixie?" he asked. "I need you to speak up," he said gently, "and tell us about whether or not that statement that Mrs. Rothstein just read is accurate."*

*Finally, Dixie looked up at her principal with tears brimming in her eyes, and said quietly, "No."*

*All eyes were suddenly on her.*

*"Excuse me?" Rothstein asked, not bothering to control her own anger.*

*"It's not true," Dixie said.*

*Principal Starr looked at Dixie's mother, who was beginning to cry herself.*

*"What is going on here?" Rothstein demanded. "Dixie, you said*

*that you were prepared to sign this statement. Why would you…"*

*"Mrs. Rothstein," Principal Starr said, cutting her off. "I need to hear what Dixie has to say before I make any decision."*

*Rothstein shut up for a moment while Dixie gathered herself.*

*"Tell us the truth, Dixie," the principal said. "Did Mrs. Hanceford force her religion on you?"*

*Dixie sat straight up in her chair and said, "No. She did not."*

*Rothstein gave a faint, exasperated flounce in her chair.*

*"Can anybody else confirm that you were simply being prayed for, and not proselytized?" Principal Starr asked.*

*"Yes."*

*"Who?"*

*"Jayce Leonard," she said without hesitation.*

*Mrs. Hanceford, who was becoming just as confused as Rothstein, albeit not as angry, sat upright in her chair. Principal Starr raised his eyebrows, turned around in his chair, and said to his assistant, "Can you find out where he is?"*

*"He's outside," Dixie said, causing the principal to turn around and face her once more. "Right outside the door."*

*The veteran educator looked surprised. "Right outside the door?"*

*"Yes," Dixie said quietly.*

*"Bring him in," Starr instructed.*

*The assistant principal got up and walked to a second conference room door, which led to the hallway in which I was sitting.*

*I immediately stood up and entered the conference room behind her.*

*"Please have a seat, Mr. Leonard," Principal Starr said, gesturing to a chair near Mrs. Hanceford.*

*I sat down.*

*"We've heard some interesting things this morning," he continued, "and were hoping you could help set the record straight."*

*I nodded, ready to do my part.*

*"Mrs. Rothstein, would you please re-read the statement you have in front of you?"*

*The stout lawyer began to read. Before she could get halfway through, though, I interrupted her.*

"It's not true," I said.

"Excuse me!" Rothstein barked at me, causing Principal Starr to put up his hand once more and wave her off. She was an out-of-town lawyer who was losing ground on his territory, and Starr knew it. He could shut her up if he wanted to.

"It's not true?" Principal Starr asked me to confirm.

"Not at all," I confirmed. "I was standing there in the doorway when the whole thing was happening. All Mrs. Hanceford was doing was praying."

I looked at Mrs. Hanceford, who gave me a grateful smile.

"Matt Danforth is lying," I said.

"Lying, huh?" Principal Starr said. He looked at Dixie's mother, who looked down and seemed to refuse eye contact with him. Principal Starr knew the history behind the Gills and the Danforths, as well as that Marty Danforth was Brenda's employer, and was beginning to see everything.

"I don't suppose," Principal Starr continued, looking at me, "that Matt would be willing to come down here and back up your side of the story would he?"

I shrugged. "I can't speak for him, sir, but my guess would be no."

Principal Starr just nodded, a look of understanding spreading across his face.

With the exception of Judith Rothstein, who wasn't from Lake Barrow, everyone else in that room was getting the picture.

Matt had complained to his daddy about how badly he was supposedly being mistreated by Mrs. Hanceford during class. When he saw her praying with Dixie that morning before the first bell, he had seen an opportunity to do something about it. After hearing from his son about what he had seen, Marty had put together a plan to get Margery (Gill) Hanceford fired from her job, ostensibly for religious proselytization of Dixie Johnson. He had enlisted the legal help of the Religious Equality Foundation, an organization dedicated to keeping religion out of schools, and used Dixie's mom's employment as leverage to gain her co-operation. He then forced Dixie and her mom to file a complaint against Mrs. Hanceford and the school district in cooperation with REF, and *threaten to file a lawsuit (something our school district could ill-afford), in exchange for which Brenda would keep her job. On the other hand, if she didn't cooperate with Marty, she would be fired.*

*The whole thing stunk, but then it wasn't really about litigation, or religion, or prayer in the first place. It was about a seven-year-old real estate deal gone bad that had started a war between two wealthy families and was now holding a helpless woman and her daughter hostage, who were struggling to remain just above the poverty line.*

*The only problem for the Danforths was that they didn't count on the fact that Dixie would have the courage to approach me about setting the record straight, since I was the only other person besides her and Matt who had seen what had actually happened; or that I would have the courage to step forward and speak up.*

*"Would you be willing," Principal Starr asked me, "to put your side of things in writing so that we can end this nonsense?"*

*"Yessir," I said sincerely.*

*"Mrs. Rothstein?" he asked, looking at her.*

*"Fine," she said, defeated. We didn't hear much out of her after that, save for some mumbling about "rednecks wasting her time."*

*Once REF had my statement on record, that was pretty much the end of the business. Judith Rothstein stormed out of the office soon thereafter and was gone for good.*

*Dixie started crying again as she approached Mrs. Hanceford.*

*"I'm so sorry," she told her teacher, who would now keep her job.*

*Brenda, also in tears, walked over, hugged Mrs. Hanceford, and began apologizing profusely as well.*

*Our teacher said nothing, but reached out and hugged both of them close to her.*

*I think, for Dixie and I, the only thing sweeter than knowing that we had done a good thing for a teacher we both loved was knowing that we had single-handedly foiled the schemes of the great Marty Danforth.*

*Later that day, Marty Danforth sat fuming in his spacious office*

*in downtown Lake Barrow. He had just received the news of his failed ploy against the Gills.*

*The door to his office swung open, and Marty was surprised to see Brenda standing in the doorway, glaring at him as if her eyes had daggers in them. Behind her, a frazzled secretary was barking about how she "couldn't just barge in here like this."*

*"It's okay, Peg," Danforth said firmly to his secretary while returning Brenda's glare. His cold blue eyes, which were framed by a head full of thick black hair, bore into her as his six-foot stocky frame towered over her frail, thin one. "I need to talk to her anyway. Come on in, Brenda, so that we can talk about your job security going forward."*

*The secretary closed the door, and Brenda strode up to her boss.*

*"Just tell me exactly…" Marty began.*

*POP!*

*Marty saw a flash of light, followed immediately by dark spots, as the blow from her fist made contact with his chin. Unable to speak as his eyes adjusted to the spinning room, he simply stared at his lowly employee, who was also carrying her uniform blouse with the words "Danforth Properties" embroidered on one breast, and her name on the other.*

*She said nothing, but threw the blouse down at his feet, turned on her heels, and stormed out.*

*Once word got out about what Marty Danforth had tried to pull, the Danforths' reputation and standing in the community took a hit. They still remained in Lake Barrow, but they definitely kept a lower profile than they ever did before.*

*A week later, Dixie's mom would show up to work at Barrow Foods, where she would be trained as an assistant manager by my mother. Not long after she began her new job, she kicked her loser boyfriend out of her life forever. After that, she and Dixie became closer than ever before.*

*Two other people who became closer after the whole incident were Jim Gill and me.*

# CHAPTER SEVEN

# Summer 2002

Deke and Ahmad came over later that evening, following the funeral and the get-together at the Gills'.

Mom was sitting on the sofa as they entered through the front door. She had seen Deke during several of his visits home since he had gone pro. However, it had been a couple of years since she had seen Ahmad. The two of them hugged as they came into the house.

Ahmad was the third member of our senior class to sign a Division 1 scholarship and had enrolled at Delta State University in Mississippi following graduation. He had starred at receiver before earning a degree in business management. After graduation, he had been hired with a company in Fort Lauderdale that sold electronics and cutting-edge software. The tech industry was booming during the early part of the new millennium, and Ahmad had jumped on the opportunity he had been given to do well for himself financially and professionally. This was no surprise given that, of the four of us, he had always been the best student. We were all fairly smart, but Ahmad outpaced us when it came to academics, largely because of his work ethic and discipline.

Mom offered to cook us something, but we declined. After the feast at the Gills earlier that day, none of us were hungry. It was just as well, given how tired she looked. Moments later, sure enough, she excused herself and said goodnight to us all before heading to the back.

"She's doing better huh?" Ahmad asked me after she had left.

"Much better," I said. "Physical therapy's helped a lot."

"She still working for Mr. Gill?" Deke asked.

"Yeah," I nodded.

"Must be a load off your mind," Ahmad said.

"It is," I affirmed.

"So what do you guys want to do?" Ahmad asked, looking around. "I guess your mom got rid of your PlayStation, 'cause I don't see it around here. Otherwise, I'd say let's play some Madden."

I laughed. "It's up in Yearwood," I said. "I didn't even think to bring it. I probably should have, though, especially since my roommate doesn't even play video games."

"Are you still rooming with the same guy?" Deke asked. "Saul, or whatever his name was."

"Soul," I said.

"Your roommate's name is Soul?" Ahmad asked with a laugh.

I nodded. "Been roommates since freshman year. He's a grad assistant with me now."

"Must be a good singer if his momma named him Soul," Ahmad said.

I chuckled. "Short for Soulemain. His dad's family's from Iran."

"One of your receivers, wasn't he?" Deke asked.

"My best one, actually," I said. "Guy could outrun a deer and hardly ever dropped a pass."

"I'm surprised he didn't go pro," Deke said.

"He probably could have if he hadn't gotten injured during

his senior year," I said, remembering our that fateful season.

"That's too bad," Deke said.

"He'll make a great coach someday, though," I said.

"You will too," Ahmad said. "Skipper gonna hire you on as an assistant?"

"I don't know," I said. "From what I've been hearing, there's a possibility that I could get offered a job, but we'll see. Never thought I'd be back here, that's for sure."

"Coach Jayce Leonard of the Sims County Spartans," Deke said. "Has a nice ring to it."

I smiled. "What about you?" I asked Ahmad. "You gonna give up the 9 to 5 soon and come join the coaching ranks?"

"Me?" Ahmad said. "No way, man. My glory days are over."

"As a player," I said, "but your coaching days might just be starting."

"He's making too much money," Deke said. "I wouldn't give it up, either."

"Easy for you to say," I needled Deke. "You're making millions yourself."

Deke grinned.

"I've thought about coaching, actually," Ahmad said. "But who knows? Maybe someday."

"So where are we going?" I turned to Deke.

"I say we get a drink somewhere," Ahmad offered.

"I got something else in mind," Deke said, with a wry smile.

Ahmad and I glanced at each other.

Deke said nothing but looked at me. "You boys feel like moving a bit tonight?"

Moments later, we pulled into the parking lot of our old high school football field house. It was pitch dark, and the lights surrounding the football field were turned off.

"Well, this was an idea," I said, as all three of us got out of Deke's 2002 Mercedes.

"What are we doing here?" Ahmad asked.

"What kind of question is that?" Deke replied, tossing Ahmad one of two footballs that he was carrying. Ahmad caught it and gave him a quizzical stare. "After all the ball you played, you don't know what to do when you see a ball field?"

"Yeah, but it's dark," Ahmad protested.

"Are we suiting up and hitting each other?" I asked.

Deke laughed. "That'd be a good way to piss off my agent, that's for sure."

Suddenly, the stadium lights flickered and began to come on.

"Who else is here?" I asked Deke.

Deke laughed. "Same person that's here all the time."

I smiled. "Ol' Beezer."

Sure enough, a shadowy figure began to emerge from the football field, and all three of us immediately recognized Frank Beezer, who had been the groundskeeper at Sims County High for as long as any of us could remember.

Beezer, as he was commonly called, was wearing the exact same thing that he had worn the last time I had seen him over four years ago; blue working coveralls that hung loosely from his wiry frame, with a green and white Spartan jacket; no color coordination whatsoever, but then Beezer's job had never called for much in the way of style points. He wore a red baseball cap that was almost too big for his head and was perched awkwardly on top of it so that it appeared as though a gentle breeze could knock it off. Additionally, he wore thick prescription lenses, reminiscent of the style in which Harry Caray, the venerable old Chicago Cubs baseball announcer, used to wear his.

It was the jacket, however, that defined Frank Beezer, in more ways than one. The fact that it was summer in Florida and the temperature was somewhere well north of ninety degrees didn't matter; Frank Beezer rarely took off his Spartan jacket, which would forever be a symbol of his allegiance to the mighty Spartans of Sims County.

"That you, Deke?" Beezer called out in his trademark nasal southern drawl as he came toward us.

"It's me," Deke affirmed. "How you doing, Beez?"

Beezer let out a chuckle and hurried toward us, moving fast for a man who was over seventy. He was small and thin but had always seemed to have the energy of a teenager, which I suppose is what made him the ideal fit for his job. His eyes, magnified by the glasses, were bright, and his expression was jovial, like a kid at Christmas, as he jogged up and hugged Deke.

"So glad you came home, Deke," he beamed. "It's great to see you again."

"It's great to be home," Deke returned with a smile.

"Sorry it had to be under such sad circumstances, though," Beezer said with a sudden frown. "Jamie was a good boy, and I know he'll be missed."

Deke nodded and agreed with him.

"And he died fighting for our freedom, so we can be thankful for that."

"I know that's right."

"Who are your friends?"

Deke chuckled. "Now come on, Beezer, I was sure you'd recognize these fellas."

Beezer turned, his bug eyes studying me for a moment. "That's Jimmy Westmore, isn't it?" he finally asked.

Deke laughed out loud, and I stifled a giggle, at the realization that Beezer had me confused with a kid that had been kicked off the team during our ninth grade year for smoking weed. He remembered everybody.

"No, Beezer," Deke said.

Beezer was skeptical, though. "Aren't you the one," he

asked, pointing a finger at me, "that Faraday kicked off the team for smoking that reefer nonsense?"

"No, Beezer, that wasn't me," I said simply.

"Beez, that's Jayce Leonard," Deke said. "He was quarterback our senior year."

"That's Jayce Leonard?" Beezer asked, surprised.

"Yep."

"Oh," he said with a laugh. "You'll have to forgive me, Jayce," he said, reaching out and shaking my hand. "My eyesight just isn't what it used to be."

"No problem," I said, feeling the sandpaper texture of his hand as we shook.

"Now you're the one who beat out Danforth's boy for the quarterback spot, aren't you?"

"That's right."

"I tell you, that was the smartest thing Faraday could have done that year," he said. "That boy couldn't break wet tissue paper with his throws, and had an even nastier attitude, as I recall."

All three of us laughed and nodded.

"Dern shame what they tried to do to Margery Hanceford," he went on. "Thank goodness that meddling group of lawyers never decided to sue us."

Deke and I exchanged a quick knowing glance.

"And who are you?" Beezer asked, turning to Ahmad.

"Ahmad Floyd," he answered, extending his hand, which Frank accepted.

"Oh yeah," Beezer said, "I remember you. Wide receiver, played for Delta State, right?"

"That's right."

"See there," Beezer chuckled, pointing to his head. "My eyesight may be going, but at least my memory's still somewhat intact."

We all laughed.

"You caught a few of this guy's touchdowns, didn't you?"

Beezer asked Ahmad, gesturing to me.

"I caught a few," Ahmad said modestly.

"Dropped a few, too," I said, causing Ahmad to beam the football at me, which I caught.

"Speaking of footballs," Beezer said to Deke, "did you bring mine?"

"Sure did," Deke affirmed, handing him the other one that he had brought out of the car. Beezer looked it over and smiled when he saw the signature near the laces.

"The great Deke Hudson," he said, looking up as though Deke had just given him a bar of gold. "Got his start out there on my field and is now an NFL running back. I can't thank you enough, friend."

Beezer beamed with pride. He had always referred to Jim Gill Stadium at Spartan Field as *his* field. And truthfully, it was hard to argue with him. Beezer had never married, though some people joked that he was unofficially married to our field, since he had devoted almost all of his entire adult life to keep it looking good as new, no matter how bad the weather turned. Frank Beezer cared for our field like most men his age care for their aging brides.

"Don't mention it, Beez," Deke said good-naturedly as they shook hands. "It's good to see you again."

"Good to see you boys, too. And she's all yours," he added, gesturing to the field. "Stay as long as you want."

"Thanks, Beezer."

# Chapter Eight

"What was Beezer's reaction when you told him we were coming up?" I asked as we made our way onto the grass.

"Almost shit a brick," Deke answered.

The three of us laughed and began tossing the football back and forth.

"Told him I was coming into town for the funeral," Deke went on. "That's when he asked for an autographed ball, and I told him I'd get him one if he lit up the field one night while I was here."

"Shrewd," I said.

"I thought so," he replied, throwing me the ball. Ahmad broke out into a medium-speed run downfield, as I planted my feet and lobbed a deep, arcing pass his way. Ahmad caught it in stride and ran a few more yards as if he were headed to the end zone. My memory bank stirred again; how many of those had we completed under these same lights?

For the next several minutes, the three of us threw the ball to each other across the field, all the while laughing and joking and feeling like kids again. We nonchalantly made our way from one end zone to the other; each yard line, it seemed, holding a memory of some kind, some good and some not so good.

And yet, Jamie's absence in the midst of it all was a hole that none of us spoke of. Truth was, none of us needed to speak of it. His not being there was like the thick mugginess that always came out during that time of year, especially at night after the sun had gone down; not able to be seen, but always palpable. For the rest of our lives, as long as Deke, Ahmad, and I kept in touch, there would always be one more empty seat at the restaurants; one less target to throw the ball to; one less beer to order; one less target to rag on with our jokes; one less confidant to lean on whenever life got any one of us by the balls; one less Christmas card to send out; and one less person to celebrate life's milestones with.

One less friend.

It was on all of our minds that evening, as the stadium lights cut through the foggy humidity and lit up the night sky. But none of us said anything. We were the same, but different, especially when it came to how we grieved. Those moments where our loss of Jamie hit closest to home for each of us would come at different times; just like our own deaths. But for that night, all that mattered was the grass of the field beneath our feet. In those moments beneath the blinding white light, we weren't big league pros, or sales professionals, or graduate assistant coaches. It didn't matter how much, or how little, money we had in the bank, or how we were struggling personally or professionally. The divergent paths that had taken us away from Lake Barrow and into the wider world, where we were now trying to find our way as men in our early twenties, had somehow led us back here for this one night. And it was here that we had temporarily shuffled off the cares of the world and reaffirmed our commitment to each other; to our unofficial brotherhood which had been forged in the fires of sports, of disagreements, of fistfights, and of child's play.

At that moment beneath the lights, all we had was each

other.

Deke caught the ball and came jogging back toward me. "Man, look at this," he said with mock indignation. "My shirt's soaked, and you've barely broken a sweat. That ain't right."

I studied him for a moment. Sure enough, a large part of his gray t-shirt with the emblazoned Florida Gator logo was darkened with perspiration.

"Don't get mad at me," I said. "It's not my fault you got lazy during the off-season."

Deke abruptly drew his arm back, as though he would beam me with the football.

"You should let me enjoy it, too," I added. "Not everyone gets to brag about being in better shape than an NFL running back."

"That's because not all NFL running backs would give you the satisfaction," Deke replied.

All three of us laughed.

"Seriously, though," he said, "I want to see you go deep for a few passes. Get some sweat on those clothes."

I thought for a moment, then finally said, "If sweat's what you want out of me, we don't need to keep playing catch. I've got a better idea."

I started making my way over to where our concrete bleachers were.

Deke and Ahmad followed me hesitantly.

"Last time I heard you say, 'I've got a better idea,'" Ahmad said, keeping up, "you and I almost broke our necks climbing up on your roof to get the Frisbee that got stuck up there. And all we had to do was go buy another one. But no, your adventurous ass almost got us killed."

"We're still alive, aren't we?" I asked, without turning around. "Didn't break anything, as I recall. And we're certainly not going to break anything tonight, though it might feel as though you did once we're through."

"Jayce, you got me worried, man," Deke said with a nervous laugh. "What exactly are we doing?"

I just grinned at him and began stretching a little. I had learned the hard way not to forget about properly warming up before doing what we were about to do.

"Just follow my lead," I said.

Twenty minutes later, all three of us lay on the asphalt of the track circling the football field as we fought desperately to catch our breath.

"Soul sprints," Ahmad gasped.

"Named after Soul Rasheed, my roommate," I barely breathed.

"Your roommate came up with that crap?"

I nodded as I forced my lungs to inhale the sticky night air. "He introduced them to our team several years ago and no one's forgiven him since."

"I can see why," Deke panted. "You just lost your free Bucs tickets, man."

"You're the one who wanted to see me sweat," I returned.

"I didn't want to die in the process."

I grinned. We had started out the exercise ritual known as "soul sprints" by running to the top of the stadium steps, running back down, and taking a lap around the entire football field. This was followed by a set of thirty push-ups, a set of thirty flutter-kicks on our backs, and finally a set of thirty "burpees"; which was a series of callisthenic movements that were probably invented by someone who liked making other people suffer…someone like Soul Rasheed, for example.

For as long as I live, I'll never forget the first day the Yearwood State Mustangs were introduced to the infamous exercises invented by Soul, who had always been in better physical shape than just about anyone else on the team. He had just recently brought them to the attention of the coaching staff, and wouldn't you know it? They just couldn't *wait* to implement them right away so that their players could get into optimal shape as soon as possible.

"Jayce, man, what were you thinking?" Ahmad asked as we hobbled toward the bleachers.

"Good question," I said, shaking my head, as we made our way up the first step, decided that was far enough, and sat down.

Taking a seat was a ginger process, which probably made us look like we were about Frank Beezer's age, rather than in the prime physical condition of our lives.

"How many times did we do that?" Deke asked.

"Whole routine?" I asked.

Deke nodded.

I thought for a moment. "About five or six sets."

"Then that's five or six more than I ever want to do again," Deke said.

I smiled, as we continued recovering from the beating we'd put our bodies through. None of us said anything for what seemed like several minutes as we gazed out at the field and let the memories wash over us in the thick night air.

There was the east end zone, where we had gathered before each game to recite the Lord's Prayer and get ready to tear through the spirit banner.

There was the spot on our sideline, right at midfield, where Coach Skipper, then our offensive coordinator, had stood with me on Friday nights as we went over plays, mistakes, and tweaks for this or that formation, even making up plays on a few occasions.

My eyes drifted back to the thirty-five-yard line; the spot from which I had thrown my very first touchdown pass as a senior, a long bullet to Ahmad, and the first of many that I would throw that season. This was despite having an all-everything running back in Deke as our star. In fact, our coaching staff's decision to open up the offense and put my decent throwing arm to use, as a complement to Deke's otherworldly running ability, had taken a lot of people by surprise, including me. Why on earth would any decent coach who had a running back like Deke Hudson reduce the number of carries he was getting? It seemed like a gamble at the time, though it certainly benefited me at an individual level, especially once Yearwood State came to town with a scholarship offer.

I looked to the other thirty-five, where I had scrambled during a play against San Mateo Catholic, just before being stripped of the ball. It was the fourth quarter with just over a minute to play, and we were tied with the Crusaders at 38. After picking up a crucial first down, all I had to do was run out of bounds, like I had been coached to do. Instead, I got greedy, and decided to run for more yardage; "be a hot-shot," as Coach Faraday yelled at me afterward. As I was being tackled, one of San Mateo Catholic's defenders knocked the ball loose, and the Crusaders recovered.

After recovering my fumble inbounds, San Mateo Catholic drove downfield, bled the clock down to two seconds, called time out, and kicked a game-winning field goal.

It was our team's only regular season loss, and it hurt; especially given that my selfish desire to be a hero had cost us the game. That moment, more than most, had taught me the importance of being a team player.

The next week we took out our frustration on Barton City, beating them by a score of 65-0, winning district, and advancing all the way to the second round of the playoffs. The fact that Barton City was our hated rival only made that victory sweeter.

For me, that's when the roller coaster had begun. Yearwood State came calling the very next week and offered me a scholarship. Mom's accident happened not long thereafter, and Jim Gill had stepped in to help us not long after that.

"Anything's possible when you're that age," Deke said, looking out at the field.

I nodded, and we were silent for another moment.

Just beyond our west end zone was the practice field, where I had taken over as starting quarterback. I'll never forget that day as long as I live, either.

I was in with the second-team offense, going against our first-team defense. As the snap from the center had hit my hands, I lost control of it and fumbled. Thankfully, however, I had picked it right back up. By that time, though, the play was busted, so I improvised; taking off to my left, I sprinted toward the sideline, got the corner, and ended up scoring one of the most unlikely touchdowns anyone had ever seen on our practice field. I had always been a decent athlete with pretty foot speed, and after dodging and eluding one tackler after another, I soon found myself in the end zone.

The coaches were ecstatic, at least on the offensive side. On defense, however, Jamie and his fellow defenders got their butts chewed pretty thoroughly by Coach Faraday for missing a tackle on the second-string quarterback.

I wouldn't be second string for much longer.

Matt Danforth soon returned with the first-team offense and proceeded to have miscue after miscue. He'd had a decent junior year, but for some reason, was having trouble putting things together on the field as a senior. On top of that, his attitude toward his teammates and the coaching staff was atrocious, just as it always had been. That afternoon, with him continually fumbling handoffs to Deke and then yelling at his center and at Deke for messing up, Coach Skipper decided he'd finally had enough. Matt was out, and I was in.

*At least Jayce can make a play with the ball when he fumbles,* I remember overhearing Skipper tell another assistant coach. *All Danforth makes are excuses.*

As I sat there on the bleachers that evening, reminiscing silently, Deke turned to me. "You ever hear what happened to Danforth?" he asked, causing me to wonder if his train of thought had been the same as mine.

I shook my head. "Last I heard, he had flunked out of college and was back here working for Pops."

"His little brother's doing well," Ahmad added. "Playing QB for Barton City."

"Morgan Danforth's starting for Barton City?" I asked.

Ahmad nodded. "Boy's good, too, from what I hear."

"Guess that's one apple that fell far from the tree," Deke said.

"Sounds like it."

"What do you have planned for the rest of the time home?" Deke asked me after a moment.

I grinned. "I'm going out with Meredith tomorrow night."

"Meredith Lee?" Deke asked with an incredulous glance. "Who else?"

"Whoo, man," Deke said, with a laugh. "There's a blast from your past. How'd you hook that up?"

"She was at the Gills' today," I said. "Asked me out."

"Listen to him," Deke said to Ahmad with a laugh. "'Asked you out.'"

"You can do better than that, though, man," Ahmad said to me. "Besides, that was high school, and y'all were only together because of the game. You need to get you a real woman."

"I don't see a woman hanging around you," I replied to Ahmad.

"That's 'cause I ain't in no hurry," Ahmad said.

"I ain't either," Deke agreed. "I gotta wade through all the gold-diggers before I settle down," Deke said, causing all three of us to laugh. "Shoot, man, I've had women throw their underwear at me from the stands."

"That's a lie," I chided.

Deke smiled. "Might as well be true, though."

"Hey, seriously, though," Ahmad said, "tell me this ain't right. Any woman Deke ends up with needs to just come home and meet his parents."

"Why is that?" Deke asked.

"Because if that woman can pass muster with both your parents, then you know she's a keeper."

"That's true," I agreed.

"Mikayla, too," Ahmad added, referring to Deke's only sister, who was a senior at UF and ran track.

"*That's* the truth," Deke said to Ahmad. "Only other person I know with a B.S. detector better than my mom's is Mikayla. She'll have it sorted out before anybody."

We went on for several more minutes, just chatting and shooting the breeze like we'd always done.

Suddenly, Deke began to cackle loudly from the pit of his stomach as he looked down at the field. Ahmad and I followed his gaze until we saw what was making him laugh.

Frank Beezer was now holding his autographed football and pretending to drop back and throw a deep pass. All the while, he was narrating his own movements as though he were both quarterback and commentator.

*Frank Beezer drops back, looks downfield, sees Jerry Rice open, fires it deep, it's CAUGHT FOR A TOUCHDOWN!!!*

"So that's what he does during the off-season when he' s up here by himself," Deke said.

"At least he's got a better arm than Danforth ever did," I quipped.

"Or Jayce Leonard, for that matter."

I elbowed Deke in one of his massive arms, as we continued watching Frank, who didn't even seem to realize that he was being watched.

After a few moments, Deke got up slowly. "Oooh," he said, "we should have done some kind of cool-down after that workout."

"Yeah, I guess so," I said, struggling as I rose.

"You should tell your roommate to come up with something like that," Ahmad said. "Call it 'Soul Chill.'"

"I'll mention it," I told him.

"And I might put in a good word for soul sprints when I get back to Tampa," Deke said.

"Yeah?"

"Kicked my butt tonight, but I could see those being beneficial, actually."

"I don't think Soul has them copyrighted yet," I answered. "Go for it."

Deke chuckled. "Who knows? They might even help us win the Super Bowl this year."

"Y'all ain't gonna win the Super Bowl this year," I argued. "Running game sucks too bad."

"All right, then," Deke said calmly. "If the Tampa Bay Bucs win the Super Bowl this year, you owe me a steak dinner."

"You're on," I said, not knowing then just how lousy a gamble I was making.

# Chapter Nine

My legs and upper body were still killing me the next evening as I pulled into the parking lot of Guadalajara Mexican Restaurant just in time to meet Meredith. It had been almost a year since I had done a soul sprint and, even at my young age, I was paying for the six I had done the day before.

I stretched gingerly as I got out of the car, and studied the outside of the only Mexican restaurant in Lake Barrow. Guadalajara had aged a little and appeared in need of some slight renovation, but other than that, it looked pretty much the same as when I had patronized it during my last visit home. Its structure was mostly yellow, save for the deep lavender-painted decorative columns that were partially embedded into the concrete. The few windows facing the parking lot were small and tinted, so as to minimize the amount of light that spilled in during the day. On the double doors leading into the restaurant were paintings of rural settings, characterized by bright colors and images which augmented the restaurant's décor perfectly, and were probably inspired by some distant village deep in the heart of Mexico.

As I approached the mural doors, I took advantage of the little bit of daylight that still remained to check my reflection in the adjacent window. After giving my button-down dress shirt and khakis a once-over, I ran my hands through my hair once more before heading inside. As I opened the door, my heart began to race.

*It's just dinner,* I told myself, trying in vain to push from my mind the memory of Meredith hugging me the day before.

Whatever renovation was needed on the outside of the building, a person wouldn't know it from inside. The dining room was as decorative and up-to-date as it could be; walls adorned with additional pictures and frescos of small Mexican towns, as well as maracas, sombreros, and other artifacts that signified that this was as close to our neighbor to the south as you would get in the heart of central Florida.

In the center of the dining area was a large fountain with multi-colored lights that illuminated the basin, into which patrons occasionally threw coins.

A few people were seated at tables interspersed throughout the dining room, but things were relatively quiet. I looked around for Meredith, but she was nowhere to be found.

*"Buenas noches, Senor Jayce,"* said a male voice. I turned and smiled as Ignacio, an older man in his early fifties who had worked at the restaurant since its opening, came toward me. His English was flawless, though he greeted everyone in Spanish.

*"Buenas noches,* Ignacio" I returned, utilizing the little bit of Spanish I remembered from high school. "Uh, *Como te llamas?"*

Ignacio laughed. *"Me llamo Ignacio,"* he said. "I thought you knew my name."

"My bad," I grinned, realizing my mistake. "Been a few years. *Como estas?"*

*"Muy bien. Y tu?"*

*"Bien, gracias,"* I returned. "How's Squat-and-Holler?"

Ignacio grimaced, causing the furrows in his weather-beaten face to deepen. "You know I hate it when you kids refer to my restaurant with that nickname."

I shrugged. "Sounds almost the same as 'Guadalajara' and it often fits, depending on what you order off the menu."

Ignacio just shook his head. "I'll pass that along to the cook," he said. "He's been known to spit in people's food if they're disrespectful."

"Explains why this place is never busy," I smirked.

Ignacio grinned and ran his finger through his thin, graying hair. "You by yourself?"

"I'm actually meeting someone," I said.

He raised his eyebrows. "Who?"

"Meredith Lee."

Ignacio grinned. "Old girlfriend, huh?"

"It's just dinner," I tried to convince him.

"Follow me to your table," he motioned with a twinkle in his eye.

A half hour later, I was still waiting. Fifteen minutes after that, I was ready to go home.

It was the first time I had ever been stood up on a date, and it stung a little. The fact that I had been looking forward to reconnecting with Meredith made it even worse.

Ignacio seemed to put two and two together when he came over to take my order.

"Want a Corona to go with those quesadillas?" he asked, trying to conceal his pity.

"No thanks," I told him. "Just the check."

Ignacio gave me a sympathetic pat on the shoulder as he walked away.

I needed to pack for the trip home the next day and get some rest, so maybe it was just as well, I thought to myself.

Suddenly, I heard a female voice behind me. "Jayce?"

I turned and saw one of the restaurant's waitresses standing a few feet from my table. She was a familiar-looking young woman who looked to be about my age, and who wore a t-shirt with the "Guadalajara" logo on it, a waitress' apron, short black shorts, and athletic shoes with ankle socks.

"You don't recognize me, do you?" she chuckled.

My mind continued struggling, as I studied her. Her curly blonde hair was pulled back into a ponytail which framed her angular face. However, it was the deep, dark green eyes that finally caused my memory to flash.

Dixie Johnson.

I got up from my table and greeted her as we hugged. "It's great to see you," I told her.

As the initial shock wore off, I studied her some more. In some ways, she still looked the same. She was still short, and her body still had the same plumpness that had always characterized her build throughout childhood and adolescence, though she definitely had matured and was wearing the weight well as she stood before me in the restaurant.

"You too," she responded with a smile, seeming to give me a look-over herself.

"How long have you worked here?" I asked.

"About three years," she answered. "Just trying to finish school in Orlando."

"That's great," I said, still not able to take my eyes off of her.

"Are you here with somebody?" she asked, looking around.

"No," I said quickly, and a little too enthusiastically. "I mean, I was, but...or actually, I was going to be...but now I'm not."

Dixie smiled.

"You look great," I said.

"Thanks," she said. "You do too. Are you still playing ball?"

"No, I graduated," I said. "Coaching some, though.

Graduate assistant; mostly just putting together game film and helping with practices."

Dixie nodded. "How's your mom doing?"

"She's good," I answered. "Doing better, thanks to physical therapy. How's yours?"

"She's doing well," Dixie said. "Still at Barrow Foods, thanks to your mom. She's also about to get married," Dixie added.

"That's good."

"Yeah, she's happy," she said. "So how long are you in town for?"

"Until tomorrow," I answered, suddenly wishing I was staying longer.

"Gotcha," she said, apparently working to conceal her own disappointment. "I guess you came down for Jamie's funeral."

"Yeah."

"I was sorry to hear about what happened."

"Me too," I told her.

"Well listen," she said, "I think Ignacio has your check ready and I should probably be getting back to work. But it was great seeing you again."

"You too," I said, suddenly wanting the conversation to continue.

"I hope I get to see you again," she said, turning to walk away. "Maybe next time you're in town, try and stop by."

"Yeah."

Dixie turned to walk away.

"Hey, Dixie," I said, my throat suddenly starting to go dry.

She turned to face me. "Yeah?"

"What time do you get off tonight?"

A half hour later, I stood outside the restaurant and waited for her to meet me. Soon, the door opened, and I was slightly disappointed to see Ignacio emerge. He put a cigarette between his lips, lit it, and chuckled when he saw me.

"She's almost out," he said with a wry smile. "Don't worry. Not even you could get stood up twice in the same night."

"You're funny," I retorted. "Getting stood up probably happens a lot in a place as nasty as Squat-and-Holler."

He laughed.

The doors opened again, and Dixie emerged, still wearing her work uniform. Her long curly hair was down now, and despite the darkness, I thought I could see fresh lipstick and some makeup as well.

"Went a little heavy on the fragrance, huh?" Ignacio quipped as she passed him.

"Good night, Ignacio," Dixie replied.

He laughed again, as we walked away.

"So how did your mom meet her fiancé?" I asked Dixie, as we sat outside a local ice cream place that was open late.

"At a health foods conference in Daytona Beach," she answered, as she took a bite of cookies and cream from a cup. "About two years ago. The store sent her there to look into purchasing a line of organic brands. Her fiancé is vice president of one of the companies that were there. They hit it off, and the rest is history."

"Cool," I said, eating a spoonful of chocolate chip cookie dough. "When's the wedding?"

"December."

"Are you going to give her away?" I asked with a smile.

Dixie laughed and shook her head. "It's going to be much simpler than that. Neither of them wants a big wedding, which is kind of nice, actually."

"Do you like him?"

Dixie nodded. "He's awesome. Treats her well, and has really helped us both get back into shape. He's a big reason why I don't look like I used to."

"You look great," I said sincerely.

"Thanks," she said. "I feel great."

"Dated anybody since high school?" I asked.

"Not seriously," she said. "Just a couple of one-timers, though I have had plenty of other opportunities since I started working at good ol' Squat and Holler."

I laughed.

"Ignacio doesn't let us call it that while we're working," she said. "Off duty is fair game, though."

I grinned. "So you get hit on a lot during your shifts?"

Dixie nodded as she took another spoonful. "You'd actually be surprised at how many of your former teammates have come in there and hit on me…several of whom were even wearing wedding rings, which was kind of sad."

"Care to name names?"

She shook her head. "Really not worth mentioning. It's just funny because they obviously don't remember me from high school."

"I certainly wouldn't have if you hadn't spoken up," I said.

She grinned as she cast a sidelong glance at me. *Those green eyes again.*

"How about you?" she asked. "Any girlfriends over the past four years?"

"One," I said. "We broke up."

"What happened?"

I shrugged. "Different paths. She's a hometown girl whose dream was to move back to her small Kentucky town after graduation, with her new husband in tow, and live on her parents' property."

Dixie chuckled. "Not a fan of hometown girls, huh?"

"Just not the ones who want me to work for their dad's concrete business for the next forty years, and take over the company one day."

She ate another bite and smiled.

"I want to coach," I said. "Been my dream for a long time now, and I might get to do it sooner rather than later."

"I thought you were already coaching."

"Yes and no," I said. "Graduate assistant work is about as entry level as it gets. I want to have my own team one day."

"What do you mean by 'sooner rather than later'?"

I then told Dixie about what Jim Gill had said to me about being an assistant coach at Sims County. "It'd be a step closer," I said.

"One step at a time," she said.

"How about you?" I asked. "What are you studying?"

"Education," she said. "I wouldn't mind teaching, but I really want to be a guidance counselor; help kids who are having a tough time."

"I think you'd be good at that," I said.

We were silent for a while. The ice cream place was located near a wooded thicket, and the crickets were the only sound that could be heard, aside from the occasional car that passed. Dixie and I had rarely spoken to each other since elementary school, and yet here we were, chatting as if that long period of middle and high school where we'd been driven apart by social circumstances had never existed. Somehow, our re-connection had been almost immediate.

"Did you see Mrs. Hanceford at the funeral?" she asked.

"Yeah," I nodded, "briefly."

"How's she doing?"

I shrugged. "Taking Jamie hard," I said, "like everybody else."

Dixie nodded, looked away, and was silent for a moment. Finally, she asked, "Do you ever think about what happened back when we were seniors?"

"Yeah, sometimes," I said, looking at her.

Dixie shook her head. "I'm still amazed that people can be that cruel," she said. "I look back at my mom's old boyfriend and how awful he was to us, as well as how bad school was for me back then." She paused. "And I just can't see any of it being as awful as what Matt and his dad did to us."

"You mean, 'tried to do,'" I clarified, glancing at her.

"Yeah," she smiled at me. "And the ironic thing is that it really wasn't done directly to me."

I kept listening.

"I just don't think I could have lived with myself if I had gotten Mrs. Hanceford fired, Jayce, no matter how much I was coerced," she said.

"But you didn't," I said smiling.

"Thanks to you," she said.

"And you," I said, causing her to smile like I had never noticed before.

Off in the distance, a jackrabbit scampered hesitantly across the grassy area and toward a nearby thicket. He then froze, almost as if he expected a fox to pounce on him at any moment.

"Small towns are strange," Dixie said. "You grow up around some of the kindest people and the most evil-hearted people all at once. Sometimes it's like you're walking a fine line between the two since you never truly know which side someone's going to end up on."

I listened as I watched the rabbit take off into the woods in a skittish scamper, never to be seen again.

"I don't think I ever really thanked you for what you did for me, Jayce," she said, looking at me.

I turned and faced her. "Sure you did."

"How?"

"By hanging out with me tonight," I said with a grin.

She smiled back, those green eyes dancing in front of me.

Several hours later, I walked into the house, still needing to pack, and still needing to get plenty of rest for the fourteen-hour drive back to Yearwood in just a few short hours.

A large part of me couldn't have cared less, though. I knew that whatever had just happened between Dixie and me earlier that evening was only the beginning.

Mom, bless her heart, was asleep in her recliner while a late-night infomercial blared through the television speakers about the latest and greatest mail-order rip-off. She had waited up for me…just like she always had.

I walked over and gently nudged her, wanting to let her know I was home. After the second or third nudge, she woke up with a start, and I felt bad for scaring her.

"I'm back," I said quietly.

"Okay, son," she said sleepily. "What time is it?"

"Time for me to go to bed," I said.

Mom looked at her watch which was on the end table by the chair. "Good heavens, Jayce, where have you been?" she rasped.

"At the restaurant, and got ice cream afterward."

Mom slowly nodded her head. "How's Meredith?"

"She didn't show up."

Mom looked at me through squinted eyes. "Well, who were you with?"

"Remember Dixie Johnson?"

Mom gingerly sat up straighter. "How could I forget Dixie Johnson?" she said. "Those Danforths should have been horse-whipped for what they did to that poor girl."

"She works at Squat and Holler now."

"You know I hate it when you call it that."

I smiled. "Sorry. Guadalajara."

"Well, how's Dixie doing?"

"She's good," I said, as I filled her in on the details.

"That's nice to hear," she said. "So what happened to Meredith?"

I shrugged. "I don't know. She just didn't show up."

For a split second, Mom looked as though she was upset, but then she smiled. "So you and Dixie hung out instead, huh?"

I nodded, as she studied me.

"Been a while since I've seen you smiling like you are right now," she smirked.

I just chuckled, as Mom started to get up from her chair. I helped her, and soon she was headed down the hallway toward her bedroom with me following closely behind her toward mine. I helped her into bed, turned out the light, and started to close the door.

"I never liked Meredith anyway," she said, just as I left the room.

Seconds later, I heard her snoring through the thin walls.

Meredith called the next day as I was making my way through north Georgia on I-75, and said she was sorry about standing me up, and something came up, and she'd love to try again next time I was home, and so forth and so on.

I listened, but I didn't care and waited until she was finished before politely hanging up with her.

My mind turned back to Dixie as I kept driving. I thought of seeing her again for the first time since high school. I thought about her laugh and her smile. I even thought of minor aspects of her personality such as how she had fidgeted and circled her spoon around her ice cream cup as she thought of how to answer a question I had asked.

And I thought about those deep dark greens.

Dixie remained on my mind as I watched the terrain become more mountainous while the Tennessee state line drew near.

# Chapter Ten

# Yearwood, Kentucky – A Week Later

**B**oth clocks went off at almost the exact same second, just as they had for almost four years. Rolling back over, I was determined to allow myself a few more precious moments of sleep before having to face the day.

My roommate, on the other hand, had a different mentality, and never seemed to waste any time answering the shrill peals of his alarm. His regimented routine was as predictable and unwavering as the red digits on the small display screen which woke him up each morning.

Soul Rasheed rose out of bed, the box springs below his mattress creating a metallic creaking as they adjusted to the movement of his weight, as he stood upright. After stretching for a solid minute, he made his way to the living room of our apartment, where he would begin the ritual of spreading out the same prayer rug he had used since high school, kneeling down in the direction of Mecca, and offering up supplications to Allah.

My roommate allowed very little deviation in his schedule

when it came to his morning *fajr*.

Soul had just finished his prayers as I was finally forcing myself out of bed. Like so many times before, I had justified sleeping past my alarm by telling myself that my roommate's ritual should not be disturbed, and therefore why not give myself a few more winks. Gradually, I emerged from our bedroom toward the kitchen area, where Soul was standing and pouring himself a glass of orange juice.

"Mornin'," I murmured, barely audible, as I headed right for the coffee maker.

Without looking up, he replied "Good morning" in a deep, northern robust tone that was entirely too chipper for my tastes at that early hour. "Blessed start to a blessed day," he said, raising his orange juice glass.

"If you say so," I grunted, pouring water into the reservoir.

He laughed again. "Of course I say so."

I ignored him as I filled the filter with coffee grounds. If there was one thing I could change about Soulemain Rasheed, it was probably his energy level in the pre-dawn hours.

"So Deke Hudson actually did soul sprints?" Soul asked, still unable to believe it.

"He did," I answered, opening a cabinet and taking out the sugar. "Probably has the Tampa Bay Bucs doing them right now as we speak."

Soul exploded into a fit of booming laughter. "That's unreal, man," he said.

I chuckled in spite of myself. At six feet, five inches tall, and just over two-hundred and twenty pounds, Soul Rasheed towered over me and had a personality that could match his physique. Born and raised in Detroit, Michigan, his paternal grandfather had settled his family in the United States after moving from Iran back in the 1950s. Soul's father had met his mother as a young adult and the two of them, despite her non-Muslim background, had married not long thereafter.

Soul was their oldest, followed by his younger brother and sister. All of them had the same dark complexion that was a combination of their father's Middle Eastern heritage and their mother's African-American skin tone. Soul's personality, combined with his athletic build and handsome features, had made him popular with the ladies around campus for the past four years; though to my knowledge he had never had a serious girlfriend. *Waiting for Allah to provide*, had always been his standard answer when asked about his love life. I had met his family during one of our winter breaks when I had accompanied him back to Detroit and had come away thinking that they seemed like some of the kindest and happiest people I had known. Soul's source of positive energy had never been a mystery.

He had majored in exercise science and, like me, was hoping to land a coaching position someday after paying his dues in the grad assistant ranks. Later that morning, as we made our way out to the practice field for the start of Yearwood State's two-a-days, we could already sense the scorcher of a day that lay ahead. Though it was barely seven-thirty in the morning, the humidity was starting to make its presence felt as the morning sun began to peek above a tree line off in the distance.

"So tell me more about Dixie," Soul inquired, as we began setting up various practice stations.

I just shook my head as I placed two tackling dummies near the goal line. "I think we've pretty much covered everything," I said.

"You sure?" Soul chuckled. "You've been talking about her nonstop, man."

Soul had a point. Dixie and I had talked on the phone several dozen times since I had left Lake Barrow the previous week, and there was talk of her coming up to Yearwood for one of the games. Things were getting serious fast, which had me scared and excited all at once.

"I gotta meet her first, though," Soul persisted, seeming to read my mind. "You're like a brother to me, man. That means you're an adopted Rasheed."

"An adopted Rasheed?" I asked, laughing.

"Heck yeah," Soul said with a smile. "'Rasheed' means 'rightly guided' in Arabic. Once you've been adopted into my family, you'll never lose your way. Because we look out for each other."

I grinned. Soul and I had hit it off almost immediately after arriving on campus together as freshmen almost four years earlier. At first, our interests had aligned primarily concerning football. His height and speed made him the receiver that every quarterback dreams of, and he quickly became my target of choice anytime the scout team found itself on the field. That relationship continued as we moved into our sophomore year and both became starters midway through the season. He could get open easily, thanks to his swift feet, and was a threat to come down with the ball, even when he was blanketed, thanks to his size. To say we made some incredible memories on Mustang Field would be an understatement.

Of course, our friendship transcended football and is a big part of what made us such ideal roommates and best friends on top of that. Our personalities fit each other; his gregariousness and flamboyance and my laid-back blue-collar approach to any task were almost perfectly complementary. I found myself hoping more and more that that relationship would continue as we both pursued our coaching careers beyond Yearwood State.

More importantly, Soul was also a guy you could count on off the field and could talk to about anything. When my former girlfriend broke things off with me during our senior year, Soul had urged me to get more serious about my spiritual life. He had gone on for several minutes about it, and I remember rebuffing him and making it clear that I was not converting to Islam.

And I'll never forget his response. He had glanced at me with a look of seriousness and asserted that he had no intention of converting me to his faith. Rather, he wanted to see me active in my own Christian faith and become the person that my own God wanted me to be.

Needless to say, I gained a new respect for my teammate and friend that day, and I even took his advice. I had grown up attending First Baptist of Lake Barrow, but like most kids who leave home, religion took a back seat in my life once I moved away to Yearwood. There were plenty of churches, but I had simply never made the time to attend any of them. My record of attendance from that day forward was not perfect, but I did begin going to church fairly often, thanks to the advice of Soul Rasheed.

What truly inspired me about that particular conversation, though, was the fact that it had taken place right after Soul had suffered a knee injury that had effectively ended his football career. I mean, here was a guy who had just lost his entire future; a potential career as an NFL wide receiver, millions of dollars, and security for life. And yet his main concern was that his best friend and roommate stayed strong, and didn't get down on himself because of a relationship gone bad.

I believe God knows what we need more than we do, and he certainly knew that I needed a friend like Soul when I got to Yearwood, Kentucky as a college freshman.

As summer 2002 moved into its last weeks, I found myself getting into a routine as the season drew closer, and two-a-days drew to a close. The days began with morning practice, followed by a shower, breakfast, and then film study of our upcoming opponents for a good part of the afternoon.

Once I had familiarized myself with the various film clips, Soul or I would copy the significant portions of them onto a disc, and show them to our coaching staff and players later that day. Oftentimes, we would finish this task just in time for the first of several meetings scheduled for that afternoon and evening before the next practice started.

After the final evening practice, I was pretty much worn out and ready for bed. Soul was too, but of course, he had to pray the last of his daily prayers before he could turn in for the night. Additionally, Soul also had to pause at various times during the day to pray, as part of his faith tradition; something the team and coaching staff had to get used to initially when he had first come to Yearwood but came to accept over time.

Before we knew it, it was the end of August and Yearwood State's first game against Indiana University was less than a week away. On Monday of that week, I got a call on my cell phone from Bud Pearlmuter, who had been my boss at the restaurant I had worked at for four years, prior to my graduation.

"Mornin', Jayce," he said in that low, Kentucky drawl of his, as I answered the phone.

"Hey, Bud."

"You and Soul coming out to the house this Thursday night?"

"Yes, sir."

"Freddy's cooking her famous gumbo," he continued, "and she'll have something that Soul can eat too, I'm sure… something without sausage or pork."

"We'd love to," I said, "but I thought that was more for the players than for us."

"Oh, nonsense," Bud said dismissively. "Just 'cause you're no longer playing doesn't mean you can't still enjoy some of the perks of being a player. There'll be plenty for everyone, too, I'm sure."

"Sounds great," I said with a smile.

The truth was that I couldn't wait to continue one of the cherished traditions surrounding our program, despite the fact that I no longer wore a blue and gold jersey for the Mustangs of Yearwood State. Each week during the season, the Pearlmuters would invite as many Mustang players as would come to dinner at their house, which was located on the outskirts of Yearwood. It was a tradition that would live as long as Bud and Winnifred ("Mama Freddy") Pearlmuter remained alive.

Bud was the owner and founder of Tootsie's Bar and Grill, where I had been employed part-time off and on since first arriving on campus. It was a typical near-campus establishment that attracted mostly students and supporters of our athletic program and had been in business for several decades, despite a few lean years. Its interior was adorned with what had to be every piece of memorabilia ever created since the founding of Yearwood State University; old pictures of Mustang legends, long since deceased, along with their jerseys and helmets; pennants bearing the name and colors of the school; and framed newspaper clippings of milestones in the athletic program's history.

Bud had accumulated all of it over a lifetime of watching and fervently supporting the Yearwood State Mustangs. Tootsie's was one of those places that fit perfectly in a town like Yearwood, Kentucky, which was only somewhat bigger than Lake Barrow, mainly because of the university's presence there. While Yearwood was growing, it still managed to keep that small-town feel that had made it such a great place for me to live, study, and play football for four years. Part of me hoped it would always stay that way.

Bud Pearlmuter had been a good boss, too. Working for him, I had always enjoyed flexible hours and decent pay, on top of the fact that he and his wife were both staunch supporters and boosters of our football program. They had both grown up in Yearwood and were fixtures in the community. Any fundraiser or civic club event that was happening in Yearwood would see at least one Pearlmuter in attendance.

"You guys bringing the Twin Tanks with you?" Bud asked me with a chuckle just before we hung up.

I grinned and shook my head. "Actually, I think we're riding with them."

Bud laughed. "On second thought, we might not have enough food after all."

"LET'S GO! GET IN!" Woody Tankersley yelled from the passenger side window of the small minivan the next day.

"You're keeping your linemen from their feeding trough, Jayce," his twin brother, Max, called out from the driver's seat, as he honked the horn. "And that's never a good thing."

I just chuckled as Soul, and I approached the car.

"Everyone knows you two have been eating all day long," I said to both of them, as I climbed in. "What you need to do is get in that weight room."

"And then run some sprints," Soul added with a grin, walking around and getting into the driver's side back seat. "Get you off that line faster."

Max glared at Soul from the rearview mirror.

"What you both really need to do is think about getting a new car," I added. "This mom-mobile needs to go."

"Girls love minivans," Woody said sincerely. "It shows them that we're serious about being husbands someday."

Soul laughed, and I just shook my head at what passed for Woody's logic.

"Hey, there goes one of the cheerleaders," Woody said, as he extended his arm excitedly and pointed out of Max's driver's side window. As he did, his hand accidentally bumped his twin brother's face and caused his prescription lenses to fall off.

"You don't have to knock my glasses off, dummy!"

"Sorry," Woody said. "It was an accident."

"Your face is the accident."

Soul and I were laughing. Woody and Max Tankersley, better known as the "Twin Tanks" had signed with Yearwood State a year after Soul and me, and had one more year of eligibility left. They were from Fort Wayne, Indiana and, except for the glasses Max wore, looked almost exactly alike. Both were just over six feet tall; both weighed around two-hundred and eighty pounds each; both had curly red hair and freckles, and both played offensive tackle. We had all become starters on offense right around the same time, so they had blocked for me almost the entirety of my time as a starter. For offensive tackles, they were small but tenacious, and every bit as dependable as any linemen I had ever played with.

"Man, I've been dying for some of Mama Freddy's cooking all summer," Woody said, as we pulled out of the athletic dorm parking lot.

"You've been eating our mama's cooking all summer long, so I don't know what you're complaining about," Max said, as he drove.

"I ain't complaining about anything," Woody protested. "And watch where you're going!" he yelled.

"I see it!" Max yelled back, gesturing to a car that had pulled out in front of us on the main thoroughfare.

Soul and I exchanged nervous glances in the back seat.

Woody shook his head. "So Jayce, did you do any surfing while you were home?"

"No," I answered, wondering if this conversation was headed in the same direction as dozens of others had gone.

Sure enough, it was.

"I thought all you Florida boys like to surf," Woody said.

I smiled and shook my head. Woody and I had been over this at least a hundred times since his freshman year, but Woody just couldn't get his head around the idea of my having lived in Florida, and yet never automatically having surfed. He was still one of the few teammates who still sometimes called me "Beach Bum," even though my hometown was not located anywhere near a shoreline.

"He doesn't live near the water, Woody," said Max.

"So what? I thought all Florida folks liked to surf."

"You have to be near a beach in order to do that, dummy."

"You're the dummy," Woody muttered under his breath. Then turning back to me, he asked, "So did you see Deke Hudson while you were home?"

"I did," I said. "He and I ran soul sprints together."

"You made Deke Hudson run soul sprints?" Max said, looking at me from the rearview mirror with a grin.

"That's right."

"That guy's a beast," Woody said with a smile.

Soon, we were out of Yearwood proper and headed into the countryside.

"I can't wait to have some of Mama Freddy's seafood gumbo, Woody said. "Every time I eat over there, I just want to slap every New Orleans chef I ever met right in the face."

"She can flat-out cook," Max agreed.

Max then turned his head to tell me something else, just as an oncoming car approached. Woody flipped out.

"WATCH IT!" he yelled.

"Oh, my gosh, Woody, would you please let me drive?" he said, turning back around and focusing on the road.

Soul and I were laughing. "It's a good thing you two block better than you drive," I chided. "Hopefully, you'll coach better than you drive someday, too."

"It's his fault," Woody said.

"No it ain't," Max protested.

Soul shook his head and continued laughing. "Are you guys still wanting to coach after you graduate?"

"Yes," they both answered in unison.

"God help whatever team they end up with," he added.

"Especially if Woody coaches with me," Max taunted. Woody punched his brother in the arm. Max returned fire.

"Your parents must be the most patient people in the world," I said.

"They had to be, with Woody," Max said.

Woody punched him again and then turned to face us. "Hey, Soul, guess what?"

"What?"

"I'm taking a Middle Eastern culture elective this semester," Woody answered.

"That's great man," Soul said, genuinely interested. "Who's your professor?"

"Dr. Brown-hiney," Woody said.

Soul laughed. "Who?"

"'Bruhani,' numb-nuts," Max said, shaking his head. "His name is Dr. Bruhani."

Soul erupted into raucous, deep laughter that was contagious.

"Shoot, I don't know how to pronounce it," Woody said, rolling his eyes. "Ask Mr. Wanna-be Brainiac here," he said, gesturing to his brother. "He's taking it with me."

"Yeah, just to make sure you don't flunk out or get kicked out," Max said. "I didn't have any other choice but to sign up."

"Shut up, Max."

"Dr. Bruhani is the faculty sponsor for our Islamic Student Society," Soul added. "Great man."

"Isn't he also the one who got attacked in the parking lot right after 9/11?" Woody asked. "By some rednecks?"

"Yeah," Soul answered, his demeanor dropping slightly at the mention. Right then, I hoped that Woody would drop the subject, which he did, thankfully.

Soon, we were headed down a dirt road that had become

familiar over the previous four years, and I realized that the remaining trips to Bud and Mama Freddy's were numbered. Once the season was over, and I moved on to whatever was next, I would miss this tradition probably more than any other.

Max turned the car off of the dirt road and onto a long gravel driveway. We began to hear the familiar "pings" of the tiny pebbles as they were kicked up by the van's tires and began hitting the undercarriage as we drove. Soon we were parked in front of the quaint one-story brick house just outside of Yearwood, Kentucky, that belonged to Bud and Winnifred Pearlmuter.

I glanced at the small, stately structure and wondered if it was even possible to count the number of home-cooked meals I had enjoyed at the Pearlmuters' home since my freshman year.

Max turned off the car, and all of us got out just as Mama Freddy walked through the front door.

"Hello, boys!" she exclaimed. "Always great to see my four adopted sons," she said.

I smiled as I saw her.

"And welcome home, Jayce," she said with a wide grin, walking up to give me a big hug.

# CHAPTER ELEVEN

"How'd you eat back home?" Mama Freddy asked, in that chirpy southern twang that I had come to adore.

"Not as good as I do when I'm here," I answered, reaching down to hug her.

She beamed as we embraced. Mama Freddy was a plump woman who was shorter than me by almost a foot, with a delightful round face, deep brown eyes that sparkled, and long gray hair which was always pulled back into a bun. In the warmer months, she often wore button-down print shirts with flowers on them and blue jeans. When the weather cooled off, she could be found in long sleeves. Usually, sweatshirts with Yearwood State's logo printed on them. My most enduring image of Mama Freddy to this day was the way in which she often stood with arms akimbo, and her head slightly cocked back with a wide grin spread across her face, usually as she waited for us to disembark whenever we pulled into her drive. She held that same warm, welcoming posture as she studied me while I spoke.

"You'll need all your strength for this weekend, I'm sure," she asserted. "Indiana, right?"

"Yes, ma'am," I said. "You and Bud making the trip to Bloomington?"

"No, I'm afraid not," she said, with a frown. "Not this trip. I've got a DAR event to go to and Bud's working. Gotta keep the locals in beer and burgers while they cheer you boys on from afar."

"Yes, ma'am."

"I was so sorry to hear about Jamie," she said, touching my arm with a look of sympathy.

"Thank you," I told her, as we made our way into the house.

Moments later, we were all seated on Mama Freddy and Bud's back porch, which they had enclosed years earlier in order to entertain guests during the colder months, especially holidays. It was hardly uncommon during those times to find at least two or three Mustang football players crashing on the large sofa in the Pearlmuters' living room, or in the back room which served as both an office and guest bedroom. I should know because I was one of them. During one particular Thanksgiving when travel money was short, they had graciously allowed me to stay with them. Many laughs and memories were shared during that time, as was the case for anyone who had ever stayed with or even spent time with Bud and Mama Freddy. Many of those memories were made on the very porch where I now found myself sitting.

Bud and Mama Freddy had married right out of high school and never left their small town. Neither had attended college, though they had both grown up cheering for the Mustangs of Yearwood State. No children of their own; though this had never stopped Mama Freddy from claiming the hundreds of young men who had gone through the YSU football program as "her boys."

That evening, she had her gumbo pot simmering on the stove, and the smell was heavenly. Bud was out back, just beyond the porch, deep-frying shrimp. Several other players showed up moments later. It would be a smaller crowd that evening which was a surprise, given what was on the menu.

Mama Freddy's gumbo was renowned in Yearwood, Kentucky and beyond.

I went out back to chat with Bud. The remaining daylight was almost completely gone as I turned on the outdoor floodlights, and the humidity was thick but tempered with the gentle breeze that rustled through the Kentucky pines which bordered their property. Off in the distance, where the backyard met the small patch of woods behind their yard, fireflies were already beginning to light up the darkness.

"Evening, boss," I said to Bud, as he ladled a metal spatula into the fryer to examine his shrimp.

"Hey, Jayce," he said kindly. "You boys ready?"

"For the season? Yes sir."

"For dinner," Bud said, almost shocked that I didn't realize what he was talking about. In his bony, gnarled hand, he held the spatula which was now full of golden fried shrimp. "Look at these babies, Jayce," he said proudly in his high-pitched Kentucky drawl. "Whoever said land-locked states like ours don't know how to do seafood needs to come visit us sometimes. Try one."

I gently picked one off of the spatula, being careful not to burn my fingers, and popped it into my mouth. Sure enough, it was still scorching from the hot oil.

"Ahhh," I said, wincing from the burning sensation.

Bud cackled as he watched me struggle to swallow the tiny sea creature. "Gotta let it cool, son," he said good-naturedly.

"Not bad," I said sincerely, as I swallowed it. "Ever think about putting seafood on the menu at Tootsie's?"

"Sure I have," he said. "It's expensive, though."

"Yeah, it is."

"Takes a lot of calculated risk to take on extra expenses this day and age," he said.

"Yeah," I agreed. "Economy's not doing real well is it?"

"No, it ain't," he answered, spooning another shrimp

onto a napkin-covered plate. He was wearing corduroy pants, a denim shirt, and work boots. His thinning gray hair was combed across the large bald spot on top of his head. "It's always something with the economy, isn't it?" he said. "If not taxes and regulations, it's people threatening to take their business elsewhere for silly reasons."

I frowned at the reference, as my memory stirred.

A year earlier, the Islamic Student Society of Yearwood State, which Soul belonged to, had approached Bud and asked if they could hold their monthly meetings in his restaurant. Graciously, Bud had agreed, which was no surprise to anyone who knew him. The downside to this decision had been the outcry from a few of the locals, who hated the idea of "potential terrorists eating at one of our restaurants." Several people stated their displeasure publicly at Bud's decision. Others sent death threats.

By and large, however, the town of Yearwood had banded together in solidarity with Bud and Mama Freddy and supported them through it all. It was during that time that I got to see the true character of this small college town that I had called home for four years. Tootsie's not only stayed in business and weathered the "bigotry storm," as we came to refer to it, but Bud's restaurant also thrived and gained more new customers in the aftermath of his decision than anyone had ever seen. The Islamic students loved Bud and Mama Freddy, as did almost everyone else in town.

Looking back, it was then that I truly fell in love with Yearwood.

"Things worked out," I said, eating another shrimp.

"Well," he responded, "you know what I always say about doing the right thing."

"It always finds its way back to you," I finished for him.

"That's right."

"Hey, Bud?"

"Yeah?"

"Where did you come up with the name 'Tootsie's' for your place?"

"From that stupid dog that Winnifred got not long after we were married," he answered with a chuckle. "She said she would only let me use the money we got from her daddy as a wedding present for the restaurant down payment if I'd let her name it after the mutt."

I laughed.

"Little tiny piss-ant, too," Bud said. "Used to bite my ankles."

"Marital bliss," I said, with a laugh.

"Oh yeah," he said, looking up at me with that twinkle in his eye. "Only true love will make a man do something like that."

I nodded.

"You see any old high school sweethearts while you were home?" he asked with a smile.

"Saw an old sweetheart who stood me up on a date," I said.

"That's too bad."

"Actually, it wasn't so bad," I added and then proceeded to tell him about Dixie.

"Dixie sounds like a keeper," Bud said when I had finished.

"We'll see what happens," I said.

Bud looked up at me. "If you can sit together in each other's presence and not feel like you have to talk the whole time, that's a pretty good sign that you've got something good. There's times when Winnifred and I will just sit on the porch and look out across the lawn to the main road. Neither of us says a word, but then, neither of us has to. It's hard to explain."

"It makes sense," I responded.

Bud scooped out the last of the shrimp and tried to stand up out of the lawn chair he'd been sitting in. "Dang knees are about to kill me. Give me a hand, here, will ya, Jayce?"

I took the platter of shrimp from him with one hand and helped him to his feet with the other. "Ever think about retiring?"

"Yeah, but who'd take over Tootsie's?" he said. "I'd nominate you for the job, but you'll probably be a big-time coach by next season?" He smiled as he scuffed toward the door with his distinctive, spry, hobble.

"Takes a while to get to the big time," I said with a laugh.

"Well, you gotta start somewhere," Bud said with a grin.

"Yep."

"First things first, though. Let's get these shrimp eaten."

"Shouldn't be a problem," I said, with a laugh, as we entered the porch and saw the table full of large men devouring gumbo and French bread.

Hours later, with full bellies, we left Mama Freddy and Bud's and made our way out to the van.

"You boys catch any girls yet with that minivan?" Bud called out to the Twin Tanks.

"Bud, cut it out," Mama Freddy said, elbowing him in the ribs. Bud smiled and put his arm around his wife as they stood on their porch, seeing us off.

"Getting girls isn't the problem," Max answered, as he walked around to the driver's side door. "Keeping them around once they've met Woody definitely is."

"Shut up, Max," Woody said to his brother, "you ain't no prize."

I laughed as I walked down the steps, just behind Soul, and got ready to leave. "Hard to believe these guys kept me from getting injured for three years, isn't it?" I said to the Pearlmuters.

Both of them nodded and smiled.

The Indiana Hoosiers beat us by a score of 24-17 that Saturday. While we were disappointed to lose the game, it was hard to be upset at the effort put forth by our guys, especially since we had played a Division I team. Jake Mossberger, our junior starting quarterback who had replaced me, was 17 of 25 in passing, with 199 yards, 2 touchdowns and 1 interception. Decent as his numbers were, his most heroic performance was leading the final drive in the last two minutes. After the Hoosiers punted and pinned us inside our own ten-yard line, Mossberger completed seven straight passes and drove the offense all the way inside Indiana's five.

From there, Indiana simply stood their ground and refused to let us into the end zone for the tying score. Once they stopped us on fourth down, their offense took over for the final ten seconds and ran out the clock.

It was a painful way to lose a game, but I was pleased to see just how high everyone's morale seemed to be as we got on the team buses and headed back to Yearwood. A lot of this had to do with Soul, who like always, was good at raising spirits no matter how dismal things became.

True to form, he was stirring up laughter as the buses pulled onto the interstate.

*"Sense of urgency, now Lloyd, sense of urgency! Get this bus moving!"* Soul chided loudly to Lloyd, our veteran bus driver. He had  transformed his voice into a high-pitched, Midwestern gravelly twang that sounded almost identical to that of Gary Carter, Yearwood State's longtime head coach. The impersonation was flawless and had the entire bus in stitches as we rolled along I-65.

Lloyd grinned and shook his thick head amidst the laughter from the players, who watched Soul's rangy, athletic frame standing in the center aisle of the charter bus belonging to the university.

*"If you're not hustling, you're costing a quality player his scholarship,"* Soul continued his mocking intonation. *"Just ask Jayce*

*Leonard, he knows what it is to piss away a scholarship."*

This drew a roar from the boys as I jumped up and punched Soul in the arm. We grappled in the aisle for a few moments, which of course, ended with me sitting back down after Soul, easily the stronger of us had manhandled me.

"Do the Twin Tanks!" a freshman called out from the back.

"Come on now!" I protested.

A chant began to rise from the middle and rear seats.

*"Twin Tanks! Twin Tanks! Twin Tanks!"* the players called out as the bus accelerated.

The rambunctious banter grew in decibel level as the entire bus began joining in.

*"Twin Tanks! Twin Tanks! Twin Tanks! Twin Tanks! Twin Tanks!"*

*"I'm Max Tankersley,"* Soul finally complied, slouching and pooching out his stomach slightly. *"I drive a mini-van to pick up chicks."*

The boys roared.

*"This is my brother, Woody,"* he said, gesturing to me. *"Woody's a homo, but don't tell anyone. He's got a crush on Dr. Brown-Hiney."*

*"Shut up, Max!"* I squealed, mocking Woody as I jumped up.

Soul and I tousled each other again to the sound of raucous laughter and cheering. When it was over, I paused and looked out over the rows of young men who were the future of the program which I knew I would one day leave…and perhaps soon. A bittersweetness came over me at that moment, and I was thankful for my time at Yearwood State. All of it.

Following the Indiana loss, we ended up winning most of

our regular season games that year, finishing 8-5 and earning a spot in the Division II playoffs, where Appalachian State, a perennial powerhouse, beat us handily in the first round by a score of 58-10. We had fulfilled one of our team goals by making it to the playoffs but were hoping for at least one post-season victory. Still, just like with the Indiana game, it was difficult to be dissatisfied with the effort our players gave, from start to finish.

On a positive note, Dixie got to come up for our game at home against Murray State. Coincidentally, that game ended up being our team's most complete performance of the season. Mossberger was almost flawless (15-16 passing, for 293 yards, 4 touchdowns, and 0 interceptions). TayShaun Foster, our running back, had almost 180 yards rushing, and our defense played lights out. We beat them by a score of 42-3.

After the game, Soul and I lobbied the coaching staff to give Dixie a game ball, claiming that she had been our good luck charm that afternoon. We were successful and even managed to get a few of the players to sign it for her.

Things were definitely headed in a serious direction where Dixie and I were concerned. We had talked on the phone at least once a day since I had left Lake Barrow earlier that summer, and during her visit to Yearwood, I had also taken her to meet Bud and Mama Freddy, both of whom ended up approving of her. *Never did like that other girl you dated*, Mama Freddy was always telling me. I guess between what Mom had said about Meredith and what Mama Freddy thought of my college squeeze, my tastes in women had never really been all that great…until Dixie.

Things were going great, but I knew that I had some decisions to make about the future, and soon. My graduate assistant contract with Yearwood State was set to expire after the season and from there, I would be out looking for work again.

I had called home as often as I could to talk with Coach

Skipper and with Jim Gill, who was president of the quarterback club, about teaching and coaching at Sims County. However, that previously-open door seemed to be closing faster than I thought it would. There simply weren't any spots that were coming open around that time, and I was getting discouraged. I had put resumes out all across the country; even as far away as Washington State.

One good thing about all of this is that while Dixie and I hadn't expressly talked about marriage at that point, she had subtly indicated to me that she would be willing to go with me wherever the coaching profession took me. She wanted to continue her degree in education at some point but also wanted to start a family.

I eventually decided to just trust in whatever God had for me after the season. I've always been taught that He has a plan and that He works in mysterious ways.

That fall, I was reminded once again just how true those words really are.

I got a call on my cell one early December afternoon, as Soul and I were putting away practice equipment for the off-season. It was Jim Gill, and he had news that nothing could have prepared me for.

"Skipper's been fired," he said flatly.

For a moment, I just sat there in the middle of Yearwood State's equipment room, too stunned to respond.

# Chapter Twelve

*Skipper out* at Sims County.

*First-year head coach fired amid allegations of player recruitment.*

The more I read as I perused the internet that night, the more surreal it seemed. A Florida High School Sports Association investigation had been triggered by e-mail correspondence between administrators at another area high school and officials at the Sims County School District. The e-mail had accused Coach Ted Skipper of improperly recruiting five players from the other school and convincing them to transfer to Sims County prior to the start of the previous season.

The investigation had snowballed quickly, and its results were clear. The article reported FHSSA findings involving campus and facilities tours that had been guided by Skipper himself, literature distributed to players and their families, and testimonies about the recruiting efforts taken directly from the players and families themselves.

Luckily, Sims County had been given the option of self-reporting and basically admitting to the wrongdoing; an option which Principal Andrew Starr had quickly agreed to in order to save the school more embarrassment (not to mention fines) than they would have otherwise faced.

In all, the school was facing a financial penalty in the

amount of just over $9,000, administrative and restrictive probation, vacated wins in games that the ineligible players had participated in, and prohibition from playing in any spring game or kickoff classic the following season. If there was a silver lining in the whole matter, it was that the Spartans could still compete for their district title, as well as playoff berths during the postseason.

I sat there in front of the computer, not knowing what to think as I became more and more engrossed in the drama unfolding hundreds of miles away in my small hometown. My mind was so far off, I didn't hear my cell phone until after the third ring.

It was Jim calling again.

"Help me understand what's happened," I told him as I answered.

"Did you read the news report?" he asked.

"I'm reading it now."

"Then you've pretty much got what happened," Jim replied. His tone was difficult to read. "Skipper left town yesterday, and he won't be back."

Both of us sat there in silence for a moment.

"The way I see it," Jim continued, "he's getting what's been coming to him for a long time. I'm glad to see him go because he never was a good fit for this school or this community."

My mind went back to the conversation that Jim and I had on their upper porch after Jamie's funeral.

"It hurts and it's put our kids and the school in a bind," Jim added. "But we've gotten through worse before, and we'll get through this."

"Yeah."

"Which brings me to why I've called you again, Jayce," Jim continued. "How interested are you in being a head coach next season?"

The words "head coach" registered with me, but I felt

as though I was still somehow missing what Jim was saying. Had he seriously just asked me about being a head coach at Sims County?

"Come again," I said.

"You heard me," Jim replied. "Say you're in, and you're automatically a top candidate for the head coaching job at Sims County."

"That's unreal, man," Soul said with a grin, as we jogged around the practice field later that evening. "A twenty-four-year-old high school head coach."

"I'm barely out of college," I told him. "Plus, it almost sounds too good to be true."

"A little bit," Soul agreed.

We jogged in silence for another moment.

"Sometimes life tosses you those opportunities, though," he told me.

"Yeah."

"So what are you thinking?" Soul asked me.

I shrugged as we ambled along. "It's not like I've got a lot of options when it comes to job prospects, but…"

I felt Soul's eyes on me.

"I just don't know if I'm ready."

The practice field lights burned brightly and illumined our way ahead.

"My high school coach during my senior season was thirty-five years old when he took over," Soul said. "First-year guy, wet behind the ears. You name it. First spring practice was a disaster. *He* wasn't ready."

"You told me this before."

"Yeah, and I also told you what happened that season."

"You went 5-5."

"And came back the next season and won district," Soul

added. "We grew as a team, just as he grew as a head coach."

"Your coach was eleven years older than I am now, and likely had more experience as an assistant."

"But not more confidence," Soul replied. "He was just as scared as you are now."

"I didn't say I was scared."

Soul stopped, and put his hand on my arm, turning me to face him. "Then what are you waiting for?"

"More experience, with less responsibility."

"Sounds like you're more scared that you're willing to admit," Soul said, fixing my eyes with his.

I resumed jogging, and Soul kept pace with me.

"If I do this," I began, "I'm going to need a quality staff."

"Yeah, you will," Soul agreed.

"You interested in coming with me?" I asked.

Soul glanced at me, and it was my turn to fix him with a gaze. He chuckled. "Man, I love the idea of coaching and especially coaching with you. But I don't know about Florida."

"No ice storms there," I said.

"I'm used to ice storms."

"You could get used to Florida," I replied.

Soul looked ahead as we moved along. "American small towns and I haven't always gotten along the best," he said.

I said nothing as we continued our workout for several moments.

"Tensions were high after 9/11," I finally broke the silence. "Not only that but for every bigot you meet these days, there are about five Bud Pearlmuters."

Soul glanced at me. "You think I'd fit into Lake Barrow?"

"Yeah, I do."

Soul thought it over for a moment.

"What about women?" he finally asked, with a smile.

"What about them?"

"Any good Muslim women down there?"

I just shook my head and grinned. "Guess that's the deal-breaker, huh?"

Soul chortled. "Could be."

"You can always convert one or two once you get down there," I said. "Who knows? Hijabs might be in style come next season."

Soul grinned. "You suck at advertising."

"Maybe so," I said, "but I could probably be a decent coach if I had the right people alongside me, which is why I'm going to keep pestering you until you say 'yes.'"

"What makes you think I'm the right person?"

"Jake Mossberger went from being sacked eighteen times during the first half of this season to being sacked only five times during the second half," I answered.

"Thank the Twin Tanks for that," Soul replied, "not me."

"The Twin Tanks didn't drill him on footwork and scrambling speed after each practice."

Soul said nothing.

"You're the only person I know with a sprint named after him," I persisted. "What's the line you're always giving the team after they run them?"

"Your soul may hurt for a while, but your strength remains forever," Soul said simply.

I kept my eyes on him. "I need a good motivator as much as a quality offensive coordinator for my team. You'd fit both of those descriptions."

"You think the boys down there will respond to my brand?" Soul asked.

"I think after what they're going through right now, they could probably use everything you bring to the table."

Soul looked at me once more. "On second thought, maybe you've got a future in advertising after all."

"Is that a 'yes'?"

"It's not a strong 'no.'"

I smiled. "Speaking of the Twin Tanks," I continued, "we could also use some quality line coaches as well."

Soul stopped and gave me an incredulous look. "You can't be serious."

"Heck yeah, I'll coach for you!" Max Tankersley exclaimed the next day, as I sat with the two of them, along with Soul, in the cramped graduate assistant office in one of the corridors of the stadium complex. "Be cool to have a job right out of college."

"Count me in," Woody added, as he sat next to his brother.

"None of us are in yet," I clarified. "I haven't accepted the position."

"When will you know?" Max asked.

I looked at Soul. "Soon as I tell them I'm taking the job, basically."

"They want you bad, huh?" Max said.

"A few people down there do," I said.

"Would this be a paid gig?" Woody asked.

"Eventually," I said. "You guys would have to get certified as teachers first. Takes a few months. Way I see it, we move down there this January together, and you guys get part-time jobs working for a close friend of mine at his car dealership. I've already talked to him about it. Study for the certification exam, pass it, and you're in school year and season. Skipper's firing left three vacancies in the P.E. department, plus a football coach. You guys, plus Soul, come with me, and you automatically get pushed to the front of the line."

"How much pay?" Woody asked.

"Not much," I answered. "But both of you guys will get experience and a chance to get your foot in the coaching door."

"So what happened to your old coach again?" Max asked.

I filled him in on as many details as I had.

Max frowned. "Sucks for those kids."

Woody nodded in agreement.

"Long as it pays enough to live on," Max continued, "I'll happily move to Lake Barrow."

I smiled.

"I guess the only question," Soul chimed in, "is who's coaching offensive line and who's got defensive?"

"We probably should put Woody on defense," Max said, "since he's not as proficient with blocking schemes as I am."

"You ain't no guru!" Woody protested, "Why don't you coach defense?"

"How many hours did you spend on PlayStation last season instead of studying the playbook?" Max persisted.

"I studied more than you did!"

"Yeah, that's why the coaches had me protecting Jayce's blind side, as well as Mossberger's."

Woody glared at him. "That's why you moved to right tackle after Jayce graduated."

"Because Mossberger's a southpaw, numbnuts," Max replied. "I moved to right so I could still be on his blind side."

Soul and I glanced at each other as the back-and-forth continued.

"You sure about this?" Soul asked me.

Things began moving fast.

I went home to Lake Barrow for both Christmas and to have my interview with Principal Andrew Starr, and the Quarterback Club of Sims County. After getting to Mom's house just before ten, I was up the next morning and getting dressed before sunup. I felt fatigued from the early hour and from the previous day's travel, but I didn't care. The more I thought of becoming the next coach of my alma mater, the more eager I became to make the best impression I could.

As I stood in front of the mirror in my old bedroom, I studied my appearance and paid particular attention to the same navy suit that I had worn to Jamie's funeral just a few months earlier. It fit well, and for the first time, I found myself noticing just how close I was to adulthood. I had graduated college, but it suddenly hit me that I was now fully capable of making my own decisions, and about to foray into the professional world for the very first time in my young life. It was surreal, and I didn't know what to think as I stood there in front of the mirror, surrounded by the juvenile environs of my old bedroom.

My thoughts were interrupted by a knock at the door. It opened, and Mom stood in the doorway, bracing herself against her walker. She smiled as she studied my appearance.

"You look wonderful," she said with a proud look on her face.

"Thanks," I smiled, as I walked to the doorway and stood in front of her.

"I came to see if you wanted anything for breakfast," she said.

"I'll grab something on my way out," I told her.

A bittersweet smile came to her face. "I always knew you'd get here," she continued, "but I didn't think it'd come so soon."

"Makes two of us," I told her. "Haven't gotten the job yet, though."

"I know," she said. "Are you ready to be a coach, son?"

I wanted to nod, but somehow couldn't. Faintly, I shook my head. "I don't feel ready."

"Are you having second thoughts?"

I hesitated before answering. "It's hard to say."

"I'm your mom," she answered. "You can say anything."

"I just don't get why they picked me," I told her. "I mean, I get it. 'Local boy makes good.' But…"

"You're twenty-four years old?"

I nodded.

"I was younger than you when I had you, Jayce," she said, reaching up to straighten my tie. "Truth is, I was probably even less ready to be a mom than you are to be a coach now."

She gave my tie one last brush with her hand and looked up at me again.

"And now look at you," she said, pride shining through her eyes. "Guess I did something right."

"Lots of things," I clarified.

"Well," she almost whispered. "Only because I reaffirmed my commitment each day you were growing up to do right by you."

I studied her.

"That's all you can do, Jayce. If you get this job, commit to doing right by those boys, come what may. Treat them fairly and equally no matter what, and ask forgiveness when you don't. That's all anyone can expect."

I nodded.

"Disappointment's a part of life," she continued. "But people cope better with it when those running their world run it honestly."

I smiled, gave her a kiss on the forehead, and was out the door within minutes.

The interview went well and was surprisingly easy.

Principal Starr, who was also our athletic director, did most of the questioning. He, along with Jim Gill, two other members of the Sims County Quarterback Club, and two of the current players knew most of what there was to know about my background, but asked a few questions anyway, just to have everything on record.

When it was over, Jim approached me.

"You did well, Jayce," he affirmed, slapping me on the

back. "It's looking good."

"Thanks," I answered. "Guess we'll know something soon enough, huh?"

"Yep," he said. His demeanor was upbeat, positive, and hopeful. It gave me confidence.

Jim had to leave to get back to the dealership, but Starr pulled me aside. "Let's take a walk," he told me.

Soon, we were traversing the halls of Sims County High School, each corner we rounded bringing back a memory of some kind. We made small talk, going over changes to the school that had taken place, as well as a few that were going to take place. Eventually, we found ourselves at the rear of the school's property near the field house, which housed the football team lockers and weight room. It was an old, concrete block structure which had seen better days, but was in pretty good shape for the years it had withstood. Its dark green and white paint was chipping, and there were other small-scale signs of wear and disrepair; a bent drainage pipe on one side, and a rusty door on another.

Starr and I seemed to be looking at the same things as we stood in the parking lot and gazed at the aging structure.

"We're getting a new one," he told me, not taking his eyes off of the field house.

"When?" I asked.

"It won't be before the beginning of next season, unfortunately," Starr said, pinching the bridge of his nose. "But we're hoping to break ground during the next off-season. There's a vacant classroom where we'd move the weights during construction, and the football team will share time with the basketball guys for locker room space."

"What's the new facility going to look like?"

"A lot like the current one, only slightly larger, and more state-of-the-art. It's less about size, and more about giving the place an upgrade."

"It's ambitious."

"It's necessary," Starr clarified. "And that's one reason we're pushing hard for a new coach sooner rather than later. Continuity is important, especially for the team and the boosters; especially if we want to keep Jim Gill on board."

"Is he thinking of stepping down?" I asked.

"He hasn't threatened, but if we can't right this ship, then it would almost make sense for him to do just that, given that Jordan's coming up on his senior year. Jim wants him to be successful, and rightfully so. He'll put him where he thinks he can best be in line for a scholarship, and a big part of that will hinge on the kind of program we run. Facilities are a part of that."

I nodded as we continued slowly walking around the building.

"Ted Skipper really screwed us up," Starr went on as we walked. "He made a mess, and we've got to get it cleaned up. And we need this new field house. To make that happen, we'll need Jim Gill and his deep pockets."

"Sounds like it."

"If you get this job, Jayce, coaching football will be your primary responsibility," he said. "And keeping the support of the Quarterback Club will be your second."

"Yes sir," I told him.

"You understand, don't you?" Starr asked, turning to look at me. His eyes were serious as he studied me.

"I understand," I answered, unsure of whether or not I actually did.

Two days after Christmas, I got word that I had been selected for hire as the next head coach of the Sims County Spartans, officially making me the youngest head coach in the state of Florida at that time. In the span of two years, I had gone from college quarterback, to graduate assistant, to being responsible for over forty high school age boys, all before I had reached the age of twenty-four.

Once I accepted the job, there were plenty of congratulatory calls; Soul, the Twin Tanks, Jim Gill, Ahmad, Deke, and many others. Dixie was ecstatic, of course. She and her mother were still close, and it was a definite perk knowing that leaving her mother behind would likely not be in the cards.

I also received congratulatory calls from the coaching staff and players from up at Yearwood State, as Soul passed the news.

The more I thought about what I had said to Soul during our jog around the practice field that night, the more I realized that it was probably the biggest reason why I took the job in the first place. Yes, it was my hometown, and yes, it was an honor to coach the team for which I had once played. But that was nowhere near the primary motivation for why I had accepted.

Coach Skipper had disgraced not only our program, but our town, and I wanted to help pick up the pieces. After all that Lake Barrow had done for me, I almost saw it as my duty to go home and be a part of the solution.

Thus, the first week of 2003 saw myself and my new coaching staff getting packed and ready to leave Yearwood for good. We said our good-byes to the coaches and players; one of whom dubbed us "Team Mustang," as he admonished us to do our alma mater proud.

On Monday, January 6, 2003, Soul, the Twin Tanks, and I loaded up our cars and began to caravan down I-65 just as the sun was coming up. It was the same old familiar route I had taken many times going to and from college. Once we reached Nashville, we headed southeast on I-24 to Chattanooga, where we switched interstates again and took the 75 all the way through Georgia and into Florida. Soon, we began seeing signs for Gainesville and the University of Florida, and I knew we'd be home soon.

I smiled as I drove, keeping Soul's car and the Twin Tanks' minivan in my rearview mirror, and looking forward to the future that lay ahead; bright and uncertain all at once.

The way I see it, there are things in life which you don't plan and can only chalk up to divine intervention. When I learned that Ahmad Floyd just happened to be home visiting family during my first full day back in Lake Barrow, I knew it had to be providential. As happy as I was with the way my rag-tag coaching staff was coming together, I knew it wasn't complete. And I knew where to start looking for the final piece.

"Good to see you, bro," I said to Ahmad, as I rose from the table to greet him the next day. I had only been waiting at Guadalajara for a few minutes when he walked through the door.

"You too," he said, taking a seat, and looking around to admire the Mexican décor in the building. He was wearing a black polo and tan slacks and looked every bit like a successful local boy home for a visit.

Ignacio approached and took Ahmad's drink order. Then he turned to me. "Folks are saying the team's not going to be very fast this year," he smirked.

I frowned at him. "Who's saying that?"

Ignacio shrugged. "Then again, what does it matter? It's no surprise, given how slow their coach is with putting a ring on his girlfriend's finger."

I glanced down and shook my head as Ahmad began laughing.

"You know," I said to Ignacio, "the football coach carries a lot of authority around here. You wouldn't want me starting a rumor at the health inspector's office about this place, would you?"

Ignacio grinned. "Health inspector eats here all the time."

"Fine, I'll call INS; get them to look at your papers."

"Been legal for years," Ignacio retorted.

"Then why don't you make yourself useful, and bring us some more chips and salsa?"

"Only after I spit in them, first," he returned. "Give Miss Dixie my best."

I smiled as he walked off, and turned back to Ahmad.

"Ignacio's still tripping," Ahmad said.

"Always."

"You just get back last night?" he asked me.

"Two nights ago. Still got my stuff in the car."

"You crashing at your mom's?"

"For now," I answered, taking a sip of water. "Got my eye on a few places."

"Houses?"

I nodded.

Ahmad grinned. "That can only mean one thing."

"Means Ignacio was wrong about me not proposing soon," I answered. "Just gotta get things settled."

Ahmad grinned. "Congratulations."

"Thanks."

Ignacio arrived with the drinks, chips, and salsa and set them all down.

"Another thing I've got to get worked out," I continued, "is my coaching staff."

"Thought you said you had it all together," Ahmad responded, dipping a chip in the salsa. "Soul and the twins are here with you."

"I need a defensive coordinator," I said flatly, "and I want you for the job."

Ahmad recoiled and took a sip of water.

"Ahmad, you were my best receiver in high school and went on to be even better in college. A big part of that was because you were a student of the game, especially other teams' defenses. There were times you even out-studied me during film sessions."

"I can't quit my job," Ahmad countered. "This merger falls into place, and I might be up for promotion. That's a rare thing in this biz."

""You can work from anywhere," I reminded him. "You've always bragged about that, ever since you took the job out of college. And this would be strictly volunteer, especially since the school's only open spots are about to be filled by Soul, and the Twin Tanks. You wouldn't quit your job, you'd just keep doing it here in Lake Barrow."

I knew that I was ambushing Ahmad, and it was by design. He was smart, and I knew that catching him on his heels with the proposal would improve my chances of getting him on board.

"You've always wanted to coach," I persisted. "You were even thinking of applying to be a grad assistant at Delta State before getting offered the job you have now. That desire's there, I know you."

"Yeah, but…"

"I know you," I repeated.

Ahmad said nothing and looked away. "I just can't," he finally said.

I studied him, thinking I saw some trace of regret. Maybe it was wishful thinking on my part.

"Promise me, you'll think about it, though," I instructed him.

Ahmad smiled and simply said, "Spartan pride."

"I'd like to welcome everyone to this special meeting of the Spartan Quarterback Club," Jim Gill announced the next night as he stood in front of a large gathering of players and parents in the school's auditorium. He wore a black blazer, tan pants, and a white dress shirt with the collar unbuttoned; the consummate pillar of the community. "As you all know, we don't usually meet in January, but given the circumstances, tonight's gathering is fairly important, especially with the head coaching vacancy that we've had since December. You all know about the unfortunate circumstances that involved Coach Skipper, so there's no need to rehash any of it. Bottom line is that we've been in a tight spot and needed to move quickly in order to minimize the lag between Coach Skipper's departure and finding a new head coach."

He then turned and glanced behind him, where I was seated, wearing a coat and tie.

"And found one we have," he beamed. "Stand up, Jayce."

I rose from my chair and immediately felt the gaze of dozens of eyes, followed by the entire audience rising to its feet and clapping. The applause was sincere, and I felt honored.

When it died down, Jim continued. "I think pretty much everyone in here knows Jayce Leonard from his days as a Spartan play-caller just a few short years ago," Jim went on. "He graduated in 1998 and went on to star at quarterback for the Yearwood State Mustangs up in Kentucky, followed by a season as one of their graduate assistants. He's a young guy, but plenty energetic, and has deep roots in this town."

Jim went on for another minute, describing my background and upbringing in Lake Barrow, even mentioning my mom and Dixie, both of whom were seated nearby. Mom dabbed her eyes with a tissue as I stood next to Jim. Dixie smiled at me.

When he finished, it was my turn to speak. I took the microphone, stood at the dais, and began addressing the group. Basic stuff: I was thrilled to be the new head coach, looking forward to winning seasons, and especially to beating Barton City. When I wrapped up, I opened the floor for questions, and almost immediately began to wish I hadn't.

"What kind of offense do you run?" asked a father whose son had started at fullback for the junior varsity squad the previous season. His expression was stern.

I cleared my throat. "We run a basic multiple-receiver set with a tight end and a lone tailback," I responded.

"My boy ran for over a hundred yards in several JV games last year," the father replied almost defensively.

"He's welcome to try out," I responded. "If he's a good enough ball-carrier, he'll play."

The man scowled as he sat back down. Tension filled the room, and as I looked over at Jim, he was shaking his head in frustration.

More questions followed, and it was a mixed bag. Some were legitimately good questions, but several were nothing more than thinly veiled implications that I was either unqualified to lead the team, or simply unwelcome to do so because of the changes, especially on offense, that we were about to implement. My dress shirt was sticking to my body under my coat as sweat began to pour out.

"Are there any other questions?" I asked.

"What about your coaching staff?" another father asked.

"I'm glad you asked," I answered since I had been planning to introduce everyone to the crowd. Soul and the Twin Tanks had been sitting next to Mom and Dixie, and Soul especially had drawn a few curious stares thanks to his unfamiliar face, as well as the *kufi* he wore on his head.

I motioned for them all to stand up and started with Max and Woody before proceeding to Soul.

"Soul Rasheed," I began, "will be our offensive coordinator. We played together at Yearwood State and were graduate assistants this past season. He's a heckuva motivator and great at teaching mechanics. I hope you'll welcome him to the team and to Lake Barrow."

As I introduced Soul, I turned and looked at Jim, whose

dour expression was difficult to read.

I spent a few moments afterward chatting with some of the parents and current players, several of whom I knew from having played with their older brothers.

Max and Woody attracted some attention, especially from the linemen, and spoke with several people. And while a few people approached Soul, it was not lost on me that he didn't get nearly as much attention as the rest of us.

"You did awesome," Dixie whispered in my ear later, after she kissed me.

I nodded and smiled.

"I'm so proud of you," Mom said, as she hugged me. "Don't worry about those parents," she whispered. "Emotions are still raw after the ordeal with Ted."

I smiled at her before turning to Soul, Woody, and Max.

"Nice people," Max said with a smile. "You guys think we can pull this off?"

"Word is that if we beat Barton City, we can lose about five other games before the natives turn on us," Woody added.

Soul chuckled, but not with his eyes. "Maybe less than that, thanks to my religion."

I shook my head. "Don't worry about that."

"At least I don't see a lynch mob forming," Soul grinned.

"You just worry about finding us a big target we can throw to on third and medium," I told him. "If you can accomplish that, your religion will be the least of anyone's worries."

"We'll see," Soul replied.

The Twin Tanks left for their new apartment shortly

thereafter. Their first day at Jim Gill Automotive as assistant office managers started the next morning. In the off-hours, they would study for the Florida Educators Certification Exam, which they would take later that spring.

I had just helped Mom and Dixie into the car and was saying good-bye to Soul when I saw Jim approaching.

He had a warm smile on his face as he walked up. "Don't think we've been properly introduced yet," he said, extending his hand to Soul. "Jim Gill."

"Soul Rasheed," he returned, as the two of them shook.

"Is 'Soul' your given name?"

"No sir," Soul answered. "It's short for 'Soulemain.'"

"Interesting," Jim said. "Where are you from, Soul?"

"Detroit."

"Is your family still there?"

"Yes sir."

"And where are they from originally?"

"Iran on my father's side," Soul answered.

"Iran," Jim repeated. "That explains your name, I guess."

"It's Arabic," Soul answered. "Soulemain means 'man of peace.'"

Jim nodded without taking his eyes off of Soul. "Peace," he said. "That's a good thing."

Soul nodded. I couldn't shake the uneasy feeling I had about where the conversation might be headed.

"Not too much of that in the world today," Jim followed up.

Soul shook his head. "Unfortunately, no."

Jim nodded and placed his hands in his pockets. "Well, Soul, how do you like our little town of Lake Barrow?"

"A lot," Soul responded. "Definitely different from where I grew up."

Jim smiled. "We're a pretty typical small, southern town," he agreed. "And we take a lot of pride in that."

Soul nodded.

"'A man of peace,'" Jim said once more. "You do seem like a pretty peaceful guy."

"I try to be."

I chimed in. "Only time he ever wasn't was when he was throwing blocks during our playing days."

Jim barely acknowledged my attempt at humor and didn't take his eyes off of Soul. "Peace is something we like around here, too, Soul," he continued. "In fact, most folks would say that it's one of the things that makes Lake Barrow the kind of pleasant place to live that it always has been."

Soul nodded.

"I just hope you'll help us keep it that way," Jim added.

"I intend to," Soul answered, not taking his eyes off of Jim.

Tension filled the silence that followed.

Finally, Jim glanced at me once more before turning back to Soul. "Good to meet you," he said, reaching out to shake hands once more. "Welcome to the Spartan family."

Both of us watched Jim leave before Soul turned to me. "Least of anyone's worries, huh?" he said with a grim expression.

"He just needs to get to know you," I responded.

Soul just shook his head as he got into his car.

"I hope this wasn't a mistake," he told me before closing the car door.

# Chapter Thirteen

Ahmad called my phone the next morning as I sat in my office.

"What are you doing?" I asked him, as I studied a roster and tried to put names with faces of my new team.

"Picking out furniture," he answered.

"Furniture?" I asked.

"Office furniture for my home," he said with a chuckle. "Seems this pay raise helps cover some essentials I'll be needing now," he added.

"You got the promotion," I said, sitting up.

"I got it," he said. "Now I just need to pick out items that will fit inside my new house in Lake Barrow."

I sat back in my chair, forgetting about the roster.

"Seems they're gonna let me work from home," he said, "which will allow me to coach defense for the mighty Spartans."

I beamed and pumped my fist.

"Assuming you've still got room for me," Ahmad said.

"You know I do!"

"When can I start?" he asked.

"Come by the field house as soon as you can," I told him. "You can meet the staff."

"Sounds like a plan," he told me.

"Thanks for reconsidering," I returned. "You won't regret this."

"I'm counting on it," Ahmad said. "Thanks, Jayce."

⁓

"What are you doing, Woody?" I asked as we sat in my office later that week.

My defensive line coach turned to me with a grin. He held a large framed painting of a horse galloping across a desert landscape and appeared to be looking for a place in my office to hang it.

"Setting the mood," he told me. "I found this at a flea market just outside of town."

I glanced over at Max, who was looking at his twin brother as if he were studying another species. Soul was grinning but looked equally as quizzical.

"What mood?" I pressed.

"For our Mustang Club," Woody told us.

"Mustang Club?" Soul asked.

Woody hung the picture and carefully let go of the frame, ensuring that it remained in its place. Then he turned and faced us. "We're all Yearwood State Mustangs," he announced. "It's only fitting that we name our coaches' meetings Mustang Club."

"You're an idiot," Max told his brother, causing Woody to scowl at him, as Soul and I chuckled.

"What about Ahmad?" I asked him. "He's a Delta State graduate."

"Yeah, but he's outnumbered," Woody replied easing his large frame into a chair. "From now on, he can be an honorary Mustang."

"I'm sure he'll appreciate that," Soul said with a wry smile. "Didn't we beat Delta State one year?"

I nodded, remembering.

"Of course he'll appreciate it," Woody affirmed.

"So we're calling this 'Mustang Club' now?" I asked.

Woody gave an eager nod, and Max rolled his eyes.

"Max, you're not on board?" Soul asked him.

"I'm on board with us winning ball games," Max answered. "Might be hard to do, long as we have silly-ass distractions like these."

"Nothing silly about it!" Woody protested. "It's about morale-building."

"Morale's what happens when you win," Max argued. "You can't win when you're focusing on dumb crap like this, rather than on studying for your teacher certification exam."

"Whatever!" Woody shot back.

"This knucklehead here," Max said, turning to us, and gesturing to his brother, "spent almost a whole night after we got off work playing video games."

"That's not true!" Woody snapped.

"I may need to coach offensive and defensive line since he'll likely be unprepared."

"Shut up, Max."

"Both of y'all shut up," I told them, looking up and seeing Ahmad through my office window as he walked toward my office.

"Big Jayce," Ahmad said, as he entered the coach's office. "Got the new office and everything!"

"Hey, brother," I said, rising from the desk and greeting him with a hug. We sat down after I had introduced him to everyone.

The next half-hour was spent chatting and making plans for winter workouts and team meetings. Spring practice would be here before we knew it, and we needed to be ready. Ahmad went over the kind of defense he wanted to implement; basic 4-3 set with versatile ends who drop back as extra linebackers in down-and-distance situations. Nothing fancy;

but plenty of room for adaptability depending on the offensive schemes that we would line up against. He had been a student of the game since high school, and I could sense that our defense would be in great hands with him at the helm.

He also hit it off with the guys, which was important. He laughed along with Soul and me at the jaw-jacking from Max and Woody and seemed right at home with everyone.

My staff was now complete.

Soul, Max, Woody, and I all passed the state certification exam and were officially hired as coaches and physical education teachers soon thereafter. With the red tape behind us, we could focus on getting settled into the area and begin prepping in earnest for the season.

Time began to fly by.

I closed on a small, two-bedroom, two-bath house just blocks from where I had grown up, and also put a down payment on a used truck. I was sad to part with my old car for sentimental reasons, but I also knew I needed something more dependable, and which I could use to haul football equipment if need be.

As soon as I moved into my new place, Dixie began coming over regularly and rearranging things, cleaning up, and putting her own touch on just about anything within reach. She was dropping hints all right, and sure enough, we were engaged on Valentine's Day of that year; barely seven months after seeing each other again at Squat and Holler. Mom gave me the ring that Rex had given her, which I put on Dixie's finger as I was proposing. For the engagement location, I took her to the same ice cream joint where we'd had our first date.

We were married on June 28th of that year in a small ceremony at First Baptist Church of Lake Barrow, with Dr. Blake presiding. Jenna Blake, whom Jamie had dated, sang

"Valentine," by Martina McBride, as a tribute to our engagement anniversary. Once again, she blew everyone away with her voice.

Of course, nothing blew me away more than seeing Dixie come down that aisle. Her dress was low-cut and made of silk, but that's about all I could tell you about it, given how fixated my eyes were on her. As far as I was concerned, she would have been just as stunning in anything she wore on that hot summer evening.

Soul was best man, and the rest of my staff stood as the wedding party, in addition to Deke, who drove up from Tampa.

It wasn't long after we got back from our honeymoon in Savannah, Georgia (a present from the Gills) that it was time to start getting ready for two-a-days. Dixie kept her job at the restaurant and would continue working until she finished her degree.

Summer workouts went well that year, and had brought with it plenty of enthusiasm; so much so that the *Barrow Times* had come out to cover our practices almost every day during those hot days of 2003. Biff and Greta Kilgore had been at the epicenter of journalism in Lake Barrow for several decades, and would probably run our local newspaper until their retirement.

"Thanks for having us out, Jayce," Biff told me one day late in the summer. He was a tall, stocky man in his late fifties, who always wore green Sans-A-Belt slacks and white polo shirts wherever he went. His thinning dark hair was combed over the large bald spot on his head, and he wore thin, wire-rimmed glasses that always seemed to slide down his nose whenever he spoke into the Dicta-phone which he always carried with him.

"My pleasure, Mr. Kilgore," I told him, as I stood with my arms folded. "Thanks for covering us."

"As the summer ends," Biff continued with his list of

questions, "how do you intend to manage expectations?"

"Focus on preparation," I answered. "Ignore the hype, and zero in on what we can control."

"Tell us about your coaching staff," Greta chimed in. She was a small, thin woman who, like her husband, seldom deviated in terms of her wardrobe. For as long as I knew her, she always wore print dresses with flowers and a button-down sweater, regardless of the outdoor temperature. She was a pleasant woman with short, red hair and an easy smile.

I went into detail about our coaching staff, making sure to brag on each of them equally as individuals, as well as highlighting how well we had been working together as a staff.

"And how about your new bride?" Greta followed up, with a huge grin. "How is she doing?"

"Honey, for goodness sakes," Biff scolded her. "It's a football piece, not a gossip column."

"Well, I might as well get something for *Greta's Corner* while I'm here," she retorted.

Biff shook his head, and I chuckled. While it wouldn't be fair to call *Greta's Corner* a "gossip column" in the truest sense, Mrs. Kilgore had always done a fair job of getting the goods on many of the happenings in Lake Barrow. This included engagements and weddings, and so I filled her in on as many details about Dixie and our new life together as I felt were appropriate.

The Kilgores' spread on our new coaching staff and upcoming season was a hit. In addition to me being Florida's youngest head coach, our staff members were all under the age of twenty-five, making us the youngest staff in the state.

After the interview, Biff and Greta assembled us together for a staff photo. The front page of the sports' section the next day read in bold print: *Young Guns Ready to Lead the Spartans.* In the picture, the five of us are standing side-by-side in a row, with me in the center, clutching a football.

As a present, Mom had a copy of that photo framed.

Dixie almost fainted when she saw it and made me promise that I would hang it in the garage, and not the living room.

Our roster wasn't loaded with talent, but it definitely had potential. On offense, Andrico Handler would be our starting quarterback. He was an eleventh-grader with the perfect skill set for the kind of offense Soul and I wanted to run: a good arm, quick feet, and the ability to improvise and make decisions on the fly.

Andrico also had the benefit of handing the ball off to Tre Bell, a sophomore tailback who showed promise, as well as throwing the ball to three above-average wide receivers; two eleventh-graders, Johnny Caldwell and Sammy Stromas, along with A.J. Smalls who was in the tenth grade.

Defensively, we were in even better shape. Jordan Gill had played hard and had a good spring and summer. As I watched him play and get after quarterbacks and running backs, there were times when I could have sworn that it was still Jamie out there wearing #44. Even Jordan's mannerisms and swagger were the same as Jamie's, although he had always been more reserved and quieter than his older brother. Jordan was clearly coming out of his shell and was ready to lead the defense as a senior.

As a result, he was now our starter at middle linebacker, and we were able to move Isaiah Waters, who had started in the middle the previous season, to strong-side linebacker. This often left him covering the tight end, which was ideal for him, given his speed and quickness. Ahmad wondered why the previous coaching staff hadn't made this connection.

At weak-side linebacker, we had a tenth-grader by the name of Nabeel Jefferson who would start for us. He was several inches shorter than Jordan and rail-thin, but you wouldn't know it by the way he played. What he lacked in size he made up for with his speed and nastiness…almost to a fault. Soul didn't like him because of his attitude, and justifiably so. Nabeel had a tendency to hit people late and play dirty, something I knew Soul (or I) would never stand for even before I brought him with me to Lake Barrow. Nabeel also talked back, which didn't help his cause with any of the coaches either. He was a smaller kid and needed to prove himself, but time would only tell if he could mature and play between the whistles.

Our linebacking corps was easily the anchor for the defense, but the defensive line and secondary were solid, too. They would keep us in games that year, especially if the offense didn't produce right away.

On special teams, Skyler Hemphill was a junior who handled the kicking and punting duties, just as he had the year before. He was a tall, rangy kid with an explosive leg who could easily nail field goals from forty-five yards. This year, his goal was to break fifty. I liked him, and not just because of his talent. His work ethic, especially at practice, was exemplary, and I continually found myself pointing to him whenever one of the other guys slacked off.

Soul and the Twin Tanks were slowly becoming acclimated to life in Lake Barrow, although it was obvious that they weren't too crazy about the warmer winters. Additionally, Soul had to travel to Orlando once a week to attend the nearest mosque, which I thought might wear on him some. Other than that, everyone was getting along fairly well. Ahmad seemed to be getting readjusted to living in his hometown again, too, and the Twin Tanks were just happy to be around football.

"Hey, Coach, any plans to run for class president?" Andrico Handler asked me as we jogged to the practice field on a hot August day.

"Knock it off," I replied.

"How do you like parking in the student section again?"

This time I ignored him, as the other players around him laughed.

"Does your mom still pack your lunch before you come to school each day?"

"No," I replied, "but your mom does."

This shut him up, and the other players razzed him as we entered the practice facility.

"Coach is gonna make us run soul sprints if y'all don't shut up," said Isaiah Waters.

"You better listen to 'Zay," I told them.

"It's too hot for soul sprints," Andrico tested me.

"Keep running your mouth, and you might be surprised," I said.

Youngest head coach in Florida or not, I knew I had to be careful to not let the lines between "coach" and "buddy" blur too much. Still, it was fun to cut loose with the players from time to time, even if they did rag on me occasionally about my young age.

Practice that afternoon didn't go well; for some reason, the effort just wasn't there. Consequently, just as Isaiah had predicted, soul sprints ended up being on the agenda after all.

"Everybody line up!" Soul shouted as everyone got into two single-file lines stretching from the track to the main field inside the stadium. Frank Beezer had turned on the lights for us, and we were ready to begin.

"Soul sprints!" I shouted at the group. "On the whistle. Ready…"

A half hour later, the entire team was sitting in the end zone, covered in sweat and dirt. Some were keeled over, and several were coughing as they fought to catch their breath.

"Anybody's soul hurting right about now?" Soul asked with a smile.

A few hands went up.

"Anybody's legs and arms hurting right about now?"

More hands went up.

"Anybody's legs and arms going to be hurting tomorrow morning?"

More hands.

"Anybody's soul going to be hurting tomorrow?"

"No coach," came the muffled response.

"I CAN'T HEAR YOU!"

"NO, COACH!!!"

"Why?"

No answer.

"Jefferson," Soul said, pointing to Nabeel, who was lying flat on his back against the grass. "Why is your soul not going to be hurting tomorrow?"

"I don't know," Nabeel almost whispered in a petulant tone.

"Stand up!" Max yelled at him.

Slowly, Nabeel rose to his knees and climbed to his feet.

"Answer your coach," Woody ordered him.

"Because the pain don't last," Nabeel mumbled.

Soul's eyes pierced him, his disdain for our young linebacker's poor attitude evident, as he turned his attention elsewhere.

"Gill," Soul said, pointing to Jordan. "Stand up and tell us all why nobody's soul's going to be hurting tomorrow?"

Jordan slowly got up. "Because even though your soul may hurt for a little while, your strength remains forever."

Soul nodded. "That's right," he said. "I guarantee at some point, you're going to go through things that hurt. You're going to lose jobs, lose loved ones, lose money, get sick. That's part of living life. The important thing is to come out stronger. That's why we do what we do out here."

I watched as Soul spoke to the guys, and marveled at how he had won their respect. His background, not to mention his unusual religious faith, had caused the boys to view him with some reticence during the early days after his arrival.

Now, however, I watched him as he towered over them, not just physically, but in terms of the gravitas he conveyed as he spoke. Soul had the reputation of a motivator, to whom the guys (with the exception of Nabeel) had begun to respond immediately. Once more I thanked God that he had come with me.

When Soul had finished speaking, I began to address the team. "Guys," I began, "more effort's needed if we're going to be competitive in our district this year, especially against Barton City. Morgan Danforth was All-Area last season, and is expected to have an all-state season this year."

I went on for several minutes. When I was finished, I brought everyone in. We dismissed after breaking the huddle with "Tested and tried/Spartan pride," and followed the team into the locker room.

"Nabeel's gotta change his thinking," Soul told me once we were inside the coaches' office. "Or I'm gonna change his status as a member of this team."

Ahmad frowned as he looked at Soul. "Give him time," he said. "He's young."

"We ain't got time," Soul said. "Attitudes like his will eat this team like a cancer, and it's not happening on my watch."

"You coming over tonight?" I asked Soul, when we were alone again.

"Tonight?" he asked.

"Yeah," I said with a smile. "Dixie's working late. 'When the wife's away, the boys will play.'"

Soul laughed. "Play what exactly?"

I shrugged. "Xbox; eat some pizza; watch Sports Center."

"I want to," Soul said. "But I've got to go pick up a piece of furniture at Maybon's."

"What kind of furniture?"

"A sofa."

I looked at Soul quizzically, knowing that he was still driving the same compact car he had driven all throughout college. "How in the world are you going to haul a sofa all the way from Maybon's to your house?"

"I'll figure it out."

I chuckled. "Yeah, and you better figure out some insurance, too, since that sofa's probably going to fall off the roof of that matchbox you drive."

"I already bought insurance."

"Soul, seriously, did it not occur to you to ask if you could borrow my truck to pick up your couch?"

"I thought about it," he said. "But I didn't want to trouble you. Besides, it's a new truck."

I shook my head. "You've got to get out of the city mindset and start thinking like a small-towner," I said. "Soon as we're out of here, we'll drive over to Maybon's in separate cars, load your couch in the bed of my truck, and I'll take it home for you."

Soul smiled gratefully. "Guess I just got my first lesson in small-town life," he said. "Thanks, Jayce."

Maybon's Furniture was another place that had been in business for decades and had shown no signs of slowing down. We pulled into the parking lot and went inside, where Soul would pick up his purchase. When all of the paperwork was signed, the sales associate went to the back of the warehouse to retrieve it.

"So no pizza and video games tonight," I said to Soul, as we were standing there waiting. "How about you come over this weekend? Dixie's making spaghetti."

"I can't," Soul said.

"Why not?" I asked.

He looked at me and grinned. "Because I have a date."

"A date?" I asked.

"You heard me."

I stood there for a moment, surprised by what I had just heard. Soul and I had seen each other almost every day since moving to Lake Barrow. Never before had he mentioned anything about a romantic interest.

"Who are you going out with?" I asked him.

"Mikayla," he answered.

"Mikayla Hudson," I said, "the new 11th grade English teacher, and girls' track coach...not to mention Deke's little sister?"

"You know any other Mikayla?" he asked.

I just shook my head.

"You look surprised," he said.

"Just a little," I said. "For one thing..."

"She's not Muslim?" Soul said with a grin.

"Well, yeah."

"Which is why we're just going out this Friday, instead of naming our unborn children, Jayce."

"Fair enough," I said.

"She's a nice young woman," he continued.

"She is," I agreed. "I've known her since she was a little kid."

"Smart too," Soul said. "Made the dean's list all through-out college."

"How'd you know that?" I asked.

"She told me last weekend on our first date."

Soul laughed as my jaw dropped.

"How did I not know about this?" I asked him.

"Probably because you didn't ask."

I just shook my head. "You could have told me," I said.

"There's nothing to tell. Like I said, we're just friends, and we like to hang out together. Maybe that will change, maybe it won't."

I just nodded and decided to leave it at that, especially since the sofa was now being wheeled to the front of the store.

Two men who looked to be in their late twenties were steering and pushing the large piece of furniture. When they reached us, the one who had been steering with his back to us, looked up. He smiled when he saw me, but quickly changed his demeanor upon seeing Soul, who was wearing the *kufi*.

"How's it going?" he asked in a reserved tone, taking his eyes off of Soul for only a moment before they darted back to him again.

"Fine," I said. "We ready to load?"

"We're ready," he said, still glancing warily at Soul.

"Right out front," I said, pointing at my truck. I felt my irritation level start to rise, as I began to pick up on the man's attitude toward my friend. "The Dodge Ram with the tailgate down, right by the door. Think you boys can handle that?"

The first worker said nothing.

"Where you from?" the second worker asked Soul. His expression was a condescending sneer, far from the unsettled demeanor of his co-worker.

"Detroit," Soul answered evenly. He had keyed into what was happening before I did. His expression bore the same peacefully resigned, hollow-eyed look that I'd seen too many times.

"What country?" the second man persisted with bile in his voice. "Why is that important?" I interjected, looking the second guy in the eye.

"Just a question."

"My family is from Iran," Soul said. "How about yours?"

"Right here in Lake Barrow, Florida," he replied. "U.S. of A."

"Congratulations," Soul said.

"So are you friends with any of the assholes who attacked us two years ago?" the second handler asked.

"Son of a bitch!" I snapped, slamming my Spartan baseball cap on the ground and lunging toward the second man. He backed away, and Soul sprang into action and restrained me immediately, preventing a sure brawl right there in the store.

I was seething. "You want Doug Maybon to fire your ass, keep running your damn mouth," I snarled. "I'll have your job so quickly, you won't even know what hit you until you get that first welfare check, you redneck prick!"

Several people in the store were now staring at us, and one of the cashiers had stepped forward in case a fight did break out.

"Take it easy," the cashier said, standing in front of me. I glared at the second handler who sneered and helped his partner wheel Soul's couch out the door.

Once they were out of sight, I turned to Soul again, whose expression had not changed.

Soul made sure the two of us stood far enough away from my truck as the sofa was being loaded, so as to prevent another incident from breaking out. The two rednecks didn't say another word to us as they finished up, and headed back inside the store.

Soul and I caravanned to his place shortly thereafter. After pulling into the small parking lot of his townhome complex, I helped him load the new sofa into his living room. His place was small but had plenty of space for what few belongings he owned. Moving the couch into the den was easy since there wasn't much that we could trip over.

Once we had it where he wanted it, we decided to test it out.

"Feels comfy," I said, taking in the new furniture aroma as I eased onto the faux-leather cushion.

"Always good to have something to ease the discomforts of life," he said with a faint smile as he sat across from me.

I nodded and glanced away.

"Thanks for sticking up for me back there," Soul finally said. "Guess that was my second lesson of small-town life."

"Guess so," I agreed.

Soul shrugged. "Of course, you could have done the same thing I've been doing for years," he answered. "Let it go."

I looked at him.

"You know it probably won't be the last time that happens, Jayce," he continued. "Truth is, I even warned you that it would happen; back when you were all over me to come down here with you."

"What are you saying?" I pressed him, not sure I wanted to know the answer.

"What I'm not saying is that I regret coming here," Soul clarified, seemingly reading my mind. "I love this town, and I think we've got a good thing going with the team. But it's not going to be easy, and certainly not for you. Me, I've been dealing with this my whole life, which is why I knew what to expect."

I nodded. "You were always good at keeping your head on a swivel during games," I told him. "Way better than me, at least."

"Had to be," Soul smiled, "especially going across the middle on some of those crossing routes."

"Been running dangerous routes all your life, huh?"

Soul shrugged.

"Truth is, I should be thanking you," I told him, "for holding me back this afternoon."

"Would be pretty bad if you got arrested and fired from your job before the first game just for fighting some ignorant bigot."

I nodded. "At least Skipper made it through the season before he got canned."

Both of us laughed.

"Seriously," I told him, "I don't know how you managed to stay calm tonight with that guy riding your ass like that."

"Like you said," Soul looked at me seriously, "I've been running dangerous routes all my life."

I nodded.

"Plus, I've got to live worthy of my name."

"'Man of peace,'" I said.

"Man of peace, rightly guided," Soul said, adding the translation of his family name.

"It's a good name."

Soul nodded. "Living up to it is the hard part sometimes."

# CHAPTER FOURTEEN

"Coach Jayce Leonard," a familiar voice called out the next day on the practice field. "I had to see it to believe it."

I turned away from supervising the offense as Lane Faraday, my old high school coach, strode toward me. We shook hands.

"How's retired life?" I asked him.

"Oh, I wouldn't mind being back out here instead," he answered with a smile. "Of course, Gracie wouldn't go for it in a million years; too many honey-do's."

I laughed. Coach Faraday's hair was only slightly grayer and thinner than it had been when I had last seen him, but other than that, he seemed to be in good shape and good spirits. He was of medium height with a slight build, but his presence commanded attention and respect.

"How's the team looking?" he asked me.

"We're pretty good," I answered, giving him a brief rundown of where we stood.

"Sounds like plenty of potential," he affirmed. "Defense will be the key, though, especially against Barton City. I hear FSU's been talking to Danforth's boy."

"That's no surprise," I said. "Morgan's a gamer; definitely

more so than Matt ever was."

"That's not saying much," Coach Faraday said, as both of us laughed.

"And probably has a better attitude," he added, "though again, that's not a big compliment, either."

I nodded.

"How's married life for you?" Coach asked, changing the subject.

"She hasn't kicked me out yet," I said with a smile.

Coach laughed. "Well, that's good. I enjoyed meeting her at the wedding."

"Glad you and Mrs. Faraday could come," I said. "And thanks for the gift; we've been putting that coffee maker to good use lately."

"You're more than welcome."

"I also appreciate you helping me get this job," I went on. "Several people said you were instrumental."

"Well," he said, almost dismissively, "I put in a good word for you, but you really ought to thank Jim Gill. He's the one who lobbied hard for you. 'Jayce this,' and 'Jayce that'; he practically organized a political campaign during several of the quarterback club meetings not long after Ted was let go."

"Any idea where he is now?" I asked him.

"Skipper? Last I heard, he was up in North Carolina, still trying to get on somewhere. Might be hard for him to do, though, depending on how closely his past mistakes follow him around."

I just nodded.

"You've gotten a really good break here, Jayce," Coach said, patting my shoulder. "Play by the rules, and you'll be fine."

"Yes sir."

Coach turned to walk away.

"You leaving already?" I asked him.

"Gotta get home," he said. "Gracie wants the hedges

trimmed before the sun goes down. Had to convince her to turn me loose so that I could come up here for just a few minutes and see you and the boys."

"I'm glad you did," I said.

"Just remember what I said, Jayce," he said, turning to me once more, a look of gravity in his features.

"I will," I said. "Of course, I'm not planning to recruit any players."

Coach Faraday gave me a faint smile. "Always play by the rules, Jayce. Remember that."

The sounds of Garth Brooks and Kid Rock blaring through stereo speakers combined with the sounds of splashing, shrieking, and friendly teenage banter on a hot August afternoon.

It was the last weekend of summer before school started, and the Gills were hosting members of the football team, their parents, the coaches, and some cheerleaders at their lakefront house for an end-of-summer barbecue; complete with swimming off of the dock, jet-skis, and plenty of food.

Dixie and I pulled up and got out of my truck just as we saw Jordan, off in the distance, returning to the shore on one of the jet skis. Seated behind him was a cute, blonde cheerleader who held onto him as he motored back into the shallow water. Nostalgia hit me once more. There was no way to tell how many times over previous summers that I had seen Jamie and Jenna on the back of the exact same wave-runner. I missed my friend.

Dixie had made an apple cobbler, which she handed to Jacqui, who greeted and hugged us both. I made the rounds and spoke with Max, Woody, and Ahmad, along with a few of the parents, and thought about going down to say hello to Jordan and the players. The adults were letting the kids have their space by the water, however, so I decided to pass on it.

Soul had gone home to Detroit for a week to see his family before school started, and would be back the next day.

Jim was stationed in front of the grill, where he flipped burgers and rotated hot dogs while wearing his favorite apron which read, "Killer Griller"; a Father's Day gift that Jamie and Jordan had given him together several years earlier.

"Afternoon, Coach," he told me, waving with a pair of grill tongs. "Perfect day for this, huh?"

"Wouldn't have missed it for the world," I answered. "Kids having fun out there?"

"Seem to be," he said, turning his attention to the sizzling beef patties. "Dixie come with you?"

"Yeah, she's right over there, talking to Jacqui."

"What about your college buddy?"

"Soul's home in Detroit," I answered. "Last hurrah before the school year."

Jim didn't respond to this.

"He wanted to be here, though," I added.

Jim glanced at me. "Let me ask you something, Jayce," he began. "How does it work with him?"

"What do you mean?"

Jim nodded. "I mean we don't have any mosques here in Lake Barrow, or in Barton City for that matter. So how does being a Muslim in a place like this work for him?"

"He goes to Orlando every Friday," I said simply.

"Orlando on Fridays?" Jim asked, looking at me and taking a drink from a water bottle.

I nodded.

"Seems awfully inconvenient," he added, mopping his brow, "especially once the season starts."

"It won't be," I assured him. "He'll probably cut out early on Fridays, go worship, and get back in time for the game."

Jim said nothing as he sprinkled seasoning onto a patty.

"What?" I asked, tired of dancing around the issue. "You

didn't exactly make our new offensive coordinator feel welcome after the quarterback club meeting several months ago, and something tells me part of that was by design."

"What does Starr say about this arrangement?" Jim asked, ignoring me and glancing up from the grill. "Him getting special treatment just because of his faith?"

"Special treatment?" I asked.

"He gets to cut out early and go to worship, while you work."

I shrugged. "I imagine it works the same way it would if things were reversed and Lake Barrow was majority Muslim with no Baptist churches."

Jim shook his head. "I just can't believe he's here. Was Lake Barrow the only place for him to go after last season?"

Jim's words stung me. "I wanted him here," I protested. "He's a great coach and an even better person."

"A lot of people are asking questions," Jim said simply.

"A lot of people don't know him," I shot back.

Jim focused on the grill and was silent again.

"Who's asking questions?" I demanded.

"Doesn't matter," Jim answered.

"It does to me," I replied. "Why do people have a problem with Soul?"

"That ought to be obvious."

"What's obvious is the way you're talking doesn't sound like the Lake Barrow I grew up in."

"That's probably because you never really knew the Lake Barrow you grew up in, Jayce," Jim replied. "I've been here all my life, and I can tell you first-hand that this is a great town. But it's not perfect, and people don't always like change around here. And as it turns out, Soul represents the kind of change that people might not be ready for; especially in today's world."

"Today's world being what?"

"Stop playing dumb, Jayce. I buried my oldest son barely

a year ago, and I don't like the fact that we're in the Middle East any more than you do. But the truth of the matter is that we are, and in a war, you have enemies."

"Soul is not the enemy!" I blurted.

Jim flipped two patties, then turned to look at me. "I know that, Jayce," he said. "But I also don't want you to get hurt; even if it's from you doing the right thing by your friend and a fellow coach."

"Who's going to hurt me?"

"Don't be stupid," Jim admonished. "The way people treat each other around here can leave some pretty deep scars, and I think you know that as well as anybody. Margery had to spend some time in counseling after what happened with the Danforths several years ago."

"You think you're telling me something I don't know?" I asked him. "Just about every time Soul and I hang out somewhere together, he gets at least one weird or dirty look. And that's if he's lucky. But he's still happy to be here and once we start winning games, which I'm sure is going to happen sooner rather than later, hopefully, none of it will even be an issue."

"I hope you're right."

"Regardless, though, people need to get over themselves," I said angrily. The conversation had darkened my mood.

A moment passed as we stood there by the grill.

Jim looked up from the grill, his face covered in sweat. "You're right about winning, though," he said, mopping his brow. "Beat Barton City, and a lot of this won't even matter."

"It shouldn't matter, regardless," I replied.

"And I shouldn't have brought this up," Jim said, turning from the grill and trying to smooth things over. "Let's just try to enjoy the day."

I nodded.

"Except I was serious about beating Barton City," Jim clarified with a smile.

I grinned.

"I want Jordan to stomp a mud-hole in the Danforth kid."

"You might get your wish," I said. "He's been playing hard, and if we can get him blitzing on..."

PLAP!!!

I saw a flash of light, as the sensation of being hit in the face with a soft object was soon followed by the feeling of suddenly being wet.

Then I heard laughter.

"BOOM!" yelled Jordan from a few feet away, as he held an armful of water balloons and continued laughing hysterically. "Right in the mouth, too!"

"Jordan, watch the barbecue, son!" Jim yelled angrily. The front of his apron was drenched.

I glared at Jordan, who face bore a look of petulance. Then I glanced at Jim, who was picking pieces of latex off of himself as he continued tending the grill.

Both of us looked at each other and began laughing.

"Teach that little twerp a lesson!" Jim instructed me.

"You got it," I answered, feeling the tension lift, as I took off after Jordan.

I had been wearing a button-down short-sleeve shirt and khaki shorts with flip-flops. Quickly, I lost the shirt and shoes and was in hot pursuit of my starting middle linebacker, who had bolted toward the lake. Once he reached the shore and bounded into the shallow water, he continued throwing water balloons at me as I kept up the chase and followed him in.

"Jayce, those are your new shorts!" Dixie shrieked at me from the dock. "Get your bathing suit on first!"

"Right here in front of everyone?" I asked her, drawing laughter from the players and cheerleaders; all of whom were egging on the showdown between me and Jordan. "I don't think you really want that."

Exasperated, she gave up as I reached Jordan, who had

thrown his last water balloon and was now in a dueling posture.

"Come on," he challenged. "Let's see if you've still got it."

"I've still got it," I assured him. "Question is, did you ever have it, to begin with?"

Seconds later, we were grappling. Soon, others began to pile on: Kez Coulter, our outside linebacker; Ryan Gilmore, our starting tackle; and Kyle Messina, our starting free safety all ganged up on me alongside Jordan. I was quickly subdued and pushed deeper out into the water.

Exhausted, and with the odds squarely not in my favor, I gave up not long after running into the lake.

Later that evening, after everyone else had gone home, Dixie sat with the Gills out near the lake shore and chatted with Jim and Jacqui, while I sat with Jordan down on the dock.

"Got beat down pretty bad earlier, didn't you?" Jordan smirked. "You gonna be okay, old man?"

"So now I'm an old man?" I returned. "The other day at practice, you didn't do anything but run your mouth about how I was too young to be your coach."

Jordan chuckled, and we continued listening to the din of the crickets serenading the clear night sky.

"Thanks, Coach," he said after a moment.

"For what?" I asked.

"For being a coach who gives a rip about us," he said. "I'm glad you moved back here."

His compliment moved me. "I'm glad too," I said.

Jordan didn't respond.

"Big year ahead," I added.

"Yeah," he responded.

"Thought any more about your future?"

"A little," he said. "Just not sure, though."

"College?"

"Kind of wanted to go Marine Corps, like my brother, but…" he suddenly trailed off.

"Your dad?" I asked.

Jordan nodded. "He's pretty much against it, for obvious reasons."

I nodded.

"He was against Jamie going in," Jordan continued. "Wanted him to stay in college. I think the only reason Jamie joined was just to piss him off."

I stared off in the distance and listened as the crickets continued buzzing. "That sounds like Jamie."

"Yeah."

"How's your dad doing?"

Jordan shrugged. "Hard to tell sometimes who's taking it harder; him or Mom."

I nodded.

"Jim's definitely tougher to deal with, though."

I looked at him, waiting for him to continue.

"Guess he just wants me to succeed," Jordan finally said. "I'm the only one, so it's kind of up to me now; family legacy, expectations, that kind of thing. And he's crazy about us beating Barton City this year; keeps going on and on about me needing to have my career game against Morgan Danforth."

"You doing okay with that?" I asked, trying to study him.

Jordan shrugged again. He had always been the less emotional of the two brothers. "Sometimes I come out here by myself just to get away and blow off steam if I need to."

"How often is that?"

"More than I'd like," Jordan said. "Probably won't have to do it as much if I do end up getting a scholarship after this year."

"Is that what you want to do?" I asked.

Jordan hesitated before answering. "It's definitely what he wants."

"That's not what I asked."

Jordan shrugged. "I mean, it's college football. Who wouldn't want to play?"

"It's a great opportunity," I affirmed. "But only if it's what's best for you."

Jordan nodded, and we were silent for another moment.

"You may not remember this," I finally said. "But when I first moved to Lake Barrow as a kid and started hanging out with Jamie, you used to introduce me as your 'other big brother.'"

Jordan smiled as he remembered.

"Definitely is a bit weird being your coach now, especially since I'm only a few years older than you. Sometimes during practice, it almost feels like we're still just kids playing in the backyard."

Jordan nodded.

"I guess all I'm trying to say is that if things ever get too crazy around here, just remember that I was your other big brother before I became your coach."

Jordan looked at me through the darkness. The only ambient light we had was coming from the Gills' porch lights behind us, making his face difficult to see. For a moment, though, I thought I could see tears forming in his eyes as we sat there.

"Thanks, Jayce."

# Chapter Fifteen

"He sounds like he's hurting," Dixie said to me, as we lay in bed that night. I had told her about the conversation with Jordan down by the dock earlier that evening.

"A lot of pressure there," I answered. "The whole family's under it."

"It's not hard to see why," she returned, fixing me with those green eyes, and causing me to break my train of thought for a moment. "

I nodded. "Jordan's always looked up to me, too."

Dixie laid her head on my chest and ran her fingers along my torso. "It doesn't sound like that's changed much."

"It's different now, though."

"Because you're his coach," she finished.

I nodded, and Dixie snuggled in closer. "And you deserve to be."

"Why is that?"

She returned the gaze, leveling me again with her eyes. "Only someone who will stay up late at night thinking about his players the way you do deserves to coach that team."

I ran my finger down her cheek. "I'm no saint," I responded.

"I know you."

"What do you know about me?"

"I know enough," she replied. "Ever since that night I came to your house and waited for you on your front porch, I've known enough."

I leaned down and kissed her gently. As I pulled back, Dixie placed her hand on the back of my head and drew me in for more.

Moments later, the sounds of our love-making filled the room.

"Is it just me," I shouted to Soul two weeks later over the din coming from the school's gym, "or do pep rallies create more nervousness than actual games?"

"I can't hear you," Soul answered with a grin amidst the bedlam that was echoing through the hallways.

I repeated the question, and Soul laughed. School had started two weeks earlier and the anticipation of our first game later that evening (and my first test as a head coach) could not have been more palpable. Our entire team was assembled outside the gym, all wearing their game-day jerseys over shorts and jeans, ready to make our entrance during the school's first pep rally of the season. Once inside, it would be my first major public address to the school.

I was sweating.

"That antacid working?" Max asked, sidling up to me. Like the rest of the coaching staff, he was dressed in a green polo with "Sims County Spartans" embroidered on the left breast, and cream slacks. His large belly, like Woody's, poked out beyond his waistline.

"Seems to be working," I answered him.

"Twenty-four years old, and you're already taking the same meds my dad takes," Max jeered.

"Shut up," I retorted.

"Just remember," he went on, "if you throw up, aim it at Woody."

"You just worry about blocking schemes and keeping Andrico from getting planted," I replied. "I'll worry about my digestive system."

Max chuckled and walked back to where his linemen were standing.

The doors to the gym opened, and Ahmad emerged. "We're ready," he announced.

Soul looked at me and smiled. I felt my insides churn once more.

"You okay?" Ahmad asked as he stood in the doorway.

"Yeah," I responded. "Let's do this."

Once the clamor of the Sims County High student body, faculty, and staff hit my eardrums, I quickly forgot about the queasiness in my gut and wondered if I would even be able to hear myself speak once I stood at the dais. After leading my team to the center of the gym floor, where three rows of chairs were set up, I stood in front of a microphone and looked out at the throngs of people. Gradually, the noise died down, the team took their seats, and the crowd watched in anticipation of my opening remarks.

Strangely, as the racket subsided, my ability to process my written remarks seemed to dissipate as well.

*What was happening?*

I felt as though I was locking up and unable to speak. It was Jamie's funeral all over again. Was it the size of the crowd? Was it the fact that the noise was quieting? For goodness sake, the notes were *right there in my hand!* Why wouldn't the words come?

It all took place in a matter of seconds, but it felt like an eternity.

Desperately, I looked out at the crowd and, thankfully, spotted my mother sitting next to Jim Gill, who wore a green blazer, shirt, and tie. Both of them grinned proudly at me.

Somehow, that was all I needed to see. Everything within me suddenly became calm, and I felt as though I were free to speak.

"Are y'all ready for some football tonight?" I asked, each syllable rising in intensity and volume.

The gym erupted again.

I smiled, and continued, completely at ease, and went through my speech about our team and that evening's game. Only later would I overhear one of the veteran teachers say that it was the most rousing address by a head coach he had ever heard.

"Great speech," Mom affirmed, as she embraced me outside the gym following the pep rally. Dixie, who was standing next to her, kissed me on the cheek.

I thanked them both as we embraced before I turned to Jim, who shook my hand.

"You looked nervous," he said quietly.

"It was obvious, huh?"

"Only for a minute, though," he clarified with a smile.

"Thanks for being here," I said.

"Wouldn't want to be anywhere else," Jim returned. "You grew up here, and know as well as anybody that this town shuts down on Friday nights in fall. Folks around here don't miss too many pep rallies either."

I grinned.

"That said," Jim continued, turning to Mom, "this lady and I probably need to get back to work. That car dealership won't run itself."

"We've got a busy afternoon," Mom sighed. "Lots of

work to finish up before the game tonight."

I shook my head. "I don't know how you work for this slave-driver."

"At least he's a well-paying slave-driver," Mom said with a smirk.

Jim chuckled. "You didn't tell him yet?"

"Tell me what?"

"I got a raise," Mom said, turning to me and beaming.

I beamed. "Mom, that's awesome!" I exclaimed, hugging her.

Jim smiled. "Business has been good, and she deserves it."

I walked Mom and Jim out to the lot, where Jim's Suburban was parked and waiting. After we both helped Mom get settled in the front passenger seat, Jim turned to me.

"Ready for tonight?" he asked.

"Ready as we're going to be," I answered.

"Spartan boys are always ready to hit someone once fall rolls around," Jim added, as we made our way around to the driver's side. "The season's all Jordan can talk about."

"He's a product of Lake Barrow," I grinned.

Jim paused briefly before speaking again. "How is the coaching staff? Think those young guns are ready?"

"They're ready."

Just then, Soul walked up to me. "I'm out," he told me, gesturing toward the faculty parking lot.

"Sounds good," I said.

"I'll be back in time for the team meal," Soul clarified, "unless Orlando traffic is unusually bad."

"Take your time," I told him.

Soul nodded and then turned to Jim. "Mr. Gill," he said politely.

Jim nodded, as Soul walked off.

"Headed to his prayer service?" Jim asked.

"Yeah," I answered, noticing the thinly-veiled consternation on Jim's face.

"You sure he's going to work out?" Jim asked.

"We talked about Soul," I said to Jim. "He's going to work out. And he's a great coach."

"I'm not worried about his coaching ability," Jim clarified.

"Then what are you worried about?"

"You getting hurt," Jim said, looking me in the eye. "Same thing I've been worried over."

"I'm not worried," I said.

Jim said nothing as he cranked the car.

"Thank you for taking care of my mom," I said to him.

Jim glanced at me. "Loyalty never goes unrewarded in this town, Jayce. You know that."

While no official "pecking order" existed at the school among the faculty and staff, there was no mistaking the fact that I was the most observed, and in many ways the most popular, teacher on campus. This translated into a few perks when it came to my role as an actual teacher within the school. As a physical education coach, who just happened to also be the head football coach, as long as my students showed up, behaved, and didn't wander the halls during class periods, there was an unofficial "wink-nod" rule that basically said I didn't have to make them do anything.

My P.E. class took place on the outdoor basketball courts during the final period of the day. There, students could shoot hoops, toss a football, run, or simply socialize. As long as they were present and accounted for, my job was easy. I sat on a chair in a shady area under a corridor awning and kept a casual watch on everyone as I studied plays and went over, for about the hundredth time that week, our first opponent who we were playing on our home field that evening.

The Benfield High Broncos ran a straightforward variation of the Veer offense and loved to pound their stocky fullback inside as much as possible. As such, Ahmad and Woody had been working all week on getting the right men inside the box and stacking the line of scrimmage. The only potential problem, as with any offense like Benfield's, was the possibility of them throwing it downfield if we crowded the line too closely in the wrong situations. I was not overly worried about this, as the Broncos' quarterback was only a marginal passer at best. According to the scouting film we had seen, their receivers had decent speed, but nowhere near enough to burn our corners and safeties.

"Good speech today, Coach," a female voice called out, interrupting my focus.

I looked up and smiled as Mikayla Hudson, Deke's sister, approached me. Like me, she was a first-year teacher who had moved back home after graduating from the University of Florida the previous spring. Like her brother, she was tall and athletic, having run track for both Sims County and UF. Her muscled frame was tucked neatly into a blue pantsuit, and her dark hair was straightened and cut to just above the neckline. Her facial features were squared and regal-looking. Mikayla was smart and beautiful, and it was not hard to see why Soul was interested in her, despite the differences in their religious faiths.

Mikayla walked over, and I noticed that she was accompanied by Quinton Leeds, an eleventh-grader who often kept to himself, wore black clothes, and was generally considered a loner, if not an outcast, by most of the teachers and students at Sims County High School. He was tall with shoulder-length dark hair and a pale, subdued expression that rarely changed.

"Thanks," I grinned at Mikayla. "What are you doing out of eleventh-grade English?"

"Well," she sighed and glanced at Quinton, "I had to go and collect Mr. Leeds here from the Dean's office."

Quinton stared off into space and did not acknowledge either of us.

Mikayla continued, "He decided that he didn't want to attend school today. Thankfully, our resource officer was off-campus and just happened to notice him coming out of a convenience store. I had to leave Mrs. Hanceford in charge of my class while I went down and escorted him back here. Now, why did you make me do that, Quinton?" she asked, her tone a balanced mixture of serious and playful.

The boy didn't answer. Quinton's story was one that was becoming all too common around Lake Barrow. Neither parent was in the picture, and a distant relative whom he supposedly lived with was the only point of contact listed on any record of his that could be found. Beyond that, very few details were known about Quinton's life.

I watched Mikayla as she interacted with Quinton. Though she was a rookie teacher, there was no doubt that she was born to teach and mentor teenagers. Mikayla Hudson, like both of her parents, had always been passionate about education, even as a student. And she had always loved helping people, especially her teammates. Her firm, caring spirit was what drew many people to her.

"Is the team ready?" Mikayla asked, turning her attention back to me.

"We'll be ready," I answered. "Benfield's tough, but I think we'll be solid."

Mikayla smiled. "That's good."

"Question is, are the Tampa Bay Bucs ready?" I returned.

Mikayla laughed. "Last I heard, they were getting there."

"Sounds like the pre-season grind's got your brother pretty busy."

"That's the truth," she answered. "How's the staff getting along?"

I shrugged. "We're fine. Rarely a moment where the Twin Tanks aren't having at each other, but other than that, everyone's doing well."

Mikayla chuckled again. She had already seen plenty of

Woody and Max during a few of the faculty meetings. "Those two are a trip," she said.

"You have no idea," I replied.

"How's Coach Rasheed doing?" she asked, averting her eyes and pretending to be nonchalant.

"He's fine," I said, looking at Mikayla with a faint smile. "Of course, I figured you might know that answer better than me."

A slight trace of bashfulness came over her as I said this.

Almost on cue, the rear doors to the field house opened, and Soul emerged, having just returned from prayer service earlier than expected. He strode out onto the court as the hot, mid-morning sun shone against his bald head, and smiled and waved when he saw Mikayla and me.

"Miss Hudson," Soul greeted her politely.

"Coach," she returned.

I began laughing.

"What's so funny?" Soul demanded, glaring at me.

"It probably ought to be obvious to you," I replied with a smirk.

"You need to pay more attention to our opponent," Soul lectured, "and less attention to me and my personal life."

I just shook my head, as Soul turned back to Mikayla.

"Who's this?" he asked her, gesturing to Quinton.

Mikayla introduced them both, and Soul extended his hand, but Quinton ignored him and stared off into the distance, a look of contempt plastered across his face.

"Quinton, why don't you head on into class," Mikayla instructed her student, gesturing toward the double doors just off of the basketball court.

The three of us watched as Quinton shuffled in a languid gait toward his destination. As I watched him go, I wondered if Mikayla was saying the same silent prayer for him that I was. There was no question that Quinton needed help.

"I'll make sure he gets there," Soul volunteered, jogging

in Quinton's direction. We watched as both of them disappeared through the double doors to the main building, Soul
escorting Quinton like a bodyguard.

"Jayce, why do you have to put my business out there like
that in front of a student?" Mikayla asked the slight playful-
ness back in her voice.

"Because you're the little sister, I never had, and it's my
job to annoy you."

Mikayla scowled. "You just better remember that I knew
you back when."

"Before I became a big shot around here, you mean," I
answered, as a basketball bounced my way.

Two ninth-graders came running over, chasing after it.
I retrieved the ball and bounced it back to them. "Thanks,
Coach," one of them said.

"Guess it's a good thing you're here to remind me," I told
Mikayla.

"And I've got some stories to remind you of," she continued. "Like that time you and Deke got up on the roof of the
elementary school and almost fell off."

"Got our butts whipped for that, too," I reminisced.

Mikayla smirked. "Anyway, the answer is, yes, Coach Rasheed and I have been hanging out. But just as friends."

I arched my eyebrows as I studied her.

"Friends for now," she clarified. "We're taking it slow."

"There's a whole lot of guys you could do worse to take
it slow with," I affirmed.

"That's the truth," she agreed.

"Soul's a wonderful guy," I continued. "But I'd be lying
if I said I wasn't surprised to hear about you two, especially
since…"

"The religion thing?" she finished for me.

"Yeah."

Mikayla shrugged.

"You don't have any reservations about dating someone

from a different faith?" I followed up.

Mikayla looked away for a moment. "Did I ever tell you about the first semester after I moved to Gainesville for college?"

I shook my head.

"I joined a large church midway through the semester and went on five different dates, all with guys from the college ministry there. Out of those five, guess how many tried to get me into bed on that first date?"

I studied her.

Mikayla held up five fingers. "Contrast that with dozen times that Soul and I have been out. That man hasn't pressured me even once."

I had no answer as I looked away toward a game of "HORSE" that was being played between several of my students.

"So to answer your question about the so-called 'faith issue,' as far as I'm concerned, there isn't one, especially given how slowly we're taking this."

"One thing about Soul," I said, turning back to her. "Relationships with the opposite sex are about the only things he's ever taken slowly."

"And I respect that," Mikayla responded.

I nodded. "There's definitely a lot to respect about him."

Mikayla smiled. "Listen, I better go, but good luck tonight."

"Thanks," I said, as she started toward the double doors. "You gonna be at the game?"

"Where else is there to go on a fall Friday night around here?" she said.

"That's not your only reason for coming, I hope."

"I also like the head coach," she replied, as she headed into the building. "And the offensive coordinator is pretty cute, too."

"See you around, Mikayla."

"These pants don't fit," Woody complained, tugging at his waistline.

"Because you keep putting on weight," Max answered his brother from the chair next to mine as we sat in the office. "And you never exercise."

Ahmad, being the last one to arrive, closed the door and our first pre-game Mustang Club meeting of the season unofficially commenced. Woody had once again placed the framed Mustang on the wall of my office. Once we were done, it would come back down. A new ritual had been born.

"Yeah, well, you don't exercise either," Woody replied, glaring at his brother.

"Which is why I had the good sense to go out and *buy a new pair of pants* before the season started," Max explained. "You're lucky I'm not the head coach. Otherwise, I'd probably bench you for the first game for not dressing properly."

"Actually, the whole *team's* lucky you're not the head coach," Woody chuckled.

"All right," I cut in. Ahmad managed to chuckle. He had only begun to get used to the constant back-and-forth between Woody and Max, whereas Soul and I had listened to it for over four years.

I continued, "At the risk of setting off another storm between you guys, can someone tell me which side won the Hog Challenge this week?"

"10 sacks, 8 pancakes," Woody blurted.

"12 pancakes to 5 sacks," Max cut in quickly.

"That's a lie!" Woody exclaimed.

"How's it a lie?" Max responded. "Every lineman on *both* sides of the ball, plus most of the linebackers, were counting and they all said the same thing. It's 12 and 5. Even your own defensive guys confirmed it."

I raised my hand. "Let's put it to an independent counsel!" I intoned, pointing at Ahmad.

"I counted 9 pancakes and 7 sacks," Ahmad said.

"Told you!" Max sneered at his brother.

"If that's the verdict," I said, "then Max, you get the Trough Prize this week."

I pulled out an envelope and handed it to him. It was another new ritual we had started. Both the offensive and defensive lines had begun competing each week during practice to see who could out-perform the other. Max's offensive line was graded on how many times they put defensive guys on the ground (known as "pancake blocks"). On the other side of the ball, if one of Woody's defensive lineman got to the quarterback, it was a point for them. Whichever side won that week got a gift card with a small amount of money to spend on anything any of the players needed; socks, mouthpieces, tape, the list went on.

"Carl's Sporting Goods here I come again!" Max celebrated, accepting the gift certificate.

"Careful how you spend it," Ahmad grinned.

"Oh, I'll be careful," Max boasted. "I'll be careful to buy Woody a pair of pants that actually fit him, assuming Carl's even has a pair big enough."

Woody grabbed his crotch. "I got something big enough for you right here," he retorted.

I let the laughter die down for a moment before turning the conversation back to the game.

"You guys think we're ready?" I asked.

Everyone seemed to glance at each other before anyone answered me.

"Yeah," Max said. "Boys have worked hard."

"Defense is set," Ahmad returned.

For the next several minutes, we made small talk about this and that; defensive schemes, receiver sets, and the like. Soon, it was time to go out and begin making pre-game preparations. As we all got up to exit, I overheard the brothers talking quietly.

"I wear a size 50," Woody told his brother.

"I know," Max answered. "Only time you were never the same size as me was back when we were eleven."

"You don't mind hooking me up?"

"We'll go to the store tomorrow morning and get you a new pair of pants. Meantime, I brought an extra pair of slacks you can borrow for tonight."

"Thanks," Woody told his brother.

I just shook my head. As an only child, I still had a hard time understanding the relationship that the Twin Tanks shared; all over each other one minute, and best friends the next. But at the same time, I could only admire them.

The doors to the field house opened before we got there and Soul appeared, having just returned from helping finish the final details of the pre-game team meal.

"Welcome back," I told him.

"Thanks," he said.

"Meal ready?"

"Of course."

"You don't miss many meals, do you?" I told him.

He grinned.

"And I forgot to ask; how did prayer service go this afternoon?"

"Great," he told me. "Loving the community down there, even though it's a drive."

"That's good," I told him, as we walked toward the cafeteria, where the pre-game meal was being set up. "Do you all do anything besides pray on Fridays?"

"What do you mean?" he asked.

"I mean, what else does the mosque do? Any community service or anything like that?"

Soul nodded. "Yeah, we're pretty active," he said, without adding anything else.

"Man, I'm ready for that pre-game meal," Ahmad told

me, as we neared the cafeteria. "I'm getting hungry."

"Who's catering tonight?" Max asked.

"Kyle Messina's mom made lasagna and salad," I answered, referring to our starting free safety. "And she's Italian, so you know it's gonna be good."

"Don't they cook with wine?" Ahmad asked.

"Sometimes," I said with a grin. "They put wine in everything, I think."

Suddenly, it hit me, and I slowly turned and faced Soul.

"It's not *halal*," I said, referring to Soul's strict dietary requirements.

"Already ahead of you," Soul returned with a laugh.

I studied him.

"Mikayla's bringing me something."

"Seriously?"

"Yeah," Soul nodded. "Best *halal* chef in Lake Barrow."

"Does she know how to cook that way?"

"She does now that I taught her."

"The two of you have a really strange definition of the term 'taking things slowly.' You know that, right?"

Soul just shrugged and laughed.

As I look back on that season, that first series of pre-game rituals from week one is still burnished in my memory. I remember the pre-game meal like it was yesterday, largely because Mrs. Messina's lasagna, as expected, tasted superb.

I remember the final offensive and defensive film study sessions in our weight room.

I remember getting the team rounded up in the locker room when it was time to get dressed.

I remember the nervousness.

I remember the fans whooping and cheering for us as we took the field for pre-game warm-ups. And I recall laughing to myself as I considered just how hungry for Friday night football this community had become. Here we were, over an hour away from kickoff, and the stands at Jim Gill Stadium were already filled with green and white-clad citizens from across the county. At that moment, Lake Barrow was like every other small town in America, ready to ring in the start of football season once more.

I remember the pre-game warm-ups on the field; Andrico throwing the ball to his receivers; Ahmad overseeing Jordan and the linebackers and defensive backs as they warmed up; Soul throwing passes to the receivers and running backs; the Twin Tanks inspiring intensity in their linemen as they conducted one-on-one drills.

I remember wondering, right there on Spartan Field, if I was going to suddenly wake up at any moment and find myself back in my dorm room in Yearwood, Kentucky, having suddenly realized that it was all just a crazy, wonderful dream.

My thoughts were interrupted by the faint sound of a familiar voice calling out my name.

I turned, and couldn't believe my eyes when I saw who was standing at the foot of the bleachers.

"Get over here, boy!" Mama Freddy demanded, beaming as she stood next to Bud.

I jogged over and embraced both of my old friends, who had driven down from Kentucky to see our first game. Evidently, Mama Freddy's shrill, southern burr had carried, because Soul and the Twin Tanks were right behind me, leaving poor Ahmad to supervise the whole team. Each of us got tight hugs from Mama Freddy and Bud both.

"When did you get into town?" I asked them.

"Not long ago," Bud answered. Both he and Mama Freddy were wearing white t-shirts that said "Sims County Spartans" on the front. "We cut it close, but at least we had time to visit the merchandise store and get us these snazzy shirts."

"Left early this morning from Yearwood," Mama Freddy

added. "Been planning this trip for months, but we wanted it to be a surprise."

"You succeeded," Max beamed.

"Long drive, huh?" Soul said.

"All day long," Bud answered.

"It's easier when you do it in style," Mama Freddy clarified with a grin. "Bud and I bought an RV two weeks ago."

"You're kidding," I said.

"We thought to ourselves, 'Other people buy RVs to go see their kids,'" she said, "why don't we do the same?

I grinned.

"And since we missed your wedding," Bud added, "I told Winifred, 'there's no way on earth we're missing his first game as a head coach.'"

"I'm glad you came."

"You boys better get back to warming up, though," Mama Freddy said. "Bud and I are going to be in the stands, but after the game, we'd love it if you all would come by the RV and check it out."

"Did you bring any shrimp?" Woody asked.

"Seriously, Woody?" Max scowled at his brother. "You just ate, and on top of that, you were complaining earlier about your pants not fitting."

"Shut up."

Mama Freddy chuckled. "You boys haven't changed a bit," she smiled. "And yes, we brought shrimp, which there will be plenty for everyone, as well as your sweet wife, Jayce, and anyone else you boys want to bring to the camper afterward."

I glanced at Soul, who grinned and looked away.

We hugged the Pearlmuters one more time before heading back to the field.

Warm-ups finished, and it was time to head back into the locker room for last-minute preparations. Once those were completed, I would deliver my final remarks.

After that, it was time to go to war.

To this day, I keep my pre-game remarks from that first season-opener in a special drawer in my house.

*"Guys, we made it through spring, we made it through one of the hottest summers on record, and we've managed to stay together through all of it. But on a deeper level, you guys have managed to stay together through one of the biggest betrayals this school has ever experienced at the hands of a football coach. What Coach Skipper did was wrong, and it hurt us. But we're beyond that now. You guys are an army that has persevered. I couldn't be prouder of a team than I am of you for making it to this point. You pulled together, rather than fall apart, and you did this school and this community proud in the process.*

*Go out there tonight, play hard, play smart, play to the whistle. Finish every play!*

I improvised some of it and threw in a few extra remarks about both our offensive and defensive schemes. As I spoke, I looked out at our team, most of whom seemed to be listening to every word I said, and I felt a large part of the nervousness I was feeling dissipate. And it was at that moment that I knew, beyond a shadow of a doubt, that I was where I was supposed to be. All of the uncertainty that had come and gone up to that point seemed irrelevant. And at that moment, I was never more certain of my calling as a football coach.

"Men," Soul addressed the team after I had finished, "the expectation is that you play hard, play fast, and play with abandon. But play disciplined; hit the other team hard, but do not..." he paused, ready to drive home his next point with extra emphasis, "do *not* hit someone late. Late hits will not be tolerated. If you hit late, you come out, and you don't play again."

Soul's usual jovial expression had been replaced by a look of gravity that conveyed dead seriousness. More than anyone else in that room, I understood why. I glanced down at his surgically-repaired knee and knew that, in addition to the physical scar that snaked its way down the skin covering the patella, there was also an emotional scar that no one could see, but which everyone could hear at that moment.

"No late hits," Soul intoned once more. "I'm not screwing around. You hit late, for any reason, you're off the team."

"Let's get going!" I called out when Soul had finished.

Just as it had been during my days as a player, the sound of over forty young men rising up, donning helmets, and snapping them into place amidst the sounds of cleats scratching the stone tile floor surface seemed to immediately elevate the energy level in the room. I felt the first tinges of adrenaline as my heart began pumping in anticipation.

"Play hard, play intense, play to the whistle," I loudly reminded the men, as we all slowly started moving toward the field house double doors.

Jordan then gathered all of his teammates in a huddle in the center of the locker room. "'Tested and tried' on three, 'Spartan pride' on six!" he commanded. "One two three…!"

"TESTED AND TRIED!"

"Four, five, six…!"

"SPARTAN PRIDE!"

Intermittent whooping and hollering followed as the team began to exit. Max and Woody held the doors open as all forty members of the team burst out and began jogging toward the field. Our field house, which housed our locker room and weight room, was located directly behind the stadium. Several fans in the bleachers caught sight of the team and began cheering and applauding, intensifying the energy level even further. I brought up the rear with Max and Woody and overheard someone yell out my name and wish me well. I tried to keep my eyes focused in front of me, rather than on the adoring fans.

*Execution, not excitement*, I told myself, remembering Coach

Faraday's words during my days as a Spartan player. I knew I was one losing season, if not one defeat, away from hearing the well wishes fade and be replaced by calls for my resignation. That steeled my concentration as I ambled toward our east end zone, where we would run out onto the field as a team.

"Jayce?!" I heard a voice that could have broken me out of a coma.

I looked up into the stands as I passed by them and smiled at my wife, who kissed two of her fingers and placed them near her heart. Mom stood next to her and waved. I could not see very well for the stadium lights' glare, but I was certain there were tears in her eyes.

My heart beat faster as we made our way toward the end zone with the rest of the team. As if the atmosphere needed any more fervor, I saw a faint beam of light shoot up into the night sky and explode in a pyrotechnic burst of color.

*Fireworks.*

The green and white-colored explosions continued as we reached the field. Once we were gathered in the east end zone, Biff Kilgore, who also served as our veteran play-by-play announcer, called our attention to the fifty-yard line. The stadium became quiet and still as a senior chorus student stood there, faced the large flag in the end zone opposite ours, and belted the national anthem. The regal notes and lyrics of our nation's signature melody echoed through the humid night sky, as adults held baseball caps over their hearts, and players stood with their helmets in one hand and their hearts covered by the other. As the singer crooned the final note, more fireworks detonated in the crisp night air, and I fought to keep my breathing under control.

*Execution, not excitement,* I repeated in my mind.

# Chapter Sixteen

"Our Father, who art in heaven, hallowed be thy name..."

I've always compared old traditions to the long stretches of rural highway that lead into and out of Lake Barrow. They have a beginning somewhere; you know they do, even if you can never see where that beginning starts. At that moment in the east end zone, I had no idea how the tradition of reciting the Lord's Prayer had come to be in existence. Nor did I care. My mind was still on the fact that forty young men in the prime of their lives were depending on me to lead them into a Friday night battle that would be the talk of the town for at least the next week. Though I was only twenty-four years old, the fact was not lost on me that how I led them, and how they performed, would set the tone for the rest of the season, and quite possibly for my future as head coach.

The fireworks that had erupted overhead might as well have detonated inside my gut as we concluded with "the kingdom, and the power, and the glory forever, amen."

I stood behind the team at the goalpost as Jordan Gill and Jeff Crocker, our offensive and defensive captains, rallied the team once more behind the large banner that the cheerleaders held up. The rest of the pep squad chanted as a tunnel was formed through which the boys would charge once the banner was ripped.

We had won the coin toss and elected to receive. That meant that Soul, who was already in the press box up above the stands, would be calling offensive plays to me via headset early on.

A wave of energy hit me again as the banner was torn in two and the team bolted forward amidst cheers, and the upbeat notes of our fight song reverberated from the band section. The energy was palpable such that I remember feeling as if I were riding a roller-coaster for the first time as I ambled behind the team alongside Woody and Max. Ahmad was in the booth with Soul. We reached the sideline, and one of our trainers handed me my headset, which I donned right away.

My mind was riding a wave of stimulation as I heard Soul's voice through the earpieces.

"You read me?" he asked.

"Loud and clear," I said. "You got the first call."

"Actually, you do."

"What?"

"It's your first game, Coach," Soul returned. "You call the first play."

"Are you sure?"

"Positive," Soul answered.

"You're not going to run to the papers after the game and complain about me micro-managing the offense, are you?" I joked with him.

"If we score, you can micro-manage it the rest of the season," he answered.

I grinned. "Sounds good."

"Hey, Jayce?"

"Yeah?"

"I appreciate you bringing me here, man," Soul said. "Didn't think I'd enjoy this anywhere near as much as I am right now."

"Me too," I told him, as our receiving unit took the field.

I was amazed at Soul's cool deportment, which was almost always evident no matter the circumstances, and which helped alleviate my nerves as we got closer to kickoff. Johnny Caldwell and Tre Bell stood back near the goal line and waited to receive the kick.

My heart kept racing as I watched Benfield's wiry kicker place the ball on the tee at their own forty-yard line while the kicking team got set. Another tense moment before I heard the referee's whistle, signaling the opening kickoff. Slowly the kicker ambled forward and picked up speed as he neared the ball. The energy and noise level in the stadium continued rising as he drew his foot back, and connected, sending the pigskin catapulting through the night air. A hush fell over Jim Gill Stadium as hundreds of spectators watched the ball sail in an arc toward Johnny, who caught it at the five-yard line, and began sprinting upfield.

He crossed the twenty, found a seam in the Benfield jerseys, and looked as though he might take it to the house for an early score. The kicker, however, who was also a starting defensive back, had good speed and was able to trip him up by the shoestrings as he reached our forty-yard line. Johnny fell to the ground, and the play was whistled dead.

Immediately, I heard jeers and yells rumbling from the other side, which were accompanied by the sight of a yellow flag flying up in the air. I glanced out and instinctively began running downfield at the sight of one of our guys fighting with a Benfield player. The referees, players, and even a couple of coaches fought to separate the two, and I strained my eyes to see who was involved.

Nabeel Jefferson.

Several of our guys finally pried Nabeel away from the Benfield player and shoved him in the direction of our sideline. The worst part was that this barely fazed Nabeel, who stormed back, looking for more action.

I reached the fracas, grabbed Nabeel around the collar, and yanked him back. "Cool it!" I yelled.

Nabeel was back on our sideline and in front of me, but his eyes were still on the skirmish, as he screamed obscenities at our opponent.

"Shut up!" I bellowed at him. "You want to get kicked off before the first game?!"

My tone of voice had gotten his attention, and he now leveled his contempt-filled eyes at me. "Coach, he grabbed my facemask!"

"I don't care!" I yelled.

"Man…" Nabeel exclaimed, jerking away and uttered more profanities under his breath.

"Get him out of here," Soul immediately instructed over the headset. "Nabeel hit late, and I'm sick of his attitude. He's finished for the year."

While the referee was assessing the penalty, I grabbed Nabeel again as he flounced near the water coolers, and spun him around.

"You're done," I told him. "Hit the showers, and turn in your uniform."

Nabeel glared at me.

"Coulter," I shouted, without taking my eyes off of Nabeel. Right away, Kez Coulter, an eleventh-grader who had been a reserve linebacker the previous season, came up beside me. "You're starting at Will, now."

Nabeel unfastened the chest strap of his shoulder pads, pulled them over his head, and threw them down at my feet before storming off the field for the last time.

The season had barely begun, and we had already lost a player; nothing even close to how I had hoped to start the season.

I tried to shake it off before going back to where our offensive huddle stood. The boys leaned in and waited for me to give them the play.

"Strong right, cross-buck 30," I barked to them, fighting the crowd noise and band music, as well as my own emotions as I compartmentalized what had just taken place.

The offense jogged onto the field, the sheen of their helmets glistening under the stadium lights. The play would be a quick draw up the middle, with Rico handing the ball off to Tre.

The fight, combined with Nabeel being kicked out of the game and off the team immediately following the opening kickoff, had sapped some of the energy out of our stadium as well as our sideline, and I became concerned.

"What are we running?" I heard Soul ask through the earpiece.

I relayed the play, to which Soul didn't respond.

The offense got set, and Rico stood about three yards behind Jeff Crocker, our senior center.

"Check it!" Soul barked with urgency over the headset.

"Check it?" I asked.

"Have Rico switch it up, and throw it deep to Caldwell," Soul clarified. "They've got their slow corner on him. Do it now!"

"Soul, are you sure?" I questioned.

"Jayce, do it!" Soul exclaimed in a tone of voice reminiscent of a kid daring his friend to do something crazy. "It's the perfect mismatch, and we need a spark after what just happened. Go for it!"

Some people say that football is a game of seconds, but in reality, it's more like milliseconds. And at that moment, I only had a few of those to quickly examine the defense, confirm that Soul was right about Benfield's cover scheme, and shout out to get Rico's attention to call the audible.

I did so, and watched as our quarterback changed the play, and moved Tre Bell up a step or two to get in position for blitz protection once the ball was snapped. Our receivers spread out wider, and Handler bent down and clapped once, indicating he was ready for the snap.

My breath caught in my throat as Crocker snapped the ball and the play began to unfold. Handler dropped back a few yards and looked downfield, having good protection from the line. Though one of Benfield's defensive ends was giving our right tackle a run for his money, Handler was unfazed as he stepped up in the pocket, avoided the rush, and launched a perfect spiral down the sideline. Johnny was streaking past Benfield's slower cornerback, and the crowd erupted as they watched him make the catch in stride, and accelerate toward the end zone. Our sideline was going nuts, a chorus of inharmonious encouragement as Johnny reached the ten-yard line.

However, at the last second, Benfield's free safety caught up with Johnny just inside the five-yard line and knocked him out of bounds.

Soul had been right. The play had absolutely been the right call and had restored the energy inside Jim Gill Stadium.

"Now run cross-buck 30," Soul relayed through the earpiece.

Benfield's defense was back on their heels now, and the draw play made more sense. I signaled the play to Rico from the sideline, who nodded and relayed it to the huddle. The team got set, and the ball was snapped. Rico handed it off to Tre, who barreled forward, but could not find the open hole over center that he needed. Benfield's defense had pinched inside, leaving their outside wide open. Tre saw this immediately and bounced outward. He accelerated around right end, picked up a block from A.J. Smalls, who had his man sealed off inside, and strolled four yards untouched into the end zone for a touchdown.

I was tempted to jump around and celebrate, just as I had done as a player. But I had to remind myself that I was the coach now, and composure was key. I held up a finger, signaling that we would kick the extra point, as the field goal team jogged onto the field.

Crocker snapped the ball to our back-up quarterback, Jadon Wilkes, who set it down and placed it for Skyler. The rangy kicker booted the ball, which sailed off of his foot and through the uprights for the extra point.

Sims County – 7, Benfield – 0.

"That was almost too easy," I told Soul.

"Guess I'll be the one micro-managing the offense now," he replied.

We both chuckled.

"Micro-manage away," I told him.

At halftime, we sat on a 35-7 lead.

As a graduate assistant, I had learned early on that successful coaching had a lot to do with how you handled your team between the halves. If you were down by a lot, then it was up to you and your staff to dig deep for that extra motivation. If the game was close or tied, emphasizing focus and discipline in the second half was key. And if you were destroying the other team, keeping energy and emotion in check was the trick, and was arguably the hardest ploy in the unwritten coaches' handbook. A large lead at halftime could mean the emergence of complacency, not to mention, an overabundance of ego. Too often, this could mean derailment of not only a sure victory, but left unchecked, an entire season.

Fortunately, the majority of the team seemed to still have their heads in the game even though we were up by a lot. The mood in the locker room was upbeat and business-like as we went over some minor adjustments on offense and defense that needed to be made in the second half. The second team and third team guys were also already relishing the thought of playing time.

I felt good about where we were.

In the second half, Andrico scored a touchdown early in the third quarter, and as he jogged off the field, I heard Soul say through the headsets, "He's done."

"You think so?" I responded, turning and looking up at the press box where Soul sat.

"Yep. Give Jadon the ball and let Rico rest."

I walked over to where Andrico was sitting and told him the news. He nodded and took it well, and I was grateful. As a player and a coach, I had seen too many prima-donnas who never took it well being sat in favor of the second-team guy. Andrico was a team player who often showed great leadership. And Jadon, who was standing nearby, lit up when I told him he was going in on the next offensive series. He was a tenth grader who was playing in his first varsity game. My mind went back to the first game I played in as a Spartan, and I could only imagine the elation he was feeling. It was rewarding to see.

I don't think it would be fair to say that the offense struggled under Jadon, though they did fail to reach the end zone again. Skyler Hemphill kicked two field goals, and that closed out the scoring. Still, in all, Jadon did an effective job of managing the offense and protecting the ball.

As the final seconds ticked off the game clock that evening, I felt proud of our team's performance. We had won 48-7 and had amassed over four-hundred yards of total offense while balancing both the running and passing game. Andrico had a career game, throwing for 245 yards, and three touchdowns. He also did a great job of spreading the ball around and getting different receivers involved in the action. On top of that, he also ran for 66 yards and a touchdown. Tre Bell was equally impressive, running for 110 yards and two touchdowns.

Even without Nabeel, our defense played lights-out, limiting Benford to 120 yards of total offense. Jordan led the

way with 10 tackles, 4 sacks, and a forced fumble.

"Proud of you," Dixie beamed as she gave me a hug after the game.

Dozens of parents and other fans had assembled outside of our field house as they waited for the team to come out. One-by-one, individual players emerged, carrying duffel bags and backpacks as they greeted their parents, girlfriends, and other well-wishers with sweaty hugs.

Mom gave me a hug. "You did phenomenal," she whispered.

I smiled at her.

The Pearlmuters were next. I hugged them both, and they greeted both Mom and Dixie.

Moments later, Soul, Ahmad, and the Twin Tanks joined us. Mikayla soon walked up and kissed Soul on the cheek, and Mama Freddy once again invited us back to the RV for a post-game celebration.

"Will all of us fit in there?" I asked.

"There's plenty of room," Bud scoffed.

"Let's go, man," Woody said. "I'm starving."

"No surprise there," Max quipped.

"Hey, my line kept Benfield out of the end zone. I coached my butt off, and I'm starving."

"Benford scored a touchdown, dummy."

"On a pass play," Woody retorted. "My line kept the running game in check and was in the quarterback's face all night long. Your line's the one that couldn't get Jadon in the end zone in the fourth quarter."

"My line paved the way for over 200 yards of rushing…" Max began.

"Blah blah blah," Woody interrupted.

The rest of us chuckled and rolled our eyes, as we made

our way toward the parking lot.

Out of the corner of my eye, I spotted Jim Gill walking toward us. He wore a dark green polo and a pair of slacks with a white baseball cap that bore our school's logo.

"Phenomenal job," he affirmed to me, as he walked up. "Sorry about Nabeel, though."

"He had it coming," I shrugged. Jim nodded in agreement.

"Jayce," Jim turned serious, as he changed the subject. "I don't want to keep you from Dixie and the rest of your guests, but I wanted to ask really quickly if you'd be willing to meet with me and Starr tomorrow at Guadalajara for lunch."

"Sure," I answered. "Is everything all right?"

"Everything's okay," Jim said.

"What's this about?" I asked, feeling uneasy.

Jim hesitated "It's about Soul," he finally said.

"What about him?"

Jim reached into his pocket and pulled out a folded piece of paper. "Someone gave this to me today," Jim said, his tone of voice similar to a father about to punish his son.

I took the paper from him, unfolded it, and began reading. The headline caught my attention immediately: "FLORIDA MUSLIMS PROTEST OVERSEAS ACTION OUTSIDE MACDILL AIR FORCE BASE." As I scanned the embedded photo, I noticed a man in his late thirties who appeared to be of Middle Eastern descent holding a microphone and gesturing as he spoke into it. Behind him was an assorted group of men and women, most of whom wore headscarves and kufis.

Soul's face was in plain sight.

Jim studied me as I studied the page. "Notice the date?"

I looked just below the byline: August 2, 2003.

"Barely a month ago," Jim said without prompting.

I sighed and read on. The story detailed the specifics of the demonstration; on a Saturday, just outside of MacDill;

peaceful and without incident, though police had to be called due to traffic being obstructed at one point. My mind went back to the brief conversation I'd had with Soul just before the team meal earlier. "Pretty active" was how he had characterized his religious community. Strangely, I found myself getting angry at Soul, but only for a moment.

"They had the cops called on them Jayce," Jim told me.

"For standing too far out in the road," I replied, looking up.

"Do you really think that's the issue here?" Jim returned. "The people of this town don't give a rip about whether or not one of its coaches threw a punch at a cop or, God forbid, a Molotov cocktail."

"Then what is this about?" I demanded.

"Protecting this town's image!" Jim replied.

"From a peaceful demonstration?"

"From the perception that one of our coaches is against the same military that our boys have fought and died in," Jim said, his voice tinged with bitterness.

I hesitated to respond as the pain in Jim's voice hit me. "They were protesting the war," I countered. "Not the boys…and not Jamie."

Jim appeared to be seething. "You really think this town will see it that way?"

"The question is, do you see it that way?" I retorted.

"Jayce," Jim said, fighting to maintain an even tone of voice, "I helped get you here. I've wanted you here since before Ted was fired. Your age never mattered to me, nor did it matter to most other people. You're a quality young man and a great fit for this community."

I kept my eyes on him.

"That's why I'm trying to stop you from jeopardizing what you've got going here by allowing your loyalties to be misplaced."

"My loyalties are to this town, this team, and to my

friends."

"Including my family?" Jim asked.

"Of course."

"Then prove it," he said.

I glowered at him. "How?" I asked. "By firing Soul?"

"By being willing to if it comes down to that, yes," Jim confirmed. "And it may come down to it if there are any more incidents like this."

I couldn't believe what I was hearing.

"Guadalajara," Jim said, turning to walk away. "Tomorrow at noon."

Everyone was upbeat and happy as I climbed into the Pearlmuters' RV.

"There he is!" Bud beamed, as I entered. "The man of the hour."

I managed a grin and sat down in a chair, as everyone clapped. There were two benches on either side of the large vehicle's interior, and everyone except Mama Freddy and Mom was seated on them. Mom sat in a chair, and Mama Freddy was busy serving food and drinks. I tried to stay upbeat as I caught up with Bud, and listened to Woody and Max harangue each other. Soul and Mikayla sat next to each other like two love-birds. I should have been happy, but the conversation with Jim hung over me like a cloud.

The chicken wings and other fare were passed around, and I managed to eat a few bites.

Dixie caught my eye, and I smiled at her, before looking back down at my plate. I felt her gaze remain on me.

After the gathering was over, we said our good-byes to the Pearlmuters and our friends before walking Mom to her car. When she was off, Dixie and I headed toward ours.

"Well?" Dixie asked as we made our way across the field.

"'Well' what?" I countered.

"Are you gonna tell me what's bothering you," Dixie asked, "or do I have to read about it in the papers?"

I didn't answer, as Dixie kept watching me, reading me like a book. We had only been together a short time, yet she already seemed to know every nook and cranny about my personality, which was a blessing and an aggravation all at once.

The stadium lights were still on, but wouldn't be for much longer. Beezer was nearby somewhere and was probably putting the finishing touches on his duties for that evening.

"Jim wants to meet with me and Starr tomorrow," I told her.

"For what?"

I pulled the news clipping out of my pocket and showed it to her. She read it before folding it and handing it back.

"So they want to meet with you because of a peaceful demonstration that Soul was involved in?" she asked.

"A demonstration, and a black eye for the town, Jim thinks."

Dixie chortled. "That's crazy."

"Jim doesn't think so."

"Does Soul know they have this?"

"I don't know what Soul knows," I answered, as we neared the stadium exit, which opened to the parking lot. "What I do know is that Jim doesn't like Soul, and consequently, neither do a lot of other people in this town."

"Why is that?"

I took a deep breath and then told Dixie about the barbecue and what Jim had said about Soul as we had stood near the grill.

"Small-town life," she almost whispered, reminding me of our conversation outside the ice cream parlor just over a year earlier.

"Soul had nothing to do with Jamie's death," I said, "or

9/11, or anything, but that doesn't stop some people in this town from hating him just the same."

Dixie frowned. "That's their problem."

"Which could be a problem for me."

We walked on in silence for several moments.

Dixie put her arms around me. "Come on, Coach," she said. "You deserve to be happy. Don't sabotage it."

I glanced down at her and managed a faint grin. Her face shone like an angel's under the stadium lights and her blonde curls bounced with each step. She was beautiful; and radiant. I couldn't tell if it was all due to the big win, or if she was just in a better mood than usual.

I leaned in for a kiss and savored the taste of her mouth.

"While you're having lunch tomorrow," she finally said, as our faces broke apart, "I may go check out the Pop Warner game."

I chuckled as I looked back at her. We were in the parking lot, nearing my truck. "The Pop Warner game? Why?"

"I just think it'd be fun to watch the little ones running around," she answered. "The boys playing ball; the little girls cheering; makes me think of what our kids might look like in one of those uniforms one of these days.

"Are we talking about kids already?" I asked her with a grin.

Now Dixie was beaming. She turned and faced me, as tears began to come to her eyes.

"We need to be talking about it," she said, "since our first one will be here in less than nine months."

I felt the fireworks in my stomach again. My jaw must have hanging wide open because Dixie laughed as tears rolled down her face and her eyes remained fixed on me.

I tried to speak, but I failed.

"We're going to have a baby, Jayce," she beamed.

Just then, the stadium lights went out.

I felt the bed move the next morning, as I awoke from a deep sleep.

I looked over as Dixie sat upright and glanced at me with a pained expression. Then, without warning, she sprang from our bed and rushed into the adjoining master bathroom. Seconds later, I heard retching.

*It's really happening,* I thought to myself, as the prospect of fatherhood hit me once more. I rose from the bed and was headed to the bathroom to tend to her when I heard the doorbell ring.

"Just go," Dixie managed to say through intervals of spitting and vomiting.

I exited our room, hesitant to leave her. As I reached the foyer, I peered through the spyglass in the front door and saw Soul on our front porch.

He gave me a faint grin as I opened the door. "Sorry to wake you up," he said.

"How do you know I was sleeping?" I asked, rubbing my eyes.

"You look the same way you've always looked after game day," he answered with a grin. "Only worse."

"Thanks," I told him, standing on the porch and closing the door. We walked out onto my narrow driveway and leaned against the truck. Soul was wearing basketball shorts and an old Yearwood State Mustangs t-shirt with athletic shoes. His shaved head gleamed in the early morning sun, and his expression was serious.

"I'll get right to it," he said. "I know about the MacDill story."

I looked at him. "Jim talked to you?"

Soul shook his head. "Jim's not the only one with that story, Jayce."

I sighed and looked out at our street. My neighbor was

raking leaves and pine straw in his front yard. "You want to tell me more about what happened?" I asked him.

Soul paused for a moment. "There's not much to tell," he answered. "Our community down in Orlando joined up with some other groups. We organized a demonstration. That's it."

"Why a public demonstration?"

"A lot of people are upset about the war."

"And a lot of people around here support it," I countered, looking at him.

Soul's face became somber. "Jayce, do you think I'm trying to hurt this town?"

"No, but I don't think it takes much trying, considering what some people in this town have been through?"

"Or do you mean what one particular person has been through?" he replied. "Is this about appearances or appeasement of the one person who got you here?"

"Jim's pissed," I said. "But it's hard to argue with his position."

"Which is what?" Soul asked. "That free speech applies to some people, and not others?"

"You don't understand."

"I do understand," Soul corrected. "It's loyalties. We're friends, but Jim's the one who got you here. Believe me, Jayce, I see your predicament. But my rights as an American citizen shouldn't be in the middle of this."

"It's not about your rights," I persisted.

"So what, then?" he challenged. "Raise your voice, lose your job? I didn't come here to apologize for protesting, Jayce. But I owe you an explanation because of the tough spot I put you in. I even told you something like this might happen the day you asked me when we were still in Yearwood."

Soul paused and looked away.

"And then I let you talk me into coming here," he continued. "And when I got here, I fell in love with Lake Barrow. Sure, it's had its rough parts. People looking at me funny when they see the *kufi*, people saying hateful things. There's always been that element, everywhere I've gone. But it all disappears under those Friday night lights, man. All that negativity, bigotry, and discord over the war; it's gone once that opening kickoff flies through the air."

"So what are you saying?" I asked.

Soul paused. "I'm saying I want to be here, but that it shouldn't come down to a choice between my convictions and my job."

"Then don't give them the power to force that choice on you," I responded. "You're a hell of a coach, Soul, and I want you with me. Just don't jeopardize it by misplacing your priorities."

"My priorities?"

"Live your life," I answered. "But stay out of the papers."

"Unless someone snaps a picture of me at the annual 4th of July parade," he quipped. "Then it's okay to be in the papers."

The bitter contempt in his voice was evident.

"Let's get real," Soul continued, "this conversation doesn't happen if I don't belong to a mosque, right? Or if that protest takes place somewhere else."

"That's not fair," I replied.

"You're going to lecture me about what's fair now?" he retorted.

I took a deep breath, stood up from my leaning position on the car, and let things cool down.

"None of it's fair," I finally said. "I can't change people's beliefs and attitudes, or how they perceive you. All I can do is try to live and operate within reality, for better or worse. That's the way it is."

Soul said nothing.

"You've been my best friend since Jamie died," I told him. "You were best man in my wedding. And I would never ask you to compromise who you are or what you believe.

But..." I hesitated.

"Stay out of the public stuff."

"Yes."

Soul glanced at me. "I'll do it for you," he said.

"Thanks," I told him.

"Only for you."

We stood there for a moment, neither of us saying anything.

"Sorry to wake you up on a Saturday," he finally said.

"You didn't," I responded. "Dixie did."

"She okay?"

"Other than morning sickness, yeah" I answered.

I waited for the implications to sink in, and chuckled as Soul's face finally lit up.

"No way, man!" he beamed.

I nodded. "There's a way," I answered playfully. "And we found it."

Soul guffawed as he bear-hugged and congratulated me.

"Summer baby, huh?" he said.

"May or June," I answered.

"Can't wait to meet him," Soul said.

"Him?" I asked.

"Don't you want a boy?" Soul said.

"Of course," I answered.

"Just helping you think positive."

"Thanks," I said.

"Man," Soul said, leaning against the car again. "Jayce Leonard, Junior."

I laughed. "Another reason for you to keep your nose clean," I told him. "I don't want you run out of town before the birth. My kid's gonna want to know his adopted uncle."

"Uncle Soul," he said, grinning, as the sun beat down on both of us.

# Chapter Seventeen

"He's getting an unofficial reprimand," Starr told me later that afternoon as we sat in a booth at Guadalajara. My boss was sitting across from me, while Jim sat on the bench next to me and sipped sweet tea. We waited for our order.

I remained motionless and tried to keep my emotions in check.

"Have you spoken to him?" Starr asked me, as I drank water from a plastic cup.

"I have," I assured them. "And he's agreed to stay out of the spotlight."

"Is that a promise?" Jim said, dipping a tortilla chip into a small dish of salsa.

"Yeah," I said, unable to hide the annoyance in my voice. "Soul promised, and he doesn't lie."

Jim didn't look at me, but I noticed the disdain on his face as he took a bite.

"You have to understand, Jayce," Starr went on in a fatherly tone, smoothing back his thinning gray hair and pushing his wire-framed reading glasses up on his nose, "people take integrity very seriously around here."

"I do understand," I told him. "But how has Soul's integrity been compromised?"

Jim cut in. "By him putting his own desires ahead of the needs of this community and your team," he said, glaring at me as if I should have known.

Starr cut back in before I could respond. "No one's losing their job, Jayce, and we don't want to stop anyone from living their lives outside of work. But at the same time, care needs to be taken so that the wrong people don't get the wrong idea."

"Wrong people?" I asked, looking at Starr for clarification.

"The same people who won't hesitate to fire both you and your principal," Jim spoke up again and gestured to Starr, "if they get the wrong idea about you and your staff."

I glanced back at Starr, who said nothing and saw no need to clarify what Jim had just said.

"And who are those people?" I persisted.

Neither of them said anything. The conversation was at a stand-still. The restaurant was alive with the sounds of people coming in for lunch, along with dishes and silverware clanking in the background, and the swishing of the fountain in the middle of the restaurant.

Just then, Ignacio walked up with our order.

"Great game last night, *Senor Jayce*," he said, placing three hot platters of food down in front of us.

"Thanks, Ignacio, but I'll need a box," I told him. "I'm not staying."

"You sure?" Starr asked.

"Need to get home to my wife."

"Right away, *Senor*," Ignacio affirmed. "How is Miss Dixie?"

"Great," I told him. "Food's actually for her."

"You're not eating?" Ignacio asked.

"I'll grab something later," I told him. "Dixie's eating for two, though."

Starr and Jim both looked at me.

"She's pregnant," I confirmed.

The tension that had been hanging over our table lightened, as all three of them congratulated me.

Ignacio walked away with my plate and would return moments later with a Styrofoam box. None of us said anything as both Jim and Starr dug into their fajitas and tacos.

As Ignacio reappeared and headed toward our table, Jim leaned over to me. "I'm happy for you, Jayce."

"Thanks."

"I only want the best for you," he said, "and your growing family."

Things settled down over the next two weeks, following the newspaper incident with Soul. We won our next two games, but neither was anywhere near as easy as the Benfield game. We struggled on offense in our second game and couldn't play with any consistency on defense in week three. Still, it felt great to be 3-0, especially considering that the Barton City Bearcats were our next opponent and were also undefeated. I felt good about where our team was as we prepared to take on our biggest rival in what was also our district opener.

Football season in Lake Barrow is always marked by a spike in the overall energy level of the town. During Barton City week, though, it goes to a whole new level. The anticipation was high as Monday rolled around, and banners and other decorations began to appear in store windows, encouraging us to "Tame the Bearcats" and "Beat Barton." Shoe polish messages and designs on rear windshields bearing the same messages materialized as well, as students pulled into the parking lot each morning and were seen driving around town.

On the practice field, however, it was a different story. Complacency after going 3-0 to start the season seemed to dominate our level of performance and preparation., With the exception of Jordan, Andrico, and a few others, the guys were lagging on the field. For the life of me, I couldn't understand why. That Monday during practice, my mind kept going back to my years as a Spartan player, and the intensity that Jamie and I always played with when we would scrimmage against each other, especially during rivalry week. Then again, maybe I was looking at those memories through rose-colored glasses. Maybe we were just as complacent but were just too young and cocky back then to realize it.

The only time the complacency was broken was when a fight broke out during practice that day.

"Break it up! Break it up! Cool out!" shouted Ahmad, as he and Woody rushed into the center of the scrum and tried to separate two players who were tangled up.

It was Jordan and Kez Coulter, the young linebacker who had stepped in at weakside linebacker for Nabeel. He had missed an easy tackle on the previous play.

"Get your shit together!" Jordan screamed at Kez, as Woody grabbed him and drug him away. "I'm sick of this half-assin' on the field!"

"I'm sick of you actin' all king shit," Kez shouted back. "Privileged-ass white boy!"

There were catcalls and other remarks, some of which egged on the confrontation, while others urged both players to relax.

I rushed over. "Calm down," I admonished. "Jordan, pick that helmet up!"

He glared at me, nostrils flaring, but gradually retrieved his headgear which had been ripped off and thrown to the ground.

The sudden burst of intensity actually had me smiling on the inside, and hopeful that this was the spark that would get our team into gear as we prepared for our cross-county rival.

"Jordan, listen," I said, grabbing his shoulder pad and turning him to face me. "You have to channel the aggression."

Jordan said nothing as he stared forward, and I suddenly became concerned. Something wasn't right, and Jordan was not himself. I knew right then that this was not just a sudden burst of aggression, but was instead coming from a deeper rage that was just below the surface, and which showed in Jordan's eyes.

"Jordan, you're the team captain and a leader on this team," I almost whispered. "We need you. Leaders set the tone, they don't tear down."

Jordan shifted and looked away for a brief moment. Then he faced me again. "We're not going to lose to Danforth and Barton City my senior year," he almost growled at me. "I'm making sure of it."

"Man, that fight was about all it took to get things hoppin' again," Max said, as he lowered his large frame into a chair in the office after practice. "Energy level was good the rest of the day."

He had a point. The guys had seemed to play with a bit more fervor after Jordan and Kez had gotten tangled up. My mind, however, was still on Jordan. I barely listened as my assistants talked among themselves. At one point, I made eye contact with Soul, who I figured knew that something was eating at me. When the Mustang Club had dispersed, he remained behind and closed the door.

"You worried about Jordan?" he asked.

"Aren't you?"

Soul nodded. "Very."

I studied him.

"He hasn't been playing dirty, but he's toeing the line," Soul told me. "Getting in those piles, twisting limbs, trying to hurt people. I haven't seen it, so I can't confirm it and have him yanked, but I hear things."

I shook my head. "I wish you could have seen Jordan's eyes today."

"I don't have to," Soul answered. "That anger's been eating him up since the season started, and what's more, I'm pretty sure I know where it's coming from."

I looked at Soul.

"And so do you," he told me.

I sighed and glanced away, knowing that my friend was right as usual. What I had seen in Jordan's eyes went way beyond adolescent intensity on the field of play, and had everything to do with Jim Gill.

Even more fundamentally, it had everything to do with the same controversy which had, for years, bubbled just below the surface in Sims County.

Friday night's game was shaping up to be the latest chapter in the Gill-Danforth saga, and Soul and I both knew it.

Jim was standing on our sideline later that week. He was supervising the team of parents who had volunteered to help Beezer line and decorate the field the night before the big game, though he had never, to my knowledge, personally applied a drop of paint himself.

I walked up beside him. "Looks like more volunteers this week than usual."

Jim kept his eye on the field and nodded. "Barton City week," he said. "Always gets us a few more than usual."

"Hey there, Coach!" Beezer exclaimed, jogging toward me. He was wearing his trademark coveralls with the green jacket and red baseball cap. We shook hands and hugged.

"Ready to whoop them whipper-snappers from Barton City tomorrow?"

"I think so."

"Man, I wish I could be out there!" Beezer looked like a ten-year-old kid at Christmas. "Did I ever tell you about the one tackle I made when I was a player?"

*Only a hundred times*, I thought to myself.

Sure enough, Beezer began regaling us about the game-saving tackle he had made against Barton City decades earlier when he was a student there. He rehashed, in perfect detail, the memory of Barton City being pinned inside their own ten yard line with ten seconds to go; of their star quarterback throwing it deep; of their best receiver catching it at the 50 and breaking free; of Beezer running full-speed to catch him from behind, which he did just as the receiver crossed the 5-yard line; how the crowd went wild; how Beezer was the hero; on and on it went.

"And I'd do it again if I had the chance," Beezer oozed, the eyes framed by his large spectacles bright as stars.

I couldn't help but smile.

"Hey, Beezer," Jim said, "I see a parent about to mess up the goal line over there. Think you better take care of that."

Beezer turned. His ebullient smile turned to a frown. "See you later!" he said. "Go Spartans!"

"Goal line looks fine to me," I told Jim.

"It is fine," Jim confirmed with a smirk. "Hearing that same story for the millionth time isn't fine, though, especially since it's not true. Beezer never made that tackle, and everyone in this town knows it."

I smiled and felt sorry for Beezer.

"'S' is really messed up," I changed the subject, gesturing to the 50-yard line where our logo was painted in white. "Been that way since the Benfield game."

"They'll fix it," Jim assured.

"You sure?"

Jim turned and looked at me for the first time. "You can cover anything with the right amount of white paint."

"Long as it's on a grass field," I clarified.

"The rest of life is definitely a bit more complicated," Jim responded. "In the world of football, though, you know the rule as well as anybody. Wins cover sins."

"Does that include protest rallies?"

Jim said nothing.

"Remember that first play against Benfield?" I asked.

Jim turned and looked at me. "The sideline pass to the Caldwell kid."

"We were supposed to run Tre up the middle," I continued. "Last second, though, Soul saw a mismatch, called down for an audible, and we changed it to a sideline pass, which Johnny ended up almost taking to the house. Next play, Tre scored."

"What's your point?" Jim asked.

"He's a hell of a coach, Jim," I said. "And an even better person."

Jim hesitated and shook his head. "Jayce, no one in this town wants to hurt anyone, least of all you. And I know Soul's proving to be a great coach, but he can't simultaneously be a distraction."

"He won't be," I replied, "especially with the town on his side."

Jim faced me again.

"If you're serious about no one wanting to hurt anyone," I told him, "then why not use your leverage to get the town behind him, rather than against him?"

Jim said nothing for a moment. We continued watching the field, as Beezer continued haranguing anyone who didn't do their job according to his wishes. He berated a parent about the *precise length* that the hash mark stencils needed to be placed apart before spraying the paint on them. He chastised another for not applying the paint evenly. Everyone knew that the field was Beezer's life, but having to deal with him each week had left Jim needing to twist arms to get parents to sign up for field duty.

"Do you really hate Muslims that much, Jim?"

Again, Jim paused before answering. "Beat Barton City," he responded, "and you won't have to worry about the answer to that question."

With that, he walked onto the field toward where Beezer and the group were working.

Even as a high school player, I always wondered if Jim Gill Stadium was the only illuminated place in Lake Barrow on nights when we played Barton City. With almost every business shutting down during the week of that heated rivalry, it was definitely within the realm of possibility

I walked with the team out to the field right before kickoff that Friday night and took in the sight of what had to be every resident of both towns lining both sides of the stadium.

Dixie signaled me just as I reached the field, and I walked over and kissed her on the lips.

"Don't be nervous," she instructed.

"How do you know I'm nervous?" I asked with a grin.

"Because I'm nervous," she answered. "And I'm the calm one in this marriage."

I chuckled. "Wonder which temperament this one's going to get," I said, gesturing to her belly.

Dixie thought for a moment. "If he gets your work ethic and my temperament, he'll be a winner."

My eyebrows arched. "He?"

She nodded. "It's no secret you want a boy. Just trying to be supportive."

"I love you."

She pressed two fingers to her lips and blew me a kiss as I headed out to the field.

The fireworks would be starting any moment.

I watched the ball catapult off the foot of Skyler Hemphill as he booted it deep for a touchback that Friday, and could not tell if the crowd noise was the culprit of my insides churning, or if it was the sheer nervousness and pressure of the game that was causing them to roil. Regardless, I found myself fighting against nerves once again as our defense took the field against Morgan Danforth and Barton City.

The Bearcats spread the field with four receivers, per their usual offensive set, and with Danforth and their tailback in the shotgun.

Danforth called "hike" three times before the center snapped it. He received the snap, stood upright as if he might throw it, and quickly handed it off to his running back. The scatback was short and wiry, but fast, and he hit the hole right in the middle of our defense with no hesitation. We were expecting a pass, but after seeing that exact play at least three or four times on film during the previous week, we should have known better. The Bearcats had caught us off guard, as their shifty running back tore up the middle and gained ten yards on the opening play.

"Jordan!" I heard Ahmad call out. "Jordan!"

Ahmad was on the sideline that night against Barton City and had to scream three more times over the din of the fans before Jordan finally looked over.

"Stay home!" Ahmad yelled, referring to Jordan's assignment. "Stay home and spy! Don't leave the middle open!" He gestured wildly with his arms, his frustration palpable at the fact that Jordan had moved out of position on the previous play.

Jordan nodded and watched Ahmad as he signaled the next set, which Jordan relayed as he got the rest of the defense in position.

We managed to halt Barton City's first drive, but only after they had driven about ten yards beyond midfield. Their punter tried to pin us near the goal line but was unsuccessful as the ball rolled through the end zone and was whistled dead. We started from our own twenty, but quickly went three and out and had to punt.

And that was pretty much how the entire first half went. Neither team could do much with the ball on offense, and both sides gave up one turnover. Andrico was intercepted by a linebacker when one of his short passes was tipped at the line of scrimmage. Danforth then came onto the field and, on the very next play, hit his best receiver on a crossing pattern, only to have Kyle Messina, our free safety, strip the ball and recover it near the fifty-yard line. The turnover gave us an emotional boost, but other than that, it was stalled drives and punts for both sides right up until the last sixty seconds of the second quarter.

Barton City had the ball with a minute remaining and was facing third and twenty after a ten-yard holding penalty. Danforth took the snap, looked downfield, saw no one, and peeled out of the pocket to his left after feeling the pressure from our line. Jordan had blitzed and was shedding his blocker right as Danforth escaped the collapsing pocket. He chased the nimble quarterback like a man possessed, as Danforth scampered to his left and looked downfield for an open guy. Jordan was about to close on him for the sack when something unbelievable happened.

Danforth adroitly moved the ball to his non-throwing left hand and used his right to stiff-arm Jordan to the ground like a rag doll. He then spun around once again, looked deep, and heaved the ball downfield. It hung in the air for what seemed like minutes, and I remember thinking that it must have traveled at least half the length of the field before falling into the hands of their best receiver. The tall, lanky wideout caught it over the head of our cornerback, who had him blanketed, shook free, and sprinted to the end zone for six points.

I felt the air go out of the home side of the stadium as the visitors' section roared.

Jordan trudged back to the sideline. Humiliated and furious, he took off his helmet and slammed it against our aluminum bench. He was seething; his roiling rage even more evident than it had been throughout the previous week. I thought about going over, but Ahmad beat me to it; just as well, since I had to ensure that we had the right personnel on the field for the extra point coverage.

Barton City's kicker booted the ball through the uprights to make the score 7-0.

We got the ball back but could do nothing with it. We even dialed up a Hail Mary for the last play of the half, but Andrico was sacked before he could even get the pass off as time expired.

I felt frustrated as our team jogged off the field and made our way into the locker room. However, my irritation was soon replaced by dread as I noticed Jim Gill standing down near the foot of the bleachers. He wore a look of fury that was almost identical to what I had seen displayed by Jordan moments earlier, and it was unsettling. I looked away and refused to make eye contact as I ambled past him. And yet somehow, I could still hear him growl through clenched teeth: "Get it together."

*Gill v. Danforth*, I thought to myself as I ambled past him.

"It's a war!" I bellowed in admonishment to the guys in the locker room moments later. "You lose battles in a war, but you keep fighting until you win!"

I went on for several moments about how we were still in it, just like we were always in each rivalry game that we played, and could not be counted out until that final whistle blew.

Soul took over after a few moments.

"Whose souls are hurting?" he asked.

Several hands went up.

"Whose souls are getting stronger?"

Only a few hands were raised.

"EVERYBODY'S HAND SHOULD BE IN THE AIR!" he bellowed, his usual cool demeanor suddenly replaced by an intense fury that I had only rarely seen. "This game is testing you, this game is bringing out what's inside you, and if you push forward, you're going to be standing in the end!"

Spirits began to rise again, along with the overall energy in the locker room, as the guys responded to this abrupt outburst of emotion from their offensive coordinator. They stood and began slapping shoulder pads, encouraging one another in anticipation of the second half.

Jordan was a picture of intensity. He rose with the rest of the team and was adjusting his helmet when I approached him.

"Jordan, you good?" I asked.

He nodded, and his eyes confirmed that even though he had calmed down, that rage was still there.

"Jordan," I began, "you've got to shake that last play off."

"I'm good."

"Look at me," I said, gently nudging his shoulder pad so that he turned to face me. His eyes met mine. "Shake it off. This is your time."

He said nothing.

I continued, "This isn't about your dad, or Marty Danforth, or anyone. It's about you and this team. We need you. We need you on that field, but most of all, this team needs your leadership."

Jordan said nothing.

"I need more from you," I said.

Jordan fixed me with cold eyes, and said simply, "You'll get more."

He fastened his helmet as he walked past me and joined his teammates who were headed out the door of the locker room.

The same dread I had felt earlier as I had passed Jim in the stands now resurfaced as I watched #44 make his way out to the field.

We got the ball to start the second half and seemed to get a spark of energy when Johnny ran the kickoff past midfield. The crowd roared and was back into it, as the offense jogged on. Andrico threw a perfect strike to A.J. Smalls on the first play, putting the ball just inside the thirty-five. Then on the next play, he added six more yards on an option run to put us inside the thirty. From there, however, the drive sputtered, and we ended up sending the field goal unit onto the field.

Skyler was usually money from anywhere inside the thirty-five, but he missed this one as his kick sailed wide left.

I could not believe how quickly our luck seemed to be running out.

Barton City took over at the twenty-nine, and on the first two plays, I was proud of our defense. We stopped a run up the middle for no gain and sacked Danforth for a loss of six.

On third and sixteen, Danforth signaled for one of his receivers to go in motion. The center snapped the ball just before the wideout crossed in front of Danforth, who caught the ball and immediately handed it off to the sprinting receiver. The receiver then tossed it to another receiver who was bolting in the opposite direction.

Our defense had seen this play on film. Double-reverse

jet sweep, which required us to seal off the outside and prevent a sideline run. And our guys were ready for it. There was nowhere, for either receiver to run, regardless of who had the ball…

…which is why what happened next took us completely by surprise.

The receiver with the ball stopped, planted his feet, and lofted the ball down the sideline to a streaking Morgan Danforth, who had slipped out of the backfield uncovered.

It was a new wrinkle which we had not seen, and we were about to pay dearly for it. Danforth caught the ball in stride and was sprinting toward the end zone. Not even our defensive backs seemed able to catch up with him.

That's when I saw Jordan.

He was running like a maniac, faster than I had ever seen him run in his entire life. Best of all, he had an angle and looked as though he might actually catch Morgan, who had crossed the fifteen and neared the ten.

Morgan turned, saw Jordan, and accelerated just enough to give himself the distance he needed to reach the end zone. As he crossed the goal line, the referee held up his arms, signaling a touchdown. Barton City's bleachers and sidelines went berserk, as ours grew silent.

My eyes, however, were still on Jordan who, despite the play being whistled dead, was undeterred in his pursuit of Morgan.

"JORDAN!!!! NO!!!!" I heard myself scream, knowing that it was already too late.

Jordan closed on Morgan and launched himself at his legs just as he came to a stop in the end zone. The massive hit at the knees that followed caused Morgan to buckle like a cheap doll and collapse to the turf.

The Barton City side went from jubilation to fury as they watched their quarterback blind-sided from behind.

It was a blatant personal foul, and I took off onto the

field in a fury. Sure enough, yellow flags were landing every-where.

Ahmad threw his headset on the ground and ran out onto the field with me, just as Isaiah Waters grabbed Jordan and shoved him toward our sideline before anyone from the Barton City side could retaliate for what he had done. Ahmad beat me to the end zone began screaming in Jordan's face and gesturing wildly. Jordan ignored him and jogged with a sullenness back to tour sideline. I followed behind, seething with anger, yet unable to say anything.

I turned back toward the end zone where a crowd was now gathering around Morgan Danforth, who lay on the ground writhing in pain...and not getting up.

# CHAPTER 18

Our trainers reached Morgan first, followed by Barton City's coaching and medical personnel. Marty and Penny Danforth were close behind.

Before I went back onto the field, I turned to Max. "Have them take a knee," I instructed.

"Y'all get down!" Max yelled to the team, motioning for them to kneel.

Almost all of our team did so; all except for Jordan, who was standing near the bench.

"Get your ass on a knee!" Ahmad yelled in Jordan's face, rushing up to confront him.

Jordan did as he was told, but was nonchalant and noncommittal.

I was disgusted at him. His lack of regard for Morgan was appalling. I reached the spot where Morgan lay and watched as a trainer prodded his knee, causing the young quarterback to grimace and wail even harder. "Oh, God!" he wailed.

"Definitely a tear," I heard another trainer murmur.

"Is there an ambulance?" one of the coaches asked me.

I nodded and signaled to Starr, who had come down to the field. He summoned a first responder, who turned and signaled for the ambulance.

The trainer nudged another part of Morgan's knee and got the same response.

"Just lay still," a trainer instructed. Morgan's parents stood over him, looking helpless.

I looked up into the bleachers and surveyed the faces of our fans, many of whom were frowning, and several of whom were praying. Then I saw Jim Gill. On his face was a look of smug satisfaction and contempt for the teenaged boy lying on the field that bore his name.

"WHERE IS THAT LITTLE SHIT?!" I heard a voice bellow out.

I turned just as Matt Danforth, my former teammate, was barreling across the field toward our sideline looking for Jordan. It was the first time I had seen him since graduation, and his sudden appearance took me by surprise.

People saw him immediately and began shouting.

"Come here, you little prick!" Matt screamed as he identified Jordan.

Thankfully, Max was there and was able to stop Matt from proceeding any farther.

All hell was breaking loose in the stands as people began to scream at the mayhem unfolding in front of them on the field. A few were even starting to come down out of the bleachers.

Matt wasn't going anywhere with Max in front of him, and he didn't need to. Jordan had seen him and had immediately jumped up from his kneeling position and advanced, along with two of our other players. Using his helmet as a weapon, he slammed it into Matt's face, causing him to collapse to the ground motionless. Max immediately spun and restrained Jordan again, screaming at him to get back.

The crowd erupted with even louder, more frantic shouts at what was happening on the sideline. This was accompanied by the Danforth clan coming down out of the visitors' stands and onto the field where Matt now lay.

Jordan, along with the rest of the team, took this as aggression and rushed forward in confrontation. This act caused the Barton City sideline to rush over from their sideline toward ours. At that moment, the only people that could prevent a complete all-out riot on our field were the coaching staffs of the two teams and a few members of our administration who had come onto the field.

"Get Morgan out of here!" I shouted at Starr, pointing at him, as I restrained two of the Bearcat players. Starr, along with the paramedics and a few people not engaged in the melee, managed to get Morgan to safety. Another relative grabbed Matt and dragged him away from the fracas as well.

Soul, Max, Woody, and I were doing all we could to restrain the Barton City players, with the help of a few deputy sheriffs who had come down to the field, as well as Barton City's coaching staff.

"Get to your sideline!" I screamed at several of them.

Meanwhile, our stands were still going crazy with boos and shouts of indignation at what they were witnessing, and several more parents came down to help restore order on the field.

Slowly, things began to stabilize.

Jim Gill was still in the bleachers. I glanced at him again as Morgan's gurney was being pushed off the field. His face bore that same smirk I had seen earlier. At that moment, I hated him.

Yellow flags littered the field following the skirmish, and the referees wasted no time in assessing off-setting personal foul penalties on both sidelines. Frankly, I couldn't have cared less about the penalties.

What I had just witnessed made me wonder if I was still in the same hometown where I had grown up. I looked up at our scoreboard with the name "Jim Gill Stadium" emblazoned on the large placard at the top and began to wish right then that I was anywhere else in the world besides Lake Barrow, Florida.

"You're out," I said to Jordan, as Soul and Ahmad flanked me.

"Coach, Matt attacked me! You saw…"

Soul jumped in. "It doesn't matter!" he yelled. "You disgraced this team, and you purposely injured another player!"

"I didn't purposely…"

"Shut up!" Soul bellowed. I had never seen my former college teammate as pissed as he was at that moment. His eyes were filled with a maniacal fury that I never knew he was capable of. Soul's arms were flailing, his voice rose with each syllable, and spit flew from his lips as he continued belittling Jordan for his behavior. It was all on display for our fans to see, several of whom clapped at the spectacle that was unfolding.

Soul finished his rant and kept his eyes fixed on Jordan. For a moment, no one said anything. Then, Soul did something I never thought I'd see. He ripped the kufi off of his head and threw it at Jordan.

"I'm sick of you and your family, Gill!"

Everyone saw it, including Jim.

I took hold of Soul's arm and urged him back away from Jordan. Principal Starr had walked up during the tirade and was now leading Jordan away from the field. Things were defused, but the damage was done.

I looked into the stands and noticed Jim. He appeared to be seething.

"Get back to the press box," I instructed Soul. "Let's just get through this game."

It was 14-0 in Barton City's favor. We got the ball back, went three and out, and punted.

Our defense, even without Jordan, continued to hold fast and play solid, keeping Barton City out of the end zone and even forcing two fumbles. Their back-up quarterback was nowhere near as talented as Morgan, which helped us.

Our offense, however, continued to stall throughout the third quarter. In the fourth, our offense got a spark when Andrico connected with Sammy Stromas on a short post route, which Sammy took the distance for a long touchdown. Skyler kicked the extra point, and it was 14-7.

Later, we got the ball on our own forty-yard line with less than a minute remaining and one last chance to get in the end zone to tie the game, and force overtime.

We moved it down inside Barton City's thirty-yard line, and the crowd began to roar again as we were nearing the end zone. Andrico dropped back on the first play, looked downfield, didn't see anyone, and took off. He gained eight yards before being tackled.

The clock was ticking as Andrico rushed everyone to the line, took the snap, and spiked the ball, which stopped the clock with ten seconds remaining but cost us a down.

He jogged back to the sideline and leaned in.

"You know what to do?" I asked.

"Air raid," he answered.

"Strong right, air raid," I confirmed.

He nodded and hustled back out. Our stands were louder than I'd ever heard, as the offense got set; the din rising with each passing second, as the populations of two small Florida towns waiting for their teams' fates to unfold.

Crocker snapped the ball to Andrico, and I felt my breath catch in my throat.

Andrico looked downfield, saw no one open, and began scrambling to his right as he felt the pressure from Barton City's pass rush. He planted his feet, reared back, and launched a bullet downfield toward the goal line. Sammy Stromas was sprinting, covered by a Bearcat corner and safety, and as he neared the goal line, all three players jumped in the air as the ball hit Sammy's hands. At the last second, though, Barton City's safety knocked it away for an incompletion.

Fourth down. Four seconds left.

Andrico cast a glance my way, and I signaled to him by holding up two fingers and making an "X" across my chest. *Same play.*

The din of the crowd was at a fever pitch as Andrico lined everyone up once more for the last play of regulation; our last chance at tying the game with a shot at the end zone.

This was the ball game.

Every eye in the county was, at that moment, on twenty-two young men who were barely old enough to shave. The seconds before the snap seemed like decades.

The ball was snapped, and the linemen on both sides shot off from their stances and collided with each other. Stromas took off again downfield, and Andrico caught the snap, dropping back deep. Our linemen were blocking better than they had all game, and Andrico was able to survey the field with plenty of time and no pressure in the pocket.

He planted his feet and launched the ball once more.

As the ball neared him, Stromas catapulted himself upward at the goal line, along with the same two defenders who had blanketed him on the previous play. This time, however, the ball connected with Stromas' fingertips and stuck there… but only for a moment.

Before Stromas could secure the ball, Barton City's safety stuck his hand up and once again knocked it loose, tipping it back into the air, where the Bearcats' cornerback was waiting.

I watched helplessly as the ball was intercepted.

Barton City's side erupted in jubilation as the wiry defender ran up the field with the ball. The game was sealed for Barton City, which is why everyone, including our defenders, thought he would simply run out of bounds. However, the shifty defensive back surprised all of us by accelerating and blowing past every one of our offensive players on his way down the field.

Only Andrico had the speed and the angle to catch him. He ran like a madman after the cornerback and dove for his ankles but barely made contact. I remember being proud of him for not giving up on the play, even though the game was over. The defender, however, never broke stride as he coasted into the end zone for six points as time expired.

Our entire home side was depleted of energy at that point, as the reality of losing to Barton City, 20-7, sank in.

The skirmish following Morgan Danforth's injury still had me on edge, as our team met at mid-field to shake hands with Barton City. I kept my eye out for any behavior that might lead to another fight and congratulated the Bearcat players. Thankfully, the post-game ritual seemed to be going off without a hitch as I reached Steve Coffield.

Barton City's veteran coach shook my hand. "Your boys played hard, Jayce," he affirmed. "Nothing to be ashamed of."

"Nothing?" I asked, with a wry grin.

"That wasn't you," he said, looking me in the eye. "You know the history of this area better than anyone."

"I'm sorry about Morgan," I told him. "Please let us know if we can help."

"Sorry about our guys rushing your sideline," he returned.

Suddenly, I began to hear angry shouts from our bleachers again.

*Hey! Hey! Hey!*
*They can't do that!!!*
*Get 'em off our field.*

I spun around and was shocked at what I saw.

Barton City's entire team was on our logo at midfield, jumping up and down, and chanting.

*Danforth! Danforth! Danforth! Danforth! Danforth!*

I could not believe what I was seeing.

Our fans became incensed once more as the Barton City players continued trampling our logo out of disrespect, and I heard more shouts of indignation. Our fans were now climbing over the rails to confront the players but were stopped by the sheriff's deputies.

Things were about to get violent at Jim Gill Stadium once more.

Both coaching staffs sprang into action; ours kept our boys away from the demonstration, while Coffield's staff went over and started breaking things up. I was restraining several of our guys when out of the corner of my eye, I saw Frank Beezer barreling toward midfield like an enraged bull. As he charged, he brandished a shovel.

"Get off my field!" he screamed at the Barton City players. "Don't you dare disrespect my field!"

In all my years of knowing him, I had never seen Beezer move that quickly or with that much ferocity. Every muscle of his seemed propelled by rage and contempt as he charged at the Barton City players with no indication that he would slow down.

I had to do something.

"Beezer, stop!" I yelled, lunging toward him. Just as I moved, he accelerated and reached midfield.

One of the Bearcat players was closer to him and pounced as they saw him. The player rammed into Beezer, causing him to crumple to the ground like a broken mannequin.

I reached the skirmish and pushed the player off of Beezer. "Get off him!" I yelled.

Another Barton City player pulled his teammate up as the celebration at midfield began to subside, and the Bearcats were ushered to their side of the field.

I knelt down where Beezer lay. He was still conscious but appeared to be in intense pain.

"Frank, look at me!" I pleaded. "Are you okay?"

"It's my arm," he wailed. His face was contorted with pain as he looked up at me.

"We're going to get you help," I said, as Soul motioned for the paramedics to come forward.

"No..." Beezer began to speak.

"It's okay, Beez," I soothed. "You don't need to talk."

"Jayce..."

I looked at him. "What?"

"No..."

"No what?"

"No one...disrespects...my field."

# CHAPTER 19

S oul and I were quiet as we sat in my office later that night. Neither of us knew what to say.

"Any word on Beezer?" he finally asked.

"Max called my cell earlier," I answered. "He and Woody are up there. Said it's probably a broken arm."

Soul nodded. "How about the Danforths?"

I shifted in my chair. "Starr talked to Marty," I responded. "Matt's got a broken nose, but will be fine. Morgan's a lot worse. Probably a torn ACL."

Soul looked away and said nothing.

"He might not play football again," I added.

Soul's hand went to his own surgically-repaired knee, to which he gave a faint stroke.

The ticking sound of the round clock above my desk with a Spartan sticker on the lens was the only thing either of us heard for the next several moments. We were exhausted and still trying to come to terms with what we had just been through. Never before had either of us seen, or been a part of, such an egregious display of lousy sportsmanship by a single football team, let alone two. In the locker room, we had gone off on the entire team for their roles in what had happened, as well as their performance on the field. Soul sprints were on the agenda for Monday, as was another good tongue lashing (or two) once the team finished that.

I learned early on that as a coach, you're going to face discouragement. It's a fact which I had seen demonstrated all my life; with Coach Faraday, and then as a graduate assistant as I observed Yearwood State's coaching staff. Somehow, you just learn to handle the attitude problems, the poor performance, the lack of motivation, the constant criticism and comparison, all of it.

What had happened that evening was something more, though. Far from just a fight on the gridiron, this was the latest chapter in a decade-long fight that transcended our football field and went to the heart of a deeper rift in the community that involved two families. Looking back, I suppose that's what hurt the worst.

"Three-day suspension for the fight," I said. "That's what Jordan gets. Whether or not he stays on the team is our decision, though."

Neither of us said anything for several moments.

"What do you think you'll do?" Soul asked.

I didn't answer.

"Are you afraid to kick him off?" Soul asked, reading my mind.

I rubbed my temples. "We got rid of Nabeel for the same reason."

Soul nodded but didn't respond.

"You okay?" I asked him.

Soul shook his head. I waited for him to say more.

"When my knee got taken out in that game against Louisville our senior year," he finally said, "it cost me my career, and I wanted to kill the guy who hurt me."

Soul stared straight ahead. His face was a picture of intense disdain. Slowly, however, tears began to form in his eyes, and I watched his chest begin to heave angrily as he continued speaking.

"That Louisville boy had been talking smack all game; belittling me, insulting my family, my team, and my faith. He wouldn't shut up, and the truth was, I didn't care. Long as I could go across the middle and take that pass away from him, keep him from getting his interception, beat him, then none of it mattered."

I sat frozen as I continued to listen.

"So I went across the middle, just like I had been doing all game. Went up, got that ball, came down, broke free, and got our six points. That defender was a little guy and ran light; never flat-footed, which is why he was so fast. And that's also why I never heard him coming up behind me once I reached the end zone and scored that touchdown."

Soul looked at me with tears streaming down his face.

"I never heard him coming," he said. "Until it was too late."

He rubbed his knee again.

"After Danforth went down tonight, I didn't see Jordan jogging off that field with that smug grin on his face." Soul kept his eye on his knee. "I saw that same guy that took my knee out."

My heart went out to my former teammate and fellow coach.

"I always heard 'football prepares you for life,'" he went on. "Maybe that's true. But it does a piss-poor job of preparing you for the injustices of life."

The metallic sound of a double door opening echoed throughout the field house. Soul gathered himself, and I glanced out of the doorway to see Jim Gill making his way toward us. He wore a look of dismay and concern.

I rose as he entered.

"Jayce," he greeted me, before turning to Soul and nodding. "How's Beezer?"

I told him everything I knew. Jim was sympathetic as he listened.

Then, changing the subject, he said, "Jayce, I also wanted to see you in person and tell you how sorry I am for Jordan's behavior tonight. Rest assured, he's going to make amends for his part in what happened. And that's exactly why I wanted to talk to you about how we can make this right…together."

"Make it right?" I asked.

"I know that what ultimately happens with Jordan is your call," he said. "And I want to work with you to ensure that he's adequately punished, but that he doesn't miss any of the season."

I glanced at Soul, and then back at Jim.

"Avoid kicking him off the team," Jim clarified, "in favor of anything else you want to do to make it right. Make him run, or do those soul exercises that the team does, whatever it takes."

"You really think it's as simple as that?" I snarled.

Jim held up a hand in defense. "Jayce…"

"Best way to make it right," Soul cut in as he stood, "is to ensure that Jordan never sets foot on that field again."

Jim's temperate demeanor changed as he glared at Soul. "I was not talking to you."

"No, but you're talking to me now," Soul retorted. He moved to within an inch of Jim, whom he towered over. "I wouldn't be surprised if you put your boy up to that hit."

"You watch your mouth!" Jim hissed.

"Watch my mouth," Soul repeated. "I've been watching you intimidate and control this town since I've been here. And it's getting pretty old."

Jim's eyes glowered at Soul; his lower lip curled in fury. I had to step in before things escalated even further.

"Take a walk," I said to Soul, getting between the two of them.

Jim's face was a mixture of bewilderment and rage as he watched Soul exit the office and leave the field house, his eyes never leaving Jim as he walked away. "Jayce, you listen to me," he began. His eyes narrowed as he moved in closer to me. "That son of a bitch, Rasheed, is out of line, and you know it!"

"So are you," I returned, fixing him with a glare.

Jim took a step back and tried to regroup, but I went right on.

"And so am I if I keep Jordan on the team," I continued, surprised by the assertiveness in my own voice. "Not after what happened with Nabeel."

Jim's face became a mixture of desperation, anger, and pleading. "Jayce, after all we've been through together; our families, the history you have with us…"

"After all that, I still have to do what's right," I told him.

"Jayce, listen," Jim almost begged. "Don't worry about Nabeel. If you keep Jordan, you won't look like a hypocrite. I'll make sure of it. We'll figure out some way to spin it. I'll smooth it over with the clubs," Jim almost pleaded. "Quarterback, Rotary, all of them. You won't look bad. We'll tell them Nabeel had drugs, and that's what did him in."

"I don't care about that," I refuted. "I care what happens beyond that field out there. I care about not being disgusted at what I see in the mirror each morning after making decisions like these. I care about my unborn kid growing up with someone he can look up to."

Jim's face was a picture of indignation.

I continued, "I care about not falling into the same trap that Skipper fell into."

"So you're kicking my son off?" he glared at me.

"I have to."

"You really think that's the best thing for you?"

"I'm going to do what's best for this team. And I'm going to be consistent about it. And if it takes sidelining Jordan for the rest of the season, then so be it."

The rage in Jim's face intensified once more as he fixed me with an icy stare. "Then you just put yourself on dangerous ground, Jayce, and you'd better be careful."

With that, he stormed out of the field house.

It was after midnight when I walked through the door of our home. Dixie was asleep, and I had no intention of waking her. I was in the kitchen pouring a glass of water when I heard our bedroom knob turn, followed by the creak of a door opening. Slowly, she emerged.

Even with tousled hair and the appearance of battling first-trimester sickness, my wife was breathtakingly beautiful in the pre-dawn hours. That fact, combined with the reality that I had just completed one of the worst nights of my football career, either as a player or as a coach, is what moved me from the kitchen and toward the doorframe where she stood. We embraced for what seemed like an eternity, and I buried my face in her neck while she cradled my head.

"You okay?" she asked, as I stood upright once more. "Dumb question," she followed up.

We sat on the living room sofa.

"Were you safe?" I asked her.

Dixie nodded. "I was way up next to the press box," she answered with a smile. "Too far away to get pelted with anything."

I smiled and nodded.

"How's Beezer?" she asked, and I filled her in.

We were quiet for a moment.

"So what happens next?" she asked.

"Jordan's out," I told her. "He has to be."

Dixie gave me a sympathetic look.

I took a deep breath and rubbed my palms over both eyes. "Damned if this decision isn't killing me. Damned if my decision to let Nabeel go hasn't been killing me, too."

Dixie watched me as I agonized.

"You have to do what's right," she affirmed.

I nodded.

"If you can't live with the fact that you'd be giving Jordan a pass," she continued, "then he shouldn't get one."

I scowled and rose from the couch. "Easier said than done," I said.

"Because of Jim?"

"Yeah, because of Jim," I said, pacing around the living room. "Because Jim's the closest thing to a father that I had when Rex died because Jim helped me get this job in the first place; and because Jim might pull strings if this thing really goes south."

"So you're scared?" Dixie asked, her green eyes burning into me.

I looked back at her and felt helpless. "Aren't you?"

She adjusted on the sofa. "Jayce, you and I both know how I grew up; one foot under the poverty line, always a step or two away from child welfare. There was hardly a morning that ever went by during my childhood where I didn't watch my mom go off to work and wonder if she was going to be unemployed by the end of the day. So yeah, I'm scared. But..." she trailed off.

"But what?" I asked, coming back toward the sofa.

"But shaky job security isn't what scares me the most."

"I'm not going to put you and our kid in a bad situation," I told her. "I can't do it."

Dixie stared at me for a long moment before saying anything. "You really have no idea, do you?"

"About what?"

"About why I married you in the first place."

She hesitated before continuing. "When I first learned that you were going into coaching, there wasn't a doubt in my mind that you'd be successful. How successful still remains to be seen, but there was never a time that I didn't believe that you would make something of yourself someday, Jayce."

I studied her.

"And when you got hired back here at home, it was like a dream come true. Here we were; two kids just starting their lives together and going back to where it all started. We'd be close to family, close to our community. It was heaven…and it still is."

"What are you saying?"

"I'm saying that none of that compares to watching you stand in that school conference room, years ago during our senior year, and go toe-to-toe with Marty Danforth and REF, all so that my mom wouldn't have to choose between hurting Mrs. Hanceford and losing her job."

She took my hand and squeezed it.

"You've always played the hero, Jayce," she said. "On the field and off. That's why I married you. Because the only stability I need is knowing that we can wake up and be at peace with ourselves each day; knowing that the lessons we're going to teach our children are based on something real, instead of a false sense of job security that may not even be there the next day."

I nodded.

"You may feel like you owe Jim your life," she continued. "But you owe your family your heart. And you better damn well never forget that."

# Chapter 20

"You ready for this?" Soul asked Monday morning as we sat in my office.

"No," I sighed.

"He should be here any minute," Ahmad said.

The three of us sat in chairs facing the doorway as we waited. Another single chair was situated directly across from us.

Finally, we heard the large metal door open and watched through the glass partition as Jordan Gill entered the field house. He made his way toward my inner office doorway, just as Soul opened it and gestured for him to come in.

He appeared to be fighting to conceal his nervousness as he sat upright in the chair across from us with his hands on his knees. He wore a button-down white shirt with slacks, and it occurred to me that this was the first time all year that I had seen him not wearing his letterman jacket.

This was one meeting he wanted to make a good impression in, which killed me as I prepared to break the news to him.

"You know why we're here," I got right to the point.

Jordan shifted in his seat.

"Jordan, I don't know any other way to say this," I said as

I took another deep breath. "But you're out."

Jordan's head dropped slightly as he fought to maintain composure. Moments passed.

"Is there anything I can do?" he almost pleaded. "To make this right?"

"I wish there was," I answered. "But keeping you would be favoritism, especially after I kicked Nabeel off the team for the same reason."

Integrity has a price. As I looked at Jordan, I didn't see one of my players. I saw the kid who was too small to play tackle football with Jamie and me and our friends. I saw the younger brother I never had losing his future. Everything in me at that moment wanted to reverse the decision I was making.

Jordan said nothing as he kept his head down. When he looked up again, his eyes were brimming with tears.

He rose slowly from the chair and exited the office.

None of us said anything for a while as we stared ahead.

"You sure about this?" Ahmad asked me.

"No," I answered.

The news of Jordan's dismissal from the team did not sit well, which we expected. For the most part, however, there was very little display of emotion.

The guys practiced hard that afternoon and seemed to be bouncing back from the sting of defeat against Barton City. Still, Jordan's absence loomed large and was never far from the surface. Isaiah Waters had shifted back to the middle at linebacker and was playing well, but he had never been anywhere near as vocal a leader as Jordan had been.

Hapsburg County was our next opponent, and we spent much of that day's practice going over their offensive scheme and getting our defense ready for Friday. Offensively, we focused on the myriad mistakes that had been made during the Barton City game and zeroed in on better execution, better quarterback reads, and limiting mental mistakes. Andrico, in particular, was motivated to improve. Best of all, his attitude was infectious and seemed to raise the level of play and motivation among his teammates.

He walked beside me as we made our way off of the practice field that afternoon.

"You all right, Coach?" he asked.

"Yeah," I answered. "Why?"

"Just know it's rough," he said, "kicking Jordan off and all."

I nodded, even more, appreciative of my quarterback. "It wasn't easy," I said. "But we'll be all right."

"Isaiah's solid," Andrico continued.

"Yeah, he is."

"You know, the players respect you, Coach," Andrico said, changing the subject.

I glanced at him.

"They don't like the fact that Jordan's gone," he went on, "but they respect the fact that you're consistent."

"Thanks," I said, grateful.

"Skipper was never consistent," he said. "Always played favorites."

My mind went back to the conversation I'd had with Jim on their upper porch following Jamie's funeral.

"Hey, Coach," Andrico changed the subject again. "My car's in the shop. Think I can get a ride home."

"Sure," I told him.

A half hour later, we were in my truck as I drove Andrico back to his home near the center of town, making intermittent small talk along the way. As we turned onto a narrow, rural road that led toward the town square, I noticed a familiar-looking figure shuffling along the shoulder.

"Looks like Quinton," Andrico commented.

Sure enough, it was Quinton Leeds, the troubled kid whom I had seen with Mikayla on the day of our season opener.

I slowed down.

"We gonna give him a ride?" Andrico asked.

"We're gonna offer him one," I said. "Roll the window down and ask."

Andrico pushed the automatic button which lowered the glass partition and stuck his head out.

"Quinton, you need a ride?" Andrico asked the boy. "Coach said he can give you a lift if you want."

Quinton did not answer and continued trudging along the street. His baggy pants sagged, and the tattered shoes he wore kicked up small wisps of dust as he moved along the road. His long, greasy, dark hair bobbed with each step. I took my foot off of the brake and allowed the truck to move slowly to keep pace with him.

When I was parallel with him again, I looked out the window. "Quinton," I called. "We've got a room if you need a ride."

"No," he murmured.

That was when I noticed his eyes. They were red-rimmed and appeared as though he had been crying.

"Are you sure you're okay?" I asked.

"Go away!" he barked, in a low, guttural tone.

I glanced at my quarterback, and we exchanged quizzical glances. Andrico decided to take one more stab.

"Quinton, man, come get in the truck. You…"

"SHUT UP!" Quinton bellowed, whipping around so that he was now square with the side of my truck. "Get out of my face!"

With that, he picked up his gait and began jogging away

from us. Andrico and I just sat there, neither of us knowing what to say or do.

Fifty yards down the road, Quinton turned down another dirt path and disappeared into a thick patch of woods.

Slowly, I applied the gas, and we were off again, driving in silence for a few moments.

"Any idea what that was about?" I asked Andrico.

Andrico hesitated before answering. "Not really."

I glanced over at him, sensing that there was more.

"Quinton doesn't have many friends," Andrico finally said. "Gets picked on by a lot of people, too."

I frowned and kept my eyes on the road. "You're not one of them, are you?" I asked Andrico.

He looked at me.

"Do you pick on him?"

Andrico paused before answering. "No," he said. "But I've stood around when other people were doing it."

"Doesn't speak real well of you as a leader, does it?"

A look of shame and embarrassment registered on my quarterback's face.

"Promise me you'll step up if you see him getting ragged on again," I said. "Someone in your position should do something about that."

Andrico nodded. "Yes sir," he answered. "I promise."

As we neared his street, Andrico spoke up again. "You ever get tired of this town, Coach?"

I sighed and hesitated before responding. "Yeah," I told him. "After what happened last Friday, I definitely do. How about you?"

"All the time," Andrico said. "Things never change around here."

I nodded and slowed the car as Andrico's house came into view.

"Small towns are strange," I said. "You grow up around some of the kindest people and the most evil-hearted people all at once. Sometimes it's like you're walking a fine line be-tween the two since you never really know which side some-one's going to end up on."

Andrico glanced at me with an impressed look on his face. "That's deep, Coach."

I smiled faintly and was tempted to take credit for what Dixie had said during our first date at the ice cream parlor. Instead, I looked at Andrico and said, "At least that's what my wife tells me."

Dixie had an appointment the next morning and asked that I go with her. After seeing the doctor and getting a good report on the baby, I dropped her off at home and headed into work.

As I got out of my car and approached the field house, Jordan emerged and began walking toward me. His hands were in the pockets of his pants.

"Hey, Jordan," I said.

He nodded as he came closer, and I noticed a pensive look on his face. "Coach, you got a minute?"

I was carrying a gym bag full of practice clothes for later that afternoon but nodded. "I've got a minute."

I put the bag over my shoulder, and we began walking in the direction of the stadium. Once inside, Jordan and I climbed into the stands and found a seat near the bottom steps. It was a crisp, cool morning which signified that au-tumn had officially arrived.

"What's going on?" I asked Jordan.

He gazed out at the field that bore his family's namesake as he sat next to me. "I just wanted to apologize," he stated. "For everything."

I nodded.

"And by everything, I don't just mean the game," he said.

"I mean, for the whole week leading up to Barton City."

I kept my eyes on him. Jordan was watching the field intently. "I've seen a lot of games out here," he continued with a smile. "Seeing Jamie out there, busting heads. You throwing touchdown passes all over the place."

I waited for him to go on.

"Growing up, I always knew I had big shoes to fill," he continued. "And the truth is, I never felt more pressure in my life to win a ball game than I did last week."

I nodded.

"You remember that night out by the dock?" Jordan asked, looking at me. "What we talked about?"

"Yeah."

Jordan shook his head. "It's only gotten worse."

"The pressure," I said.

Jordan nodded. "Worst thing that could have happened was Morgan Danforth starting at quarterback for Barton City. It's not just a rivalry in our house. It's a war; it's a never-ending fight to see Marty Danforth beaten. It's sick."

I waited for him to continue.

"It's funny, Jim hates the idea of me joining the Marines like Jamie and going off to war to be killed. But he's also too blind to realize that the war happening right here in front of us is killing everyone."

Neither of us said anything for several moments.

"I never wanted to hurt Morgan," Jordan finally blurted, his voice starting to crack. "But it was the only way to get Jim to let up."

Jordan brought his hands to his face and covered his eyes, sweeping away tears.

"Is he hurting you?"

Jordan dried his face before looking at me with red-rimmed eyes. "Physically, no."

"I'm sorry," I said.

Jordan nodded, and I glanced out at the field again.

"I don't know how long I'll coach football," I told him. "But I can't imagine any decision being harder than the one I had to make about whether or not to keep you on the team. I had to do it because of Nabeel, but I didn't want to."

Jordan didn't respond. Inwardly, I was dying. He needed my help, and I felt powerless to do anything for him.

"If you still think you want to play college ball…" I began.

Jordan shook his head. "I'm not begging for help."

I studied him.

"I'm here because I let you down," Jordan went on. "And I wanted to apologize. What you said to me out by the lake that night was true."

"Which was what?"

"That you were my other big brother first," he said. "It's one thing to get kicked off a team. It's another thing to disappoint the people who care about you most."

"I still care," I replied.

Jordan reached into his pocket and pulled out something that I did not recognize.

"Coach Soul just gave this to me," he said, holding up a small string of amber-colored beads. "Right before you showed up."

I studied them.

"He called it a 'misbaha,' Jordan said, "or something. Muslims use these when they pray. Soul said he'd had them for years and they always gave him comfort, which is why he gave them to me."

"When did you talk to Soul?"

"Right before you got here," he said. "I wanted to make it right with him after the game last week."

I nodded, and Jordan glanced at me with a look of sincerity that I had only rarely seen before.

"I'm gonna miss this team."

"We're going to miss you too," I returned.

Jordan glanced away and then back at me as if he had something else to tell me.

"I was hoping," he hesitated, "that you might be willing to help me with something else."

I shrugged. "What is it?"

As the elevator bell dinged, and the doors opened to the third floor of Sims County Medical Center, I still wasn't sure that this was a good idea. Regardless of how ready Jordan was to make amends for what he had done, somehow I felt uncomfortable with what we were doing.

We reached the doorway with a placard on the outside wall that read, "Danforth, M.," and I took a deep breath.

"I'll go in first," I said to Jordan, who nodded in agreement. "You probably should wait outside until I tell him you're here."

I knocked three times, and heard a gravelly teenage voice respond, "Come in."

I pushed the metal latch forward and opened the door. As I entered, the figure of Morgan Danforth slowly came into view. He was lying partially upright in the bed and was dressed in hospital issue. His right leg was elevated and was concealed by a compression stocking and other bandaging. He was alone.

He appeared healthy overall, despite being disheveled and pallid. His eyes were slightly glazed over; no doubt, aftereffects of the morphine he'd been given, and his blonde hair was pushed back away from his face. He squinted as he struggled to take note of who had entered his room.

"It's Jayce Leonard," I announced myself, "from Sims County."

Morgan's expression turned contemptuous as he realized who was standing in his hospital room. "What are you doing here?" he rasped.

"I came to check on you," I said.

"My parents aren't here," he replied. "So you probably shouldn't be either."

I felt my insides churn. This was a worse idea than I thought.

"I understand," I returned. "And I won't stay long, but I did want to…"

"…tell me how sorry you are," he interrupted. "Or tell me you're praying for me. Or some other useless crap."

I didn't respond.

"Save it," Morgan's low voice was saturated with bitterness and violence as he glared at me, "because until prayers and apologies can repair torn ACLs, none of it really means a whole lot."

"Morgan, can I just…"

"…shove the reason you came here up your ass?" he interrupted. "Yeah, you can do that. Because the only reason you're even at Sims County now is because of your connections to Gill. To me, you're still just the same poser who took Matt's quarterback job, and then turned around and made our whole family look bad."

I fought my emotions, as his words cut me.

"You're Jim Gill's puppet," he continued. "And that's all you've ever been."

"Jordan's here," I cut him off, triggering a surprised look. "He's right outside, and he wants to apologize for everything and try to make it right."

A look of disgusted amazement came across Morgan's face as I said this.

"Jordan's right outside your room," I repeated. "Will you see him?"

The bewilderment seemed to transform into outright fury, as he gripped the loose sheets on his bed, causing them to crumple into bunch-like wads. Morgan didn't respond but glared at me as I slowly backed toward the door to let Jordan in against his wishes.

I opened it, motioned, and watched as Jordan slowly entered the room. He was cautious but confident as he approached the bed under the scathing glower of the boy he had injured the previous week.

Morgan kept his eyes locked on Jordan and slowly pointed to his bad knee. "You see that?"

Jordan nodded.

"There's a tube running that's connected to a drainage pouch; helps the fluid and blood drain from my knee. Turns out, it's also the one thing that's preventing me from jumping out of this bed and beating you senseless right now, you prick."

I took a step forward, but Jordan motioned for me to stay put.

"I deserve it," Jordan told Morgan without hesitation, absorbing all of the contempt. "I deserve all of it."

"You deserve worse!" Morgan yelled, grabbing an empty bedpan and hurling it at Jordan's feet. Both of us instinctively jumped backward as metal clanged against linoleum. "I'll never play football again!" he bellowed.

Morgan's lip was quivering. His entire body trembled, as he thought of his next insult.

"I'm sorry," Jordan repeated.

Morgan leaned back in his bed, and again crumpled the bed sheets with clenched fists. His demeanor had gone well beyond anger, and he was now a picture of impotent rage that could not be calmed except through violence, which was impossible for him. At that moment, he was a caged animal.

Jordan was a picture of stoicism as he stood in place, ready to receive the next barrage of hatred in the same manner that a soldier might accept discipline from a commander. I admired him.

Moments passed, neither of the three of us saying anything.

"Why did you really come here?" Morgan demanded, coming down from the climax of his wrath. "And don't give me this shit about apologizing."

Jordan thought for a moment. "Because it's got to start somewhere."

Morgan looked up at him. "What?"

"Don't act like you don't know what I'm talking about," Jordan went on. "Our dads, the land deal, everything that happened when we were just kids. Look at us. I'm not paying for Jim's grudge any longer, and you shouldn't have to pay for Marty's."

Morgan looked away.

"If I could do a miracle and heal your knee, I'd fix it in a heartbeat," Jordan continued. "All I've got now, though, is an apology and a desire to change what I can; about us, and about this town."

Morgan didn't look at him. Moments passed. "You can't change things," he finally said. "The town is what it is."

Jordan said nothing, but turned and looked at me for the first time since coming into the room. Then he turned back to Morgan.

"It can always change," Jordan said. "And I just hope that you can forgive me."

"How'd *that* go?" Soul asked after I told him about the hospital visit later that day.

"Jordan was a class act," I answered, sitting behind my desk.

Soul smiled.

"Tell me we did the right thing," I told him.

"What do you mean?" he asked.

"About not letting Jordan back on the team," I said. "He's

learned his lesson, and bringing him back would get Jim off my ass."

"Are you bringing Nabeel back too?" Soul asked, looking me in the eye.

"Nabeel's not Jordan," I said. "Kid's already been in trouble with the dean several times since we dismissed him."

"It'd be favoritism," Soul insisted. "That's why you can't go back."

I rubbed my temples and stared straight ahead.

"I wish some of that class would rub off on his daddy," Soul continued.

I glanced at him. "Did you give Jordan a set of your prayer beads?" I asked.

"Yeah, I gave them to him," Soul answered. "As an encouragement gift. Not much of one, but better than nothing."

"You're a better man than me," I said with a grin.

Soul chuckled and brushed it off. "Speaking of good men," he said, "have you seen who's back?" He gestured to the doorway just as Frank Beezer walked by.

I smiled and waved at him as he entered the office.

"Coach," he greeted me, carrying a dustpan and large broom in his good arm. His injured arm was in a sling.

"What are you doing here?" I asked, standing and patting his shoulder. "Aren't you supposed to be resting and healing up?"

"Can't sit still," he answered. "So I thought I'd come in here and pitch in around the field house. Doctor would have a fit if he saw me, but I figure if I can't take care of my field out there, I might as well do the next best thing."

I smiled. "It's good to see you."

"You too," he said. "Thanks again for helping get those hooligans off my field."

"Anytime."

"Speaking of hooligans," Beezer continued, "I just saw

Jordan up here. Hate to see him go, he's a good kid."

"He is," I agreed.

Beezer set the broom bristles on the floor and began pushing.

"You okay?" Soul asked me as I stood there.

"Yeah."

"Is it Jordan?"

"It's the town," I said. "Lake Barrow needs healing."

Soul kept his eyes on me. "Insha'Allah," he said. "God willing."

# Chapter 21

We beat Hapsburg County 28-14 the following Friday. I was proud of our defense, and especially of the way, they pulled together in Jordan's absence.

The following Monday, I was in my office studying game film, when the door opened. I was so engrossed in what I was doing that I barely heard it.

"Coach Jayce," said a deep voice.

I glanced up and grinned when I saw who was standing there.

"Come on in," I invited, as Coach Lane Faraday entered. I had seen him in the stands at one of our games, but other than that, he had kept a low profile for most of the season. His presence that morning was a welcome sight.

"Just came to check on you. Rough night the previous Friday, huh?"

I nodded. "Yeah."

Coach Faraday was sympathetic. "You sure seemed to get them back on the right rail against Hapsburg, though. Congratulations."

"Thanks."

"How's ol' Beezer?" he asked, changing the subject.

"He's doing well," I answered. "Hanging out around here

somewhere?"

"He's working already?"

I nodded. "Did he ever sit still when you coached here?"

"Good point," Coach chuckled. "Who you got this week?" he asked.

"San Mateo Catholic."

He grinned. "Another bitter rival," he quipped, "especially for you."

"Thanks for the reminder," I grinned, looking away and remembering the fumble that had cost us the game my senior year.

"You were always a good scrambler," Coach continued, "except for that play."

I nodded and smiled.

"It's ironic sometimes," Coach went on thoughtfully, "how the one thing that can help you is sometimes also the one thing that can bring you down."

"That's true," I agreed.

"You're a good coach, Jayce," he began. "Certainly ahead of your time in regard to your career. And I always knew you'd make it to where you are, but I never expected it to be at the age of almost twenty-five."

"Thanks," I answered.

"I remember the day I heard that Ted was fired. I had gone to a Rotary Club dinner that evening, and word was pretty much all over town at that point. I walk into the assembly hall, and it was all anyone could talk about; scandal gossip and rumors were flying all over the place."

He paused, took out a handkerchief, and dabbed his brow.

"And of course there was ol' Jim Gill," he said, looking at me, "right in the middle of it, like always; going on and on about how he could have seen this coming, how we had needed a new coach at the helm for some time, and how someone like Jayce Leonard, young as he was, would be the ideal person to lead the team."

I kept my eyes on my former coach.

"And it was at that moment I knew," Coach went on, "that you were going to be the next head coach."

I looked away for a moment and studied a portrait of my old high school team on the wall; forty or so guys in matching uniforms, with Coach Faraday right in the middle of us. Directly above our team was the scoreboard with "Jim Gill Stadium" emblazoned in bold letters.

"No man should have the kind of power that Jim Gill has over a town like ours," Coach said. "But that's the reality. The few roads to prosperity in Lake Barrow run right through that car dealership."

I glanced at him. "What are you saying, Coach?"

Coach Faraday's fatherly demeanor was replaced by an unfamiliar forlornness; as if he had bad news that could no longer wait. My mind went back to the day he visited during practice and had told me to obey the rules, and everything would work out. Somehow, I had felt at that moment that there was more to what he was saying than what I was hearing. And for some reason, perhaps for the same reason, I now felt that I was about to hear it.

"I'm saying that the reasons Ted Skipper was fired run deeper than what you were told," he answered.

"He recruited players," I said.

"So did I, Jayce," Coach Faraday said in a tone that was abrupt and rueful all at once. "We cheated."

I stared at him as shock waves ran through my gut. "What?"

"You heard me."

My tongue felt as though it was welded to the roof of my mouth, as the admission sank in.

"Everyone remembers Deke Hudson from back when you played," Coach went on, "but few people remember Carlos Powell."

"Our starting left guard," I answered, thinking back to

my playing days.

"And the biggest reason Deke ran for almost 2,000 yards that season," Coach added.

I kept my eyes on him.

"Carlos Powell transferred from a school on the opposite side of Orlando from us and was by far the biggest lineman we had that year. He was only 6'-1" but weighed between 280 and 290 pounds and had the best footwork I have ever seen in a lineman."

I said nothing.

"We recruited him," Coach continued.

I sat there stunned.

"We brought him over here, walked him through our facility, promised him the moon. I think Gill even got his mom into a job somewhere."

"You recruited him," I repeated, barely above a whisper, feeling like a kid who had seen the puppet strings at a show.

"Carlos wasn't the only one, either," Coach went on. "We brought in guys from all over. Jim kept it quiet for me. He's got connections all over the state and paid off the right people; a school administrator here, a school board member there. He's even bribed superintendents before. Silence was available, as long as the price was right. And with Jim Gill, the right price is never hard to reach."

I could only stare and wait for him to go on.

"The man's actually a lot easier to figure out than people think," Coach continued, getting up from his chair. "When you get right down to it, there really are only two things you need to know about the guy: he knows people, and his loyalty only extends so far as your loyalty to him. Thankfully, I figured both of those things out that out early on. Skipper, on the other hand, never could."

I felt my blood boiling as I stared at my former coach.

"What I'm saying to you, Jayce," Coach continued, "is that Ted Skipper refused to play Jordan Gill at linebacker, and that's what got him fired."

I was silent.

"He was a tremendous coach, and probably still will be, if he can ever find a job again. But he was also stubborn. And that's what did him in. It wasn't the recruiting violations. He would have continued pulling guys onto the team for years, just like I did if Jim hadn't outed him at the newspapers and the state athletic association. Hell, that's why I treated you and Jamie like gods. You both were great players, but above all else, I knew what the price would be for running afoul of Jim Gill."

I stood up from my desk feeling dizzy.

"That's why you had such a good senior year, Jayce," he went on. "You were always a good athlete, but everyone knew it was Deke Hudson's offense that year. Matter of fact, when Jim first approached me and 'suggested' that I put the ball in the air more because it would benefit you, I looked at him like he was crazy." He paused and smiled faintly. "And I'm pretty sure that's how most folks looked at me when we started throwing."

"Why?" I managed. "Why did he make you do it?"

Coach Faraday shrugged. "Like I said, loyalty. You proved your allegiance to the Gills when you stood up for Margery during that whole Danforth fiasco. Way I figure, Jim saw that the best way to reward you was to get us showcasing that arm of yours on the field."

"I can't believe this," I said, my disillusionment rising with my heart rate.

"Worked out pretty well for you, though, didn't it?" Coach returned, keeping his eyes on me. "Yearwood State, prosperous college career, now look at you. You're right back where you started; coaching, doing well, all courtesy of the man who's been pulling the strings the whole time."

"It was Jim," I said.

"It's been Jim," Coach clarified. "For years."

"Why are you telling me this?!" I snapped at Coach Faraday.

"Because you just kicked Jordan Gill off of the team," he answered. "And because I don't want you to wind up like Ted Skipper."

I glowered at my former coach. "I am *nothing* like you or him," I snarled through clenched teeth. "I don't cheat."

"No," Coach agreed. "You were always the most upright kid I had ever come across. And you still are. Ironically, though, it's precisely that that could get you canned in your first year as a coach."

"Get out of my office," I said, glaring at him.

The grandfatherly charm was back, and for a split second, I almost regretted the malice with which I was addressing my former coach. But then he turned as he reached the doorway.

"The way I see it," he began, "I had two choices: deny you the truth and let you continue thinking of Lake Barrow as the idyllic paradise you've always believed it to be. Or tell you the truth so that you don't end up being run out of your own hometown, Jayce. Because integrity only takes a man so far, and it's rarely sufficient to protect you when people demand loyalty at any cost."

"My loyalty is to this town."

"Save yourself," Coach said, as he exited. "Because this town won't."

"I'm sorry," Ahmad said as we sat in my office after Coach had left.

I shook my head and took a sip of water. Soul was seated against a far wall and kept his eyes on me. Woody, Max, and Ahmad were seated across the desk from me.

"I'd be lying if I said I didn't see this coming," Soul remarked.

I wanted to argue with him, but I knew it was true. The conversation in the weight room at Yearwood State continued to haunt me. "Faraday," I said to myself. "He was cheating all that time, and I never saw it."

"I did," Ahmad said.

I glanced at him.

He continued, "Carlos used to joke with me about all the perks he was getting just for playing here."

"And you never said anything," I glared at him.

"Would it have made a difference?" he glowered back. "Hell, the way Lake Barrow runs, I might have been kicked off the team."

I just shook my head. None of us said anything for several moments, each of us seemingly wondering just how much worse things could get in the small town of Lake Barrow, Florida. I sat there hunched over, elbows on my thighs, and stared out through my office window into the weight room. A few of our players were lifting, preparing, working hard so that their efforts on Friday night would do their hometown proud. I ran a finger through my hair and began to wonder when I might expect to see the first indicators of a receding hairline.

Max and Woody stood up, almost in tandem. "We got P.E. in less than five minutes," Max said as they exited. "Keep your head up, Jayce."

Ahmad wasn't far behind them. "I've got to run to the bank," he said, walking to the doorway. "But I'll be back."

Soul and I were the only two in the office. "You gonna be okay?" he asked.

I looked at him and could almost tell how haggard my appearance was based on his expression. "Yeah," I answered.

"Hell of a week," he added.

"Hard to imagine hell being much worse," I replied.

Soul grinned. "The Qur'an tells a different story."

"So does the Bible."

Soul shook his head and glanced away. "Mankind seems to have more similarities than differences," he stated. "And yet it's amazing how we almost invent things to fight over."

I rubbed my eyes and stared ahead.

"So now what do you do?" Soul asked. "Faraday's talk change your mind about Jordan?"

I had no answer. After several moments, Soul stood and made his way toward the office door. He exited, and I watched him stroll into the weight room and begin straightening it. Through all the turmoil of the past weekend, he was consistent; never rattled. He would be okay, no matter how bad things got. I envied him.

My thoughts were interrupted by the phone ringing on my desk. I answered it after the second ring.

"Jayce, it's Starr," our principal's voice came through the receiver. "I need to see you in my office right away."

For some unknown reason, my insides began to roil over again, as I left the field house and headed to the front office.

The man sitting in the principal's office was dressed in a navy suit with cropped hair and a clean-shaven face. He looked to be in his late thirties or early forties, with a pleasant and cocksure demeanor. As I entered, he rose to greet me, and we shook hands.

"Sheldon Twane," he said with a clipped accent, as Starr introduced us and we shook hands.

"Jayce Leonard," I returned.

"Let's have a seat," Starr said. I took the second chair opposite of him.

Twane reached into a brown attaché case, retrieved a stack of documents, and held them in his lap.

"Jayce, Mr. Twane here is from the Religious Equality Foundation," Starr began in an even tone. "I know you're familiar with them."

I nodded, glancing at the visitor.

Starr went on, "And I'm going to let him tell you a little more about what's brought him here." He turned to our guest and gave a faint nod.

Twane continued without missing a beat, "I'm here on behalf of a Sims County High School student, who has filed a complaint through our Florida offices with the intent to possibly follow through with a lawsuit. The student in question is alleging religious discrimination and proselytization on the part of Sims County School District, and specifically, Sims County High School."

"What?" I interjected, looking at Starr, whose face bore the look of a doctor about to deliver heartbreaking news to a patient.

"It's Jordan Gill," Starr answered. "He's threatening to sue us."

# CHAPTER 22

My mouth fell open.

"According to his official statement," Twane continued, "The student, one Jordan Gill, is alleging that he was 'strongly encouraged to alter his religion by an employee of the school district'; a Mr. Sool-Man Rasheed, during school hours on school property."

"How the hell is Soul getting dragged into this?" I seethed.

"Jayce, calm down," Starr urged.

"The statement goes on," Twane said, "to record that on one occasion, Mr. Rasheed attempted to proselytize Jordan and persuade him to convert to the Islamic faith. This overture was characterized by what Jordan is describing as an overt verbal invitation, as well as a nonverbal offer in the form of Mr. Rasheed's presenting a string of prayer beads, which Jordan has volunteered to submit as evidence favoring his case."

"Bull shit!" I yelled, jumping up. "Those prayer beads were a gift, and have nothing to do with trying to convert anyone! Jordan told me so himself!"

"Jayce, calm down," Starr admonished sternly.

I glared at Twane as he went on. "Also favoring the case will be the testimony of an eyewitness who was nearby when the alleged proselytization occurred; a Mr. Frank Beezer, who is an employee of Sims County High School."

"This whole thing is a lie!" I exclaimed. "And Beezer will verify it."

Twane seemed to recoil from my outburst but regrouped quickly. "This is a copy of the statement," he whipped out a piece of paper, and handed it to me, almost as if it were a shield.

I snatched it and glanced over it, ignoring most of the tedious black-and-white print and scanning to the bottom where, sure enough, Jordan's signature was affixed. Directly beneath it, I saw where Jim Gill had signed his name in the "Parent/Guardian" space.

"This is wrong," I whispered to myself.

Starr kept his eyes on me as he said, "Mr. Twane, if you could please step out and give Coach Leonard and me a few minutes, we'd appreciate it."

Twane rose from the chair with his attaché case and left the office. I had no intention of sitting back down. When we were alone, Starr said, "Jayce, I know how you feel."

"No," I retorted, rising and storming out of the office. "You have no idea, and I want to talk to Jordan."

I reached the Physics classroom and stared through the window of the closed doorway where another teacher was busy lecturing. After knocking, I opened and asked to speak to Jordan Gill, who was seated toward the back. Slowly, he rose and walked out of the classroom.

"Explain this!" I demanded as he closed the door, holding up the REF statement. "Your dad hates Coach Rasheed, but how could you be a part of this, Jordan? After all, we've been through?! You're gonna do this?"

"You have no idea," Jordan answered, his eyes hollow

and his voice subdued. At that moment, I noticed his appearance for the first time. He looked as though he had not slept in weeks. "You don't know what I'm up against."

I studied him.

"I came home that afternoon," he continued. "Right after talking to you in the bleachers. That's when my dad saw the beads."

He paused as I glared at him.

"He's going to use the statement I signed with REF to get you and Soul fired," Jordan confessed.

My knees felt weak, and I fought to keep the hallway from spinning.

"Jim lost it when he saw the prayer beads," Jordan said, tears coming to his eyes. "Then he began asking questions; about Soul, about the beads, about the conversation we'd had when he gave them to me, about who was around when he gave them. It didn't take long for me to realize what he was doing; putting all those pieces together so that he could finally move against Soul. And you. Sure enough, right after I told him everything, we were in the car the next day, during my suspension from school. Our first stop was to see Beezer. Dad coerced him and used his employment against him as leverage. Told Beezer he'd never set foot on that field again if he didn't sign on as a witness against you and Soul."

"He can't fire Beezer," I protested, "only the school can."

Jordan shook his head. "Which they'll do if my dad threatens to pull his funding from the new field house project."

My head was spinning again as I became overwhelmed once more at the web of control that Jim Gill had, for years, woven throughout Lake Barrow. Coach Faraday had been right.

"After Beezer agreed to be a witness, we headed to the REF office in Orlando," Jordan continued. "He made me sign the paper you're holding. Said he'd cut me off if I didn't.

That was it."

I ran my fingers through my hair and sighed.

"He'll do it, too," Jordan went on, "I've seen it happen. You probably never knew this, but when Jamie joined the Marine Corps against our dad's wishes, Jim sold his car and transferred his inheritance over to me. Truth is, he never forgave Jamie for disobeying him."

I fought to regain my balance as I stood in the hallway in front of Jordan.

"Same thing it's always about," Jordan continued. "You obey Jim, or he works his will against you. Been that way all our lives. If you're a Gill man, you get your way, and you don't stop until you do."

"What about you, Jordan?"

He glanced at me.

"Does it continue with you?" I asked. "Do you just go along with this plan of Jim's because it's required of you? Because of an inheritance?"

"I can't lose my future."

"What future?" I exclaimed. "Jordan, listen to me. I faced this exact same thing years ago; between Matt Danforth, Marty Danforth, and your aunt. Hell, you faced it like a champ when you went to see Morgan. Now you're cowering!"

"Because it's not the same thing!" Jordan countered. "Marty Danforth's powerless compared to my dad. You don't understand."

I stepped away and took a breath as things calmed down, keeping my eyes on Jordan as he continued losing his composure; tears were streaming down his face as he leaned against the wall, bent over, and put his hands on his knees.

"I understand this," I told him, stepping forward again. "It takes a hell of a lot less to be a star on the football field than it does to make this right. And you know it."

With that, I left him standing in the hallway as I strode off.

❧

Frank Beezer was by the utility shed, just off of the concession stand near the west end zone, and was organizing a pile of tools.

"Coach," he beamed, as I made my way toward him. "How are we doing today?"

I closed the gap on him, grabbed his coverall lapel, and pushed him against the shed before he could react. "Cut the shit," I snarled, "and you answer me one thing: how could you do it?"

Stunned by my sudden ambush, Beezer dropped the socket wrench that had been in his hand and gaped at me. His eyes were as big as saucers.

I tightened my grip. "And don't even think about pretending like you don't know what I'm talking about," I snapped. "Because I saw the REF statement with your name on it."

"Coach, just listen," Frank stammered, "I thought I saw Soul…"

"Don't give me that crap!" I yelled, shaking him.

"I thought he forced those beads into Jordan's hand," Frank finished, his eyes bulging as if blinded by a set of headlights.

"Bullshit," I spat, moving within an inch of his face. He was shorter than me by several inches and was powerless. "I talked to Jordan, and he told me about the conversation you had with Jim. I know he threatened your employment. My only question is why the hell is this field so much more important than protecting an innocent man whom you know damn well didn't do anything wrong?!"

My tirade had shaken the elderly groundskeeper, and he slinked down against the wall, desperate to ease away from my grip. "Jayce, listen, I had to do it!"

"Had to do what?" I knelt down and got in his face. "Stab Soul in the back?!"

"I had…I had…"

"You're gonna retract this!" I instructed.

"No…"

"Make this right…"

"I can't…"

"And you're going to fight this thing."

"Jayce, listen!" Beezer wailed. "Just listen to me please!"

The frailty in his plea got my attention, and I eased up just enough to let him know he had only moments to explain himself.

"Jayce, it's my world!" he whimpered.

I glowered at him.

"It's my whole world!" he wailed. Tears were streaming down his wrinkled cheeks as he recoiled before me. "And it's not just this field. It's this team, this community, these people!"

Beezer began sobbing like a small child.

"Jim knew best where to hit me," Beezer cried, "and he hit me good. I can't leave this field, and it doesn't have a damn thing to do with money, or employment or anything."

Beezer paused as his chest heaved with sobs.

"All my life," he wept, "I've lived as an afterthought in this town. Never had anyone. Barely any family; no friends. And worst of all, I had nowhere else to go. This place," he gestured all around him, "was my home, still is, and always will be."

I kept my eyes on him as he struggled to talk between bouts of blubbering.

"When I got this job,, it became my life. I met you, and the Gills, and everyone that's ever been around this field, this team, this community. It was like a re-birth for me. Suddenly, I was part of something. Suddenly, my life had meaning, even if it only amounted to cutting grass and spraying white paint."

He paused and brushed away tears.

"You'll never know the pain of losing something like that

if you're someone like me."

"I know about pain," I told him. "But why in God's name would you allow something like this to happen to Soul? Or to me? Especially if this is about not losing the ones you say you love?"

Beezer was silent, and I prayed in that long moment that he would see the light.

Finally, he looked at me with eyes that were as pathetic as I had ever seen on him. "Because it's me," he answered, almost pleadingly. "It's who I am, and I can't let it go, even for Soul. I'd take a bullet for you and him all at once, but I can't…I just can't…"

"You can't do what's right," I finished for him.

He looked up at me as if begging for mercy. I had no sympathy for him as my eyes burned holes into his face, and as I rose from my kneeling position. I was about to walk away when out of the corner of my eye I noticed something lying on the ground nearby. It was the football that Deke had given Beezer that night he and Ahmad and I had come to the stadium and run soul sprints. Deke's signature was still visible, and I became sick once more.

Beezer watched me as I walked over and picked it up.

"You know," I said, turning to him and holding up the ball, "you may not have much dignity left, Frank, but if you have any decency left, you'll know what to do with this ball. Because you're damn sure, not worthy of keeping it."

I whipped a spiral at him. Beezer instinctively covered his head as the ball missed him and made a cracking sound as it hit the wooden shed.

I left Beezer sitting on the ground as I stormed off again.

# Chapter 23

Soul's face was a portrait of bewilderment and shock. "I can't believe this," he managed.

He wasn't the only one. As we stood in the weight room before the final bell that afternoon, neither of us could think of words that were either useful or encouraging. We heard the commingling din of adolescent voices rise in volume outside the field house as students, on their way to the parking lot and busing area, made their way past. Both of us knew that the locker room would be packed and bustling within minutes, as the guys filtered in and began gearing up for practice that afternoon.

"Take the day off," I said to him. The news of the complaint against him was hitting him hard, and his features showed it. His brown, vibrant eyes had an emptiness to them that I had no memory of seeing before. Soul's shoulders slumped, and he seemed to be fighting against the emotions that were no doubt raging within.

Soul turned to me and managed a faint grin.

"Soul sprint," he said, without any emotion. "That's all this is. A soul sprint. Hurts like hell, but if it makes the soul stronger in the end," he shrugged. "It's probably all worth it somehow."

With that, he turned and left the field house.

"Warm-ups!" Andrico called out. "Are you ready?!"

"Always ready!" came the response in unison.

Andrico and our other seniors kicked off the pre-practice ritual with jumping jacks, which would be followed by other calisthenics before practice began in earnest. I watched the team warm up, though I may as well have been miles away in any direction. My mind was consumed with the events that had transpired throughout the day, as I watched Max, Woody, and Ahmad walk among the columns of players.

"Coach?" a voice called out behind me.

I turned and saw Starr approaching.

"You got a minute?" he asked.

"Not really," I said, tucking a clipboard under my arm.

"This won't take long," Starr assured.

I stood with my arms folded and faced him.

"Coach, I know it's been a rough day, and I wish I had better news to take the edge off," he began, "but I'm afraid that's not the case."

I glared at him.

"Jayce, you need to know that we've gone ahead and put Coach Rasheed on administrative leave."

I kept my eyes on him, despite the growing bewilderment inside me.

"It's just until we can work through this," he continued.

"You mean until Gill pulls another puppet string and changes it," I retorted.

"Jayce…"

"It's not like I don't see what's going on here," I cut him off. "I talked to Jordan, and I also talked to Faraday, and I know exactly what this is about."

"Do you?"

I turned and took a few steps away from him closer to the practice field. "This is about you playing by the rules and getting your field house."

Starr was jolted by my frankness. "Jayce…"

"I have a team to coach."

"Not if you don't fire Soul, and save your own hide," Starr said bluntly.

I turned and faced him again.

"Think about it, Jayce," he said. "Success comes from knowing what you want and knowing how to get it. And in this town, there just aren't many options for the latter. So do us all a favor, Jayce: go with us on getting Rasheed out of here. He goes, and this entire ordeal goes away."

I turned and walked back toward the team.

"You always do the right thing, Jayce," Starr called out, "but this is one of those times where you'd better be sure you know what that is."

The guys worked hard that afternoon, and I was proud of the effort. The win over Hapsburg County had reenergized the practice session and created new momentum that I hoped would carry us throughout the season, no matter what happened off the field.

Andrico's deep passes were getting better with each rep, and the rest of the offense seemed to click right along with his improvement. Tre Bell ran hard, and the line did an exceptional job blocking for him. On defense, it was an equally impressive showing. Isaiah Waters was becoming more of a leader with each practice, and the guys responded well to him.

But it was more than just solid play and good practices; the guys were having fun. Each successful play on offense or defense brought heightened energy and a greater unity than what had been there before…which is why having to break the news to the team about Coach Soul was killing me.

"Strong right, strong right!" Waters called out from the middle linebacker position.

"Down!" Andrico yelled.

"Lou! Lou! Lou! Lou! Lou!" players were shouting to each other, as defenders scrambled to adjust coverages.

"Come on, Rico, get that six!" other players shouted from the sideline. "Come on 'O'!"

"Stuff 'em, D!" I heard Woody call out.

It was the last play of practice, and the defense had kept the offense out of the end zone all day. I watched as the guys lined up, and as Johnny Caldwell got into position. The ball was going to him, and everyone on both sides of the ball knew it.

Andrico took the snap and dropped back. The line held as long as it could, before defenders started to break through, and Andrico had to scramble. He dashed to his right looking downfield, as several defenders, including Isaiah, gave chase. Finally, he stopped, planted his feet, and launched a bomb toward the east end zone of the practice field. Sure enough, Johnny was streaking toward the post while blanketed by two defenders. It was an ill-advised pass under any other set of circumstances, but it was also a last-ditch scoring effort that I prayed would go Andrico's way…especially given how the last hail-Mary he had thrown had gone.

Johnny leaped into the air, along with Kyle Messina who was helping cover him at safety.

Messina tipped it, Johnny tipped it, and the ball hung in the air for two seconds before falling back into Johnny's hands, who sprinted the rest of the way into the end zone.

The offense went nuts.

As the whole team ran downfield to congratulate Johnny and celebrate, I jogged behind with the rest of the coaching staff.

"You got lucky," Max said to his brother. "Rico would

have been sacked if he didn't know how to move the pocket."

"We did what we had to," Woody retorted, "and Rico's got skill. Quit being a sore loser."

I laughed, as did Ahmad, who was good-natured despite having to lick his wounds.

Once we got everyone huddled up and settled down, I took a deep breath before dropping the bomb on them. "Guys, I've got some bad news. And I'm not going to sugar-coat it, so here it goes. Coach Rasheed has been put on administrative leave, and won't be with us for the San Mateo game," I stated.

I watched as shock and disbelief shone on the faces of our players. For a moment, no one said anything.

"What'd he do?" Andrico asked.

"Got in trouble for putting out religious stuff," Kyle Messina answered.

I glanced quickly at Ahmad and the Twin Tanks. News had spread quickly, just as we'd expected. I began to hear sighs of indignation and other murmurings as the players began to whisper amongst themselves.

"So that means he's fired?" asked Sammy Stromas.

"No," I answered quickly. "It just means he's out of work until Mr. Starr and the school district decide on how to handle him."

"What exactly happened?" Skyler Hemphill asked.

"That's not important," I answered him.

"Man, that's bull shit!" Johnny Caldwell exclaimed, tossing his helmet on the ground.

"Watch your mouth!" Ahmad snapped.

"And pick up your helmet," Max instructed.

More chatter.

"Hey, lock it up!" Woody shouted, managing to calm the noise a little.

"Coach, can't you do something?" Ryan Gilmore, our tackle, asked. "I mean, you dealt with that same organization years ago when you played here and kept Mrs. Hanceford out of trouble. My brother told me about it."

Once again, I wished to God at that moment that there was something I could do.

"No, I can't," I admitted.

"Man, we need to do something," I heard Andrico say, turning to several of his teammates, and prompting more cross-talk.

"Listen!" I called out, getting their attention once more. "Here's the way forward: I'm calling plays, along with Coach Woody. Nothing's changing in terms of our scheme. You guys just focus on practicing and getting ready for San Mateo."

"We need some change around here," I heard Andrico mutter to another teammate just before I dismissed the team.

"Are you scared?" Dixie asked as we sat on the sofa that afternoon, her head against my chest as I leaned back.

"More than ever," I answered, staring at the ceiling.

"Me too."

I looked at my wife, gorgeous as ever, and I remembered our conversation from the night of the Barton City game.

"Think I'll keep the kitchen closed tonight," she finally said. "Baby's been kicking the life out of me all day, and I'm too tired to cook."

I glanced at her. "You sure it's not the other crazy stuff going on here that's wearing you out?"

"Could be," she answered.

"How about some Squat and Holler, then?" I suggested.

"Read my mind," she said. "We should invite your mom. She's been worried about you since Barton City, and I know she wants to see you."

I chuckled.

"Are you laughing at me?" Dixie demanded.

"No," I answered. "Just marveling."

"At what?"

I took a deep breath before answering. "At the fact that I married a gal who not only doesn't mind spending time with my mom but who actually *initiates* spending time with her."

Dixie smiled and leaned to kiss me once more. A peck on the lips turned into something more, and soon, we were falling backward onto the sofa.

"Dinner can wait," she said, unlocking her lips from mine only for a moment.

"Does Guadalajara still have that taco salad that I like so much?" Mom asked from the back seat, as we drove to the restaurant hours later.

"I think so," I answered from the driver's seat.

"Dixie, you've worked there," Mom said. "And I haven't gone there in ages. Is the food still good?"

"It sure is," she answered sweetly, as we held hands.

We pulled into the restaurant parking lot and found a spot. I got out and walked around to the rear passenger side to help Mom out, and we took our time getting to the entrance. Ignacio smiled at us as soon as we opened the door.

"*Buenas Noches,*" he greeted.

"Bony Nachos," I returned, causing Ignacio to shake his head.

"*Ay, bobo!*" he said good-naturedly. "Senora Dixie, why did you marry this fool? I was the love of your life when you worked here!"

"You were," Dixie returned with a smile. "I let him talk me into it, though. Good to see you, Ig."

Ignacio smiled and greeted my mother.

"Senora Cheryl," he grinned. "Soon to be *Abuela Cheryl.*"

"That's right," she said. "On pins and needles until I meet

my grandbaby."

Ignacio showed us to our seat and went to retrieve menus, along with chips and salsa. We were still getting settled when I became aware of someone walking toward our table.

"You just gonna ignore an old teammate, or what?" a deep, familiar voice asked.

I looked up and grinned at the sight of Deke Hudson standing next to us.

"How can I not ignore you," I retorted, standing up to give him a hug. "I can barely recognize you."

As we embraced, I noticed that Deke was wearing street clothes, and a large Spartan baseball cap pulled low over his eyes. "Trying to keep a low profile," he said, touching the brim. "That's about the only way I can get a quiet meal in this town anymore."

"It's great to see you," I said.

Deke greeted Mom and Dixie, before turning back to me.

"What are you doing back in town?" I asked with a smile. "Thought you'd be slammed with preparations for Coach Spurrier and the Redskins this Sunday."

Deke shook his head. "Ol' Ball Coach can wait," he grinned. "I had to get up here and get me some Squat and Holler, though. Had to see my sister, too."

"Mikayla's here with you?"

Deke nodded in the direction of a table in the far corner. Sure enough, Mikayla was sitting and holding a menu. She smiled and waved.

"You wouldn't know it by the smile," Deke said, "but she's not doing too well."

I glanced at Deke.

"She told me about Soul," he went on. "Shit deal, man."

"Yep," I affirmed.

"All of it's a damn shame," he frowned. "The fight during the Barton City game, Soul, every bit of it. Is he really getting fired over handing out some prayer beads?"

"He's on administrative leave," I clarified. "But it's not looking good."

"I don't envy your job," Deke cringed.

"It's this town," I said. "We need new leverage, especially funding."

"You coming to a point?" Deke gave a wry smile.

"I'm not telling you how to spend your money," I answered. "But you do make a lot of it. Truth is, a new field house with the name 'Deke Hudson' on the sign would look a hell of a lot better than the one we have now."

"You make a convincing argument," Deke complimented me. "Maybe this town could use a new sugar-daddy."

I glanced away. "Last convincing argument I made caused my best friend to have a First Amendment complaint thrown at him."

"Don't beat yourself up," Deke encouraged. "Everything I've heard about Soul is that he's been a great thing for this town, despite what all's happened."

"I agree," I replied. "Let me go chat with Mikayla."

I strode over to their table as Mikayla stood to give me a hug. "Hey, Coach," she said, as we embraced.

"You're dating my best friend," I told her. "The name's Jayce."

She laughed as Deke rejoined us.

"Soul didn't want to come with you?"

Mikayla shook her head. "He stayed home tonight."

"Can't blame him," I affirmed. "What do you think he's doing right now?"

"Probably either praying or watching Sports Center."

"Wish I was with him."

"You Muslim now?" Deke chided.

"The way some Christians in this town act," I responded, "I haven't ruled it out."

All of us laughed.

"How are classes?" I asked Mikayla.

She shrugged. "Same. Still have the same problem kids, especially Quinton."

I nodded, remembering the encounter Andrico and I had with him on the road the previous week.

"He's not getting any better," Mikayla continued. "But I'm still trying to get through to him."

We chatted for a moment before I noticed Ignacio taking our table's order. My stomach growled.

"Should I go by there later?" I asked Mikayla. "Check on Soul?"

She shook her head. "I was going to head over there myself after Deke leaves. You should probably take care of Dixie and that precious baby."

I gave her another hug, as I turned to Deke. "Headed back tonight?"

He nodded. "Gotta get back to work if I'm gonna cause Spurrier's visor to hit the ground on Sunday."

After placing my order, I left the table again and headed to the men's room. As I stood at the sink washing my hands, my body and mind must have been in preservation mode, tuning out sights and sounds that would have otherwise registered with me. Looking back, there can be no other explanation for the fact that I didn't hear the door open or notice who walked through it.

"Jayce," said a familiar deep voice.

I felt my insides lurch at the sight and sound of Jim Gill entering the restroom.

"Thought I saw you and Dixie and Cheryl over in the corner," he said, walking to a urinal and unzipping his fly. "And that looked like Deke you were chatting with."

I said nothing and focused on the sink. His willful vulnerability at that moment angered me more than anything else.

He did not perceive me as a threat, and both of us knew it.

"I should go say 'hello,'" Jim continued, with one hand down below and the other on his hip. "Always is nice when hometown boys come home. Especially when they stay loyal to their town."

"You mean when they stay loyal to you," I glowered at him.

Jim finished urinating, re-zipped his pants, flushed, and turned to face me. "Jayce, you've got no one else to blame but yourself for this mess with Soul. Both of you were standing there in your office the night after the Barton City debacle, and heard what I told you." Jim moved closer to me, and I fought to not back away. "You painted a bull's eye on your back, son."

"I'm not your son," I shot back.

"Fair enough, but you better start connecting the dots," Jim replied, as he placed his hands under a sink, and turned on the water. "I may not be your father, but you've benefited more from my benevolence than just about anybody else ever has, my own boys included."

"And that's why you think it's okay to do to Soul and me what Marty Danforth tried to do to your sister years ago."

"You really don't get it do you?" Jim sneered, turning off the faucet and flicking the excess water off his hands into the sink. He reached for a paper towel. "Do you really think there's a parallel between what's happening now versus what happened then?"

"Yes."

"Then you better ask yourself this," Jim returned, "what did Marty Danforth have to gain by hurting my family, other than and score-settling? That's the difference. There's nothing personal here, Jayce; not with you, and certainly not with Soul. He broke the law."

"You're sick," I glowered.

"Not sick," Jim shook his head. "An opportunist, sure,

but not sick."

"What do you gain from this?" I demanded.

An insidious grin crossed Jim's face. I had seen his boastful, conceited side before, but never had I seen him as sardonic as he appeared at that moment. He paused as if carefully selecting his words. Watching him was like witnessing someone take off their skin so that you could see inside their soul.

Jim looked me in the eye. "Same thing I would have gained from getting that land from Danforth," he finally said. "Satisfaction. Screw everything else that's happened, Jayce. There's nothing quite like the realization that you can bend an entire town to whatever you will."

"You're depraved," I kept my eyes on him.

"And you're about to be unemployed," he said.

I watched him toss the paper towel in a trash can as he headed for the door. "You do impress me, though, Jayce," he continued, "you always did. Being the upstanding guy you've always been, I guess I should have seen this coming, rather than just assume that you'd fold like a cheap table once I put the screws to you. You really are true to your word and your friends and your family." Jim turned to me and raised an index finger. "But know this, it doesn't stop here. Jordan stays off the team, and I won't just see Soul fired, you'll be next… and your mother won't be far behind."

I felt the acid in my stomach begin to lurch.

"Your integrity, or your career," Jim said. "It's a timeless choice, really. Just ask Lane Faraday…or Ted Skipper for that matter."

With that, Jim left. My knees and bowels felt weak, and the acrid taste of digestive juices began to surface within my mouth.

I darted to the nearest stall, collapsed to my knees, and retched into the toilet.

*God help me*, I whispered between gags. *Help my family.*

# CHAPTER 24

"Feeling any better?" Mom asked as I helped her to the front door later that evening.

"I'll make it," I told her. My stomach was still queasy after the confrontation with Jim, and I had skipped dinner altogether. Mom and Dixie had asked repeatedly if I wanted to leave, but I didn't want to spoil their evening. Instead, I had sat there drinking water while they ate, all the while glaring at Jim's table. He had been meeting with some local big-wig politicians whom he no doubt had in his pocket. At that moment, I loathed him more than I ever had.

We reached the front porch, and Mom found her house keys before facing me again. "I'm probably going to quit my job," she told me.

I gaped at her. "You can't do that."

Mom shook her head and dismissed me. "What I can't do is let Jim do this to you," she said. "And yes, he's been good to me, but using me as a pressure point to hurt my child is crossing a line."

"You just got a raise," I protested.

"I can find another job, Jayce."

"Making barely enough money to eat, Mom," I countered, "let alone keep you from being buried by medical bills."

"Let me worry about that," she said. I watched her and was struggling to find an edge.

"I'll let Jordan back on the team," I blurted.

Mom's head shot up, her eyes piercing me. "Don't you dare," she said. "Let him twist your arm to the point of breaking, but don't you compromise!"

I glanced away and felt tears forming in my eyes.

"Jayce," Mom said. "Look at me."

I couldn't.

"Look at me!" she demanded.

Slowly, I turned my gaze toward her. She reached up and slowly began wiping away tears.

"You don't remember, do you?"

"What?" I asked.

"What I said to you the day you interviewed for your job," she clarified.

I didn't answer.

"Commit to doing right by the boys, come what may. Treat them fairly and equally no matter what, and ask forgiveness when you don't. That's all anyone can expect."

I nodded.

"This world's knocked us on our asses several times over," she went on. "And I know we're due for a break, Jayce. Truth is, I thought we were out of the woods when Jim stepped in, hired me, and helped you with football and school. But life happens, Jayce. And it may break your employment, your bank account, whatever. The worst thing any of us can do, though, is let it break us. Because the one thing that doesn't always come back stronger once it's broken is our integrity."

I shook my head.

"We'll be fine," she said, putting a hand under my chin and tilting my head up. "Survival takes a while. But we'll get there."

I kissed her good-night and made sure she got into the house, before heading out to the car where Dixie was waiting. She noticed my red-rimmed eyes and held my hand as I backed out of Mom's driveway.

Neither of us said anything as we drove the rest of the way home.

Practices did not go well the rest of the week. The guys weren't focused, mental mistakes abounded, and I felt like we weren't in any shape to take on San Mateo Catholic that Friday on our home field.

No one said it out loud, but the foundational cause of the malaise was pretty obvious. I had taken over play-calling duties and knew our offense backward and forwards. We were fine in all of the technical aspects of the preparation. Yet, there was an energy that was missing. It had gone out the same day that Soul Rasheed had begun his administrative leave of absence.

Friday came, and I found myself struggling with a last-ditch effort to motivate our team against San Mateo Catholic.

"Guys," I said as I stood before them in the locker room before the game. "I need you focused on the task at hand, and on each other. Forget about who's not here, about what's going on around us outside the white lines of that field. Because all that matters tonight is what happens when you set foot on that field. Who's walking away from *your* field with the respect that's going to be earned out there tonight? It's a simple question, but it's one you need to answer."

The guys looked around at each other but said nothing.

"Let bring it in," I said, as the guys crowded together for the chant.

"I say we go out with a bang," Woody told me, as we

stood on the sideline together, "in case this really is our last hurrah here."

I donned my headset and grinned, staring ahead while the guys assembled in our east end zone behind the cheerleaders' banner. For as long as I could remember, my favorite part of any football game, as a player, coach, or spectator, was watching the team break through the pre-game banner and dash toward their home sideline to the cheers of the crowd. To me, there was never anything more pure, or more unifying, than seeing a hometown team and its community come together like that in the moment. I relished it and would miss seeing it in Lake Barrow if in fact my days were numbered here. Watching it from the sideline, it didn't matter that things were as abysmal as they were in the community. We were a team, and our community loved us. That was all that mattered.

The cheerleaders began chanting as they formed a column on opposite sides of the banner, and I felt that old, familiar energy begin to rise within the stadium once more as anticipation grew.

The paper was torn, and the players emerged.

Something was different, though.

Strangely enough, the first thing I noticed was that the boys weren't even running. They were walking, in a single-file line in a different direction from our sideline.

Where were they headed?

"What the hell…?" Woody asked, noticing it.

"What are they doing?" I heard Ahmad say through the headset.

I didn't have an answer but kept my eyes on the team as they marched in a straight line toward the large, stenciled "S" at midfield.

The crowd began to die down, as everyone in attendance also saw what was going on. Where were the Sims County Spartans headed?

Andrico led the way. He reached the "S" and took a knee,

followed by Ryan Gilmore, Kyle Messina, Johnny Caldwell, Sammy Stromas, and others. One by one, each member of the Sims County Spartans knelt down in a centipede-like formation that stretched all the way back to our east goal line.

Jim Gill Stadium was completely silent; the hum of highway traffic a mile off in the distance was the only sound that could be heard. For what felt like five minutes, but was really no more than twenty seconds, nobody moved, and not a sound was made.

Suddenly, Andrico rose from his kneeling position and bellowed, "We love Coach Soul!"

On cue, the rest of the team rose and hoisted their helmets in the air. Andrico then called, "We won't play without Coach Soul!"

The rest of the team followed suit in unison as they roared:

"WE WON'T PLAY WITHOUT COACH SOUL!"
"WE WON'T PLAY WITHOUT COACH SOUL!"
"WE WON'T PLAY WITHOUT COACH SOUL!"

With each repetition of each syllable, the team moved from their linear formation across the field to a tight cluster in the middle of it and began bounding up and down on our logo, never breaking cadence as they chanted. Everyone in attendance watched as the boys continued bouncing up and down, honoring their dismissed coach with rhythmic incantation.

"WE WON'T PLAY WITHOUT COACH SOUL!"
"WE WON'T PLAY WITHOUT COACH SOUL!"
"WE WON'T PLAY WITHOUT COACH SOUL!"

I began to realize what was happening; that this was no longer a football game, but a protest. Everyone else in the stands caught on as well, and as the recognition hit them, they began to make their displeasure known

"Come on boys!" I heard a spectator call out.

"Let's play ball!" screamed another.

"Forget Coach Soul!"

"Forget that terrorist!"

"Coach, get your players!" another fan yelled.

Strangely, at that moment, I began to think about the Barton City game and all of its insane aftermath. My first season as a head coach had been one of happenings that I never would have dreamed of facing either as a player or as a coach, and this was just the latest of them. At that moment, I had no idea what to do.

"Coach," said a referee in black and white stripes walking over to me, "what's the deal?"

I shook my head and kept my eyes on the team.

"Are they gonna play?" he asked.

"I don't know," I answered.

The chanting continued, as the players kept bouncing at midfield.

"WE WON'T PLAY WITHOUT COACH SOUL!"

"WE WON'T PLAY WITHOUT COACH SOUL!"

"WE WON'T PLAY WITHOUT COACH SOUL!"

Suddenly, they stopped.

"SOUUUUUUUUL SPRINTS!" Isaiah Waters bellowed to his teammates.

Right then, the boys broke from the large huddle and began running off the field toward the stands. Andrico climbed the steps first, followed by his teammates, and proceeded to lead them, dodging fans and weaving in and out of the crowd, as they made their way up the stadium stairs to the very top row. The whole team followed, and they were soon crossing the highest level, and heading back down another flight of steps, all while our crowd looked on.

The reaction was mixed. Some were still confused at what they were seeing. Others, who had figured out what was happening, were angry. A few had begun chanting right along with them, and there were even a couple of smaller children who were following after the players like disciples, as they jogged their way up and down the stadium steps, following the route which had been designated for soul sprints before the season had begun earlier that year. More kids followed, and pretty soon, the team was headed back to the field with a procession in tow, where they continued paying tribute to Soul with the same exercises that bore his name. They paraded around the field's perimeter, past the opposing team, who still had not completely figured the situation out, and finally back to where it had all started.

For my part, I suddenly found myself unable to hold back emotions as I watched those boys demonstrate a devotion to their embattled coach that I had never seen before; admiration and appreciation for the lessons he had taught them, and dedication to the legacy which he was leaving for them to follow. What was unfolding before the community to witness now was a symbol that signified all that Coach Soul had poured into the lives of these young men over the course of a nine-month period. The lessons, the laughs, the encouragement; the culmination of all of it was on display for the town of Lake Barrow, Florida to watch as the Spartans of Sims County High School paid homage to Soulemain Rasheed.

"Push-ups!" Andrico called.

The team, along with the kids who were now with them, began to exercise accordingly, which was followed by flutter-kicks on their backs, and burpees. When they were finished, they drew in together in a tight group once more and began chanting again.

"WE WON'T PLAY WITHOUT COACH SOUL!"

"WE WON'T PLAY WITHOUT COACH SOUL!"

"WE WON'T PLAY WITHOUT COACH SOUL!"

Slowly, the boys began to exit the field, along with their diminutive adoring fans who had accompanied them out of the bleachers. I watched as they made their way, still chanting, back toward the field house.

"I guess we forfeit," Woody said, standing next to me.

He was right, but I was concerned as I jogged off toward the field house amidst jeers and demands from the crowd.

*Make 'em play, Coach!*

*Enough showboating!*

I tried to tune it out as I ran after my team.

Reaching the field house, I opened the door and was flanked by Woody, Max, and Ahmad.

There was gleeful chatter amongst the boys, but it stopped as soon as we entered.

Andrico moved to the front and spoke first. "I'm sorry, Coach," he began, "we probably should have told you first."

I shook my head. "Do you know what you're doing?"

Andrico and a few of the players standing near him nodded.

Max chimed in. "Florida rules mandate that we play every scheduled game unless it's canceled by inclement weather. Forfeiture means not only losing the game but forfeiture of our district games also."

"We know the rules," Tre Bell chimed in. "We learned them beforehand."

"And we know what we're doing," Andrico added.

"No, you don't," Max asserted. "You're hurting the program, as well as your community."

Andrico shook his head and fixed Max with a gaze. "This community's been hurting for years, Coach" he countered, his face a picture of youthful and idealistic determination. "And I'm tired of seeing it happen. All of us are. And we're not going to be part of it. What's happening to Coach Soul is wrong. And it either stops, and he comes back, or we don't play. I don't care if we have to forfeit all of our games the rest of this season."

All of the coaches turned and glanced at one another.

"Like I said," Andrico continued, "we know what we're doing."

"And what is that?" I pressed him.

"Running soul sprints," Andrico answered.

"That's not what I meant," I retorted.

"It's not?" Andrico countered, keeping his eyes locked on mine. "Forfeiting a season hurts, Coach, especially for the seniors here. But the pain's worth it if it means standing up for Coach Soul. That's why we did this. And that's why we're forfeiting."

Nobody said anything for several moments.

"Are you guys sure about this?" I asked.

Almost in unison, every head in the locker room nodded.

"Pain's temporary," Andrico said. "But a strong soul is forever."

There had been many moments throughout the season when I had questioned whether or not any of what we were saying, what we had been teaching the boys, had even registered. At that moment, however, my questions were put to rest.

These boys were becoming men.

I exited the locker room amidst more cat-calls and orders from our fans.

*Where are the boys?*

*Get 'em on the field, Coach!*

I tried to block it out as I made my way toward the officials, who were gathered close to mid-field and near our sideline with the opposing team's coaching staff. The referee turned toward me as I approached.

"What's the deal, Coach?" he asked.

I hesitated, still unsure if I was fully on board with the decision made by our team, but also knowing that I had just witnessed something that every coach or educator in my position would kill to experience.

"We forfeit," I said.

The opposing team's head coach spoke up. "Are you sure about this, Jayce?"

"No," I answered. "But we forfeit."

A short pause, then the referee said, "I'll let the press box know. They'll want to announce it."

I nodded and left the field once more.

*There's gonna be hell to pay, Coach!* I heard a gruff voice yell out as I neared the field house.

"Hell to pay," I said to myself as I reached for the door handle. "In exchange for a strong soul."

*Spartans Forfeit as Coach's Dismissal Looms Large.*

I stared at the headline from Saturday morning's edition in my office the following Monday, which was accompanied by two large photos of the team kneeling across the field, along with a photo of Soul that Biff Kilgore had taken during one of our practices.

As I looked at it, I tried to come to terms with how I should feel about what had been written about the previous Friday's game. "Commendation or Condemnation?"

The weekend had been a tough one, and Dixie and I had stayed home and watched college football on television all day Saturday. Soul, Mikayla, and Mom had joined us for dinner at our home that evening. Soul had been touched by the show of support, and we tried to keep things light at the table that evening, but the turmoil swirling around us made that all but impossible. Dixie had gone to the grocery store that day and had gotten dirty looks from several people as she walked the aisles. Whatever good vibes had come from the boys' show of solidarity with their coach had been replaced by consternation and worry.

As I leaned back in my office chair with the paper, I heard a clanking coming from the coaches' lockers outside.

I rose and stood in the doorway as I watched Soul clearing out his storage space that was between mine and Ahmad's.

"Need help?" I asked him.

Soul turned and grinned at me. "No," he answered. "Just getting a few things."

I nodded and glanced around. "Your locker was always the neatest of all the coaches."

Soul chuckled. "Should make it an easy exit for me, then."

I shook my head. "Nothing's official yet. You might want to keep it as is."

"I can always bring everything back," he told me, as he went on packing.

Moments passed as I stood there.

"You meet with Starr yet?" Soul asked me.

"Should be any minute," I said. "Just waiting for the call."

"Word on the street," Soul continued, "is that the folks who were most pissed about how everything went down were the ticket takers."

I smiled faintly.

"Mikayla said it was like a mad dash to the windows after the game was called with people trying to get their money back."

"Dixie said the same thing."

"Starr's probably going to bring that up, too."

"I'm sure," I said.

Neither of us spoke for a moment.

"Speaking of," I finally said. "I better get down there. If I show up before he calls my office, maybe he'll go easy on me."

"Did you tell him you didn't have anything to do with the boys' decision to protest?"

"He knows."

"Doesn't matter, though, huh?"

I shook my head. "Jim Gill's pretty much convinced him that I've never had control of this team."

"Jim Gill can do that."

"Jim Gill's money definitely can."

Soul chuckled as he finished loading his duffel bag.

"You mind taking attendance for me while I meet with Starr?" I asked.

"That's against the rules, isn't it?" Soul said.

"Way the rules have been treating us lately," I returned, "I don't mind bending them a little."

"Sounds like a plan," he said with a laugh.

"Maybe I'll see you when we're finished."

Soul closed his locker and zipped his pack. "Insha'Allah."

I closed the door to my office and headed out of the field house just as the first bell rang. Walking around to the main building, I opened a set of double doors and was greeted by the monotonous, bustling sound of students heading to their first class of the morning. I barely heard any of it, dwelling instead on my impending meeting with Starr and the consequences that I was now likely facing after Friday night.

Out of the corner of my eye, I saw Jordan Gill. He was preoccupied with a female student and did not see me.

The end of the hallway opened to a more spacious common area where more students were assembled, and as I entered, I began to worry again; about Dixie, about Mom, and about my unborn child. How would I provide for them if I lost this job? What possible way forward…

POP!...POP!...POP!

A sudden burst of earsplitting cracks, like fireworks, interrupted my thoughts and pierced the still air of the building.

Instinctively, I spun around.

POP!...POP!...POP!

I heard screams; loud, horrifying, blood-curdling, terror-stricken yells that echoed down the hallway through which I had just come.

My gut seized up, and my lungs deflated, as I watched a sudden deluge of terrified students begin tearing down the hallway in my direction, as the cracking sound continued.

"He's got a gun! He's got a gun!" bellowed a male voice.

"God! He's shooting everyone!" screamed a girl as she darted past me. Her face was a picture of pure terror.

I suddenly realized what was happening, and began sprinting in the same direction as the students.

"Go! Go! Go!" screamed a male biology teacher as he ran beside me, his arms flailing wildly as he sought to direct anyone within sight away from the danger while trying to save himself.

As I ran, a new reality began to manifest itself: Sims County High School was under attack.

The gunfire became louder as it echoed through the hallway.

# CHAPTER 25

My alma mater had become a killing field.

The school shooting that gripped Sims County High School that day had students running for their lives screaming; teachers scrambling to checkpoints, trying desperately to adhere to protocols laid out in case of emergencies like a school shooting, as they shepherded the terrified teenagers to safety and feared for their own lives.

I found myself near a fire door doing the same thing, wondering all the while if I would get out alive; wondering if I would ever see Dixie again; certain that I might not meet my kid; never attend a baseball game, or a dance recital, or anything. I tried to push all of it to the back of my mind as I marshaled kids off of school property, and down the walkways toward the street. Many of these children were sobbing uncontrollably, while others looked dazed and disoriented, still trying to get their minds around what exactly was happening at their school.

At that moment, football didn't matter; nor did controversies, field houses, land deals gone bad, or any of the drama that had washed over Lake Barrow during the previous several months.

All that mattered was survival; of the kids, and hopefully, of the teachers who were trying to get them to safety.

Rick's Convenience Store was our safe haven. Its owner, Rick Bentmyer, not only opened his parking lot to our school during the shooting and its aftermath, but he also shut down business, and personally had his entire property cordoned off and designated as a safe haven for everyone. He and the two employees who were on duty that day even brought out bottles of water and other items for students who needed to cool off and calm down.

He would later be given a civic award for his actions, which everyone agreed was well-deserved.

Spacious as it was, Rick's parking lot could only hold so many, and thus, the rest of the student body and faculty had simply been directed to our practice field. It was on school grounds, and dangerously close to where the shooter was likely still wreaking havoc, but it would have to do.

"First period teachers, listen up!" Starr called out through a bull horn with a shaky voice, as he stood in the parking lot. Police cruisers, ambulances, and other first responder vehicles continued wailing as they zipped past us en route to the campus. I stood near my boss and held onto one of our cheerleaders, who gripped me and wailed into my chest, desperate for comfort. She was hardly the first one. Traumatized teenagers and adults were everywhere in that parking lot. Sobbing and lamentation could be heard for yards in every direction as students and teachers alike held onto one another, the shock and grieving almost more than anyone could bear.

How could this have happened? To us? In Lake Barrow? A shooting?

"First period teachers," Starr went on, his hands barely able to control the large megaphone he held, "get accountability of your students right away."

One by one, my colleagues began to speak up and raise

their hands, ordering students to gather with them so that they could take roll.

For me, that was weightlifting. I had to find my guys.

"Cheree," I told the young cheerleader, still desperately clinging to me. "You've got to let go, all right? You need to get with your teacher."

She continued bawling as I fought to pry her hands from my shirt. Mikayla saw us, rushed over, and managed to free the small tufts of fabric that had been wadded up in the girl's tight grip.

"Go," Mikayla told me, with tears streaming down her own cheeks, as she gently guided Cheree toward her teacher.

I made my way to the other end of the parking lot where a few of my players were already gathered. One by one, I began to call out names and panicked each time I didn't get an answer right away. *Handler, Stromas, Bell, Messina…*the list went on.

"Gilmore?!" I called out.

An excruciating moment passed, as I waited for Ryan Gilmore to respond.

"Here!" he said, after what felt like a year, whereas it was probably only five seconds. I felt a weight rise from my shoulders as they responded, and I thanked God silently.

There was one more name. "Gill?!" I called out. *Jordan Gill.*

No answer.

"Jordan Gill?!" I called again.

Nothing.

The guys began looking around and seeing if Jordan was anywhere to be found. There was no sign of him.

"JORDAN GILL?!" I bellowed, a little too loudly.

I scanned the parking lot, desperately hoping that Jim and Jacqui Gill's only living son would suddenly come jogging over toward me.

But he never came.

My insides began to churn.

"Let's muster up," Starr called out after ten minutes. "If your students are all present or accounted for, please say so. If they are not, please indicate that they are not, and then please come forward and meet me here."

One by one, he began to recite from a list of teachers, each of whom responded. Thankfully, all of them had their students accounted for. I prayed at that moment that the teachers over at the practice field were just as lucky.

"Coach Leonard," Starr called out, looking up from his clipboard. "All accounted for?"

I hesitated, feeling my throat begin to seize up. "Missing one," I choked out, fighting back emotion and terror.

"Who?" Starr asked.

"Jordan Gill," I managed to say.

I had to hold it together for the guys and the other frightened students in the parking lot. But it was hard.

Starr pulled out a cell phone and dialed a number, as an assistant principal with a clipboard wrote down his name and moved on to the next teacher. I felt nauseous and prayed for the umpteenth time since realizing that Jordan had gone missing, that he was okay, and had possibly gone to the practice field instead of the parking lot. The rift that had been between us suddenly seemed to dissipate and became infinitesimal compared to what was happening now.

I looked up and saw Mikayla approaching me. Her eyes were red and puffy, and her face bore a look that was different from the shock and bewilderment that was all around me.

"Jayce," she almost whispered. "I can't find Soul."

My gut tensed. "You haven't seen him here?"

She shook her head.

"He must be at the practice field, then."

"I called several teachers over there," she answered, holding up her cell phone. "None of them have seen him."

My heart began pounding but knew I had to keep as calm as possible.

"We can't panic," I told her, fighting to keep my own voice calm. "There's probably a bunch of folks missing, and until we get everyone sorted, and hear from the authorities, we won't know anything for sure. I'm sure Soul's fine."

I watched Mikayla as I said this and hoped to see some reassurance in her face. Instead, my words seemed to cause even more concern for the man she loved.

"Are your kids are accounted for?"

Again, she shook her head. "Quinton's missing."

I ran my fingers over my head.

"We'll find them," I tried to reassure her again.

An hour passed.

At one point, a deputy sheriff walked over and began speaking with Starr. I tried to get as close as possible so that I could hear, but the hushed tones in which they spoke kept me from deciphering anything. Starr had already told the teachers not to bombard him with questions. When he knew something definitive and relevant, we would know when he passed it to us.

"Coach," Ryan Gilmore said, breaking my concentration. "Your wife's here."

I glanced over to where he pointed. Sure enough, Dixie was at the police cordon near the edge of the parking lot, scanning it as she searched for me.

Ignoring the rules, she ducked under the yellow tape as I began jogging over. Both of us picked up the pace and, reaching me, she almost knocked me over as she jumped into my arms and buried her face in my neck while she sobbed.  A moment later, she looked up. Her eyes and cheeks smeared with tears and mascara.

"Thank God," she bawled.

"I'm fine," I said.

We embraced again and held on for another minute. Reluctantly, I broke apart from her and said, "Jordan's missing."

Dixie placed her hands to her mouth.

"Soul is too."

Another hour.

Details began to slowly trickle in. The shooter was a lone operator, carried one rifle, high-capacity, along with several magazines. Multiple casualties, though there was still no news about the exact number; certainly nothing about their identities, which only kept the panic and worry at a fever pitch. Prayer circles were formed, as students and teachers alike began to offer up pleas to the Almighty on behalf of their friends and colleagues. Students continued weeping and grasping each other for comfort. Dazed teachers tried to comfort their kids and make sense of it all. Starr looked as haggard and burdened as I had ever seen him as he intermittently spoke with the law enforcement officers who came and went.

I continued praying silently for Jordan and Soul, searching the crowd, fearing the worst, while hoping for the best. The only good news I had received was that Woody and Max had made it to the practice field and were fine. Knowing that they were okay, along with the rest of the team not in my first-period weightlifting, was a load off.

Mom called my cell phone multiple times. I called her back just to let her know I was safe, before hanging up again. She needed reassurance and had calmed somewhat by the time we ended the call. I wanted to talk to her more, but the students needed me. New information was at a premium, but very little was forthcoming. All we could do was wait with each other and pray.

As proud as I had been of our football team on Friday, words still can't describe how much pride I felt as I watched them in the aftermath of the shooting. They were just as shaken and shattered as the rest of the student body, but they took it upon themselves to walk around and be comforters and encouragers to their fellow students. Andrico, Tre, Ryan Gilmore, Kyle Messina, and others; they all chose to be leaders of their school and community. They chose, in those moments, to be men and decent human beings.

"Where's my son?!" I heard a voice scream, breaking my focus.

I spun around and saw Jim Gill being restrained by a police officer as he tried to break into the safe area. Jacqui was beside him.

"Where's my son?!" he yelled. "I want to see Jordan!"

I immediately went over.

"Jayce!" he exclaimed. "Where's Jordan? I heard he was missing!"

"We don't know," I said, drawing near.

"You don't know?!" Jacqui exclaimed.

"Jayce, find him!" Jim pleaded, tears forming in his eyes. His round face was contorted into a mixture of fear and bewilderment. I had never seen him as petrified as he was at that moment, and it frightened me. "Find my boy!"

"The police are doing all they can," I tried to reassure him.

"Find my boy!" Jim began to sob, as his demeanor broke down. "Find Jordan! Find my boy! Find my boy!"

The officer on the perimeter stood his ground as Jim's resistance slowly gave way, and he turned to embrace his wife. For a moment, they stood upright but slowly began to collapse to the pavement in each other's arms. Once again, all of the consternation of the past several weeks seemed to fade against the reality that Jordan Gill might never be seen again, and that Jim Gill, with all his faults, could likely have lost his only remaining son at the hands of violence.

My heart broke as I watched one of the pillars of our community sit on the ground like a wino in the arms of his wife.

At just before 10AM, we got the call.

Jordan Gill was alive.

He had been found in a classroom closet, taking refuge along with the same female student with whom I had seen him talking right before the shooting. They had ducked in following the first shots and managed to barricade themselves in the storage room as the assault continued. Both were found uninjured but badly shaken up and in need of first responder care. An ambulance had taken them to the hospital. Jim and Jacqui were on their way to meet them there.

About ten minutes later, the news took a turn for the worst. The shooter was identified as Quinton Leeds, a Sims County High School student. He had calmly walked into the same hallway that I had entered only moments earlier, wearing a trench coat with an AR-15 rifle hidden underneath. He then proceeded to open fire, killing seventeen human beings, before turning the gun on himself.

As Mikayla heard the news, she clasped her hands to her face and crumpled in a heap upon the asphalt. Dixie and I rushed to her and held her, as she sobbed harder than I had ever heard her sob in my life.

"Jayce, he killed them, and he's dead!" she wailed, as Dixie and I grasped her around the shoulders. "Why? Why? Why? Why?"

All three of us were weeping.

Moments passed. Soon, Starr walked over and beckoned me off to the side. I walked over to him after I managed to pry Mikayla's hands from my shirt.

"Jayce," he began, looking as though the weight of the world might push him through the ground at any moment, "I can't read this now, but I wanted you to see the list of the victims first."

I studied his troubled face, as he held out a piece of paper and handed it to me.

"It's only fair," he told me.

Reluctantly, I took it and began reading. Sure enough, there were seventeen names, the first sixteen of which were students. My heart broke as I carefully read each name, recognizing several of them; kids whom I had interacted with on a few occasions, and a few who had P.E. with me. Tears came to my eyes, as I scanned the list all the way to the bottom; to the last name…which belonged to the lone member of our faculty who had been killed.

I felt my world collapse as I read it.

Soul Rasheed.

Starr reached out and grabbed me as I began to wobble, fighting to steady myself.

"Jesus…" I half-prayed, half-cursed, as I fought back tears. I bent down and kept my hands on my knees, struggling to regain composure.

When I felt that I was strong enough to stand again, I rose upright and turned. Dixie was watching me as she comforted Mikayla who was still sobbing.

I knew from my wife's face, a dreadful, pleading look, that she was nonverbally begging me for it to not be true. *Not this*, she seemed to beg, *not him. Anything but that.*

Both of us knew, though.

Slowly, I walked over to her once more and knelt down where they both were sitting.

"No, Jayce," Dixie whispered.

Mikayla looked up in horror, waiting, praying for me to deliver something other than what we were all now expecting.

"Jayce," Mikayla said.

"He…" I stammered. "He's gone. Soul's gone."

"No," Mikayla screamed. "NO!"

I reached for her.

"No, no, no, no, no!" she bawled. "Noooo, no, no no!"

All I could do was hold her and cry with her.

# CHAPTER 26

Surreal. Numbing. Exhausted. Sleepwalking.

When you live through a tragedy, words can only take you so far in describing the experience. Only a combination of miscellaneous phrases and clichés seem to even come close to summing up what you're feeling; the bewilderment, the despondency, the anger, the sorrow. All of it.

You don't feel a sense of loss, though; at least not initially. That comes later. And it comes at you with a vengeance.

I went to the city morgue that night, after the shooting, to identify Soul's body. Dixie didn't want me to; said I'd been through enough hell in one day. But I insisted...as did Woody, Max, and Ahmad. All of us wanted to see our friend. I can't speak for them, but I imagine a big part of it was sheer disbelief. Could he really be gone?

We arrived at the morgue and were escorted inside to where Soul's body was being kept, where it was confirmed for us that yes, he was gone...at least physically.

He looked as though he were sleeping. His eyes were closed, and his mouth was turned downward, though not in a scowl or frown. Other than his chest not moving, his demeanor looked the same as it had many times before; during our days as roommates, when he would fall asleep on the sofa watching Sports Center, or another show.

I was thankful for the opportunity to see him like this. Morose as it seems, I'm still grateful to this day that the bullets from Quinton's rifle had gone in through Soul's torso and not his face or head. Soul's handsome features were still intact, enabling us to watch him truly rest in peace at that moment.

Woody began crying.

"That's him," I told the mortician. "Soulemain Rasheed."

The short, balding man nodded. "I'll give you a few moments," he said.

We each stood there, just watching our friend in repose, none of us knowing what to say…none of us wanting to say anything.

I drove toward the Gills' home the next day, not knowing fully what to expect. My mind was awash in emotion and thoughts that I wished would disappear.

I still heard the gunshots and the screams, especially Mikayla's wails. In my mind's eye, I saw Soul's name at the bottom of that God-forsaken list that Starr had given to me.

I needed some noise.

Turning on the radio to a national talk show, all anyone could talk about was the little map dot that we called home.

I changed the station.

*"Sims County High School in Lake Barrow, Florida…"*

I turned the dial again.

*"The shooter was a student by the name of Quinton…"*

*"Damn,"* I said under my breath, as I turned the knob once more.

The next program featured a radio host down in south Florida. He was reading from what appeared to be a list of statistics that seemed unrelated to anything that was unfolding here.

*"And I have here,"* he began, *"hard, irrefutable data that points to a trend. These shooters, these children, have access to weapons that have no business anywhere in society. And until we get serious about gun control, then the question will remain, how many more Quinton Leeds imitators will we see?"*

Disgusted, I turned the radio off. *"Fucking pricks,"* I hissed. *"Politicizing a damn tragedy."*

I was sick to my stomach as I turned onto the dirt road leading to the Gill property, wondering how low someone had to stoop to turn what had happened in my hometown into a political weapon. I tried to push it from my mind, as I passed the Hancefords' house and came closer to the Gills'.

Moments later, I parked the car and got out. The day was crisp and clear, and Barrow Lake appeared more serene than I had ever remembered it looking; a far cry from the turmoil and anguish that had enveloped the town just over twenty-four hours prior. The rays of the sun shimmered atop the water's surface, creating an atmosphere that made the mayhem, death, and destruction of the previous day seem worlds away, even though it was fresh in the collective mind of the town, and probably would remain so for years.

As I neared the large, two-story white home, the screen door opened and Jim stood in the doorway of the spacious porch. He wore an old t-shirt and sweatpants.

"Jordan's resting," Jim told me.

I nodded as I looked out at the water again, wondering if simply running out and jumping into the cool water (clothes and all) would somehow wash away the detritus of the previous day off of me.

"Can I see him?" I asked Jim.

"If he's awake," Jim affirmed, as he re-entered the house and kept the front door open.

I walked up the steps, and it occurred to me that I had not been to the Gills' home since before the season had begun; before the controversy over Soul; before Soul's death; before everything that had shattered the world I had previously known. Life in Lake Barrow had been harmonious, or at least I had believed it to be. But then maybe harmony, safety, idyll, and all of the other savory aspects of life which I had taken for granted had simply been illusory. Maybe that was the lesson here.

Maybe that was my soul sprint.

I walked in the house and was hit with the memories once more; of Jamie, of our video game duels, of the games played inside the house and out in the yard; of Jordan tagging along with us. All of it weighed on me as I struggled to push the previous day's events out of my mind.

The house was quiet.

"We've been keeping the televisions off," Jim said as he led me upstairs to Jordan's room. "Damn news crews. Least they can do is get the story right if they're going to traumatize people with re-telling it."

Jim had a point. Our local news team had done a decent job of accurately reporting the events of the shooting. Cable news, however, had been a different story. True to form, they had blundered horribly and repeatedly; everything from mishandling names of key figures, including those of several victims, to giving inaccurate information about the type of gun Quinton had used in the massacre. One outlet even reported that he had utilized "machine guns," which was absolutely ludicrous. It was a nauseating display of agenda-driven politics if ever there had been one.

We reached Jordan's bedroom door, and Jim knocked gently. There was no answer, but Jim quietly turned the knob and pushed the door open.

Jordan was lying on the bed, but was awake and sat up when he saw me. I nodded to him, as Jim backed away. "I'll leave you two," he said, pulling the door closed.

As I sat down on the edge of Jordan's bed, he said in a

raspy voice, "Thanks for coming."

I nodded. "How are you feeling?"

"Can barely sleep," he answered.

"Yeah."

"Jayce," he began, after a few moments. "I'm sorry."

I studied him.

"For what I did to Soul…and you."

Tears began to form in his eyes.

"I don't think that matters now, Jordan," I said.

Jordan nodded, wiping his eyes.

"You've got your whole life to live," I continued, "and Soul would want you to live it, and not be hung up on the past."

"I know."

"He never held any grudges," I went on.

"I know."

Neither of us said anything for several moments.

"Do you know what happened?" Jordan asked.

I shook my head. Details were still trickling out about what exactly transpired in that hallway, but I had seen no official report. And until I did, it was all rumor-based as far as I was concerned.

"I think you should know," Jordan added.

"Only if you want to tell me," I responded.

Jordan hesitated. His face was a mixture of concentration and dark reflection. He was fighting to remember details, while simultaneously wishing that he could forget everything. It was a look I would always remember.

"Me and the girl I was with, Kacie," he began, "we were about to go into Biology. That's when the shots came. First, we hit the ground, because we didn't know what it was exactly. Then Kacie saw Quinton. He had his gun pointed in our direction, had that trench coat on. Looked like he was stoned or something; a blank stare on his face. Just popping away on that trigger, like it was nothing. Meanwhile, kids were scrambling, trying to get out, a few were falling over, blood coming out…" he paused, and closed his eyes.

"You don't have to do this, Jordan," I said.

He ignored me and continued. "Somehow, I managed to grab Kacie and pull her into that classroom. It was empty, but for some reason, I knew it would be enough to cover us, and that's when I made us run toward that closet. We got in and closed the door, but could still hear the shots out in the hallway. Quinton seemed to be going up and down the hallway, firing and picking off whoever he could, just going back and forth. Then we began hearing him enter classrooms. Doors were locked, but he'd kick them open, come in, and shoot whoever was there. He got closer and closer to us, and we knew it was just a matter of time."

Jordan paused and glanced at me. "I prayed," he said. "Prayed harder than I have in years. Prayed for a miracle. Prayed for God to send someone to save us."

Jordan stopped once more and fought to maintain his composure.

"That's when we heard the door open. The closet door had a window that was mostly covered with paper, but we managed to peek through a small hole in the covering. When we did, we saw Quinton coming toward us. I'll never forget it. He had that same blank, crazy stare on his face. Had that gun in his hands, ready to kill the first thing he saw move. And he was moving right toward us. He wasn't going to leave any door unopened. He wasn't going to leave any person alive. Everyone was going to die that morning if he had his way."

Jordan paused.

"What happened next?" I asked.

"Quinton reached the door. He was about to open it. Kacie and I were bawling at this point, stacking stuff against the door, whatever we could do. Both of us thought it was the end. But…"

"But what?"

Jordan looked at me. "Something crashed against the door," Jordan said. "Or someone. We heard this loud bang, followed by what sounded like a fight or wrestling match just outside the door; Quinton wrestling with whoever it was out there with him. Kacie and I couldn't see anything, because it was right in front of the door and underneath the window, too bad of an angle for us to peek at. Then we heard gun-shots, followed by two guys screaming out...and then after that, we didn't hear anything."

Jordan shook his head as if the memory was devouring his brain.

"Me and Kacie were too terrified to move after that," he went on, "We just figured that someone had come in and fought with Quinton, and whoever it is was probably dead. But there was no way we were opening that door. Finally, the police came. It was several minutes before they could get the door open because the bodies were right there. But...when they did..."

I waited for him to continue.

"They opened the door," he said. "And they began help-ing us get out."

"Go on," I encouraged.

"And that's when we saw him."

"Saw who?"

Jordan looked away and began wiping away tears again. He fought to compose himself before answering.

"Soul," he answered.

I was frozen and could say nothing in response.

"He was the one." Jordan continued. "He had to have come in and knocked Quinton against the door; fought him for the gun. He couldn't get it out of his hands before Quin-ton shot him three times."

I just sat there in disbelief.

"Right after that was when Quinton killed himself."

Suddenly, Jordan broke down sobbing. "I'll never forget

that sight as long as I live," he bawled.

I reached over and hugged him.

"He took a bullet for me," Jordan said. "He took a bullet…and died for me; gave his life up for me."

Jordan was limp in my arms, like a crestfallen child whose parents had abandoned them. I held him, unable to control the tears that were now streaming down my own face. For what felt like an hour, we just sat there, mourning in reverence the man who had saved Jordan's life.

Soon, Jordan pulled back and reached for something on his bedside table. "Here," he said, handing me the same set of prayer beads that Soul had given him. "You deserve these more than me."

"No," I insisted. "He would want you to keep them."

Jordan shook his head and was adamant. He took my hand and pressed them into my palm. "Someone else will need them more than I will."

I left Jordan in his room and made my way back down the stairs and out the front door.

"Is he okay?" Jim asked from a rocking chair on the front porch. I had no desire to see or speak to him but turned as he addressed me.

"Yeah."

"I appreciate you coming."

I gave a slight nod and turned to get back into my car.

"Jayce?"

I stopped again as Jim rose from the rocker and slowly made his way down the steps. As he drew closer, it occurred to me for the first time just how old he looked. The last twenty-four hours seemed to have aged him more than the last ten years combined.

"Did Jordan tell you what happened?" he asked. His eyes

appeared hollow as they studied me.

I nodded. "Yeah. Soul died saving your son's life."

Jim hesitated before saying anything else. "Jayce..." he began, "...I really don't know how to..."

"Apologize?" I interrupted.

I turned and opened my driver's side door.

"Only way you can make any of this right, Jim, is to take care of my mother."

I got in the car without another word and drove off. As I neared the end of the Gills' long drive, I began to feel it hit me again. Tears were coming, and a great mass of emotion welled up within my chest.

Before I turned onto the main road, I was bawling once more and struggling to see the road ahead through my tears.

The next week was a blur.

Candle-light and memorial vigils of every kind were held for the seventeen victims who died at the hands of Quinton Leeds, and a special memorial service for Coach Soul Rasheed was in the works also. The tragedy had put the tiny town of Lake Barrow, Florida squarely in the spotlight, and we were getting more attention than we ever wanted. Churches were packed, as people poured in to pray, mourn, give and receive love and support, and generally try to make sense of what had happened.

The latter, however, was impossible.

It was no secret that Quinton had led a troubled life, and this fact alone caused hand-wringing and "what-if" reflections on the part of more than a few people, me included. *We should have seen this coming, we should have done more for him, I could have reached out*...were the general attitudes. Still, there was no established motive for why this had taken place. Quinton left no note and made no remarks to anyone about what his plans were. His reasons for taking seventeen lives would likely remain a mystery and be left to speculation forever.

Aside from the news coverage of our town's tragedy, there was much debate and discussion about gun control, mental illness, and a host of other peripheral issues that were suddenly on everyone's mind. Most everyone in town ignored it, as we fought desperately to mourn and seek closure in our own ways.

That's not to say that all of the attention we received was bad. Hundreds of cards and well-wishes poured in, and we even received visits by a few high-level dignitaries and celebrities. The governor visited, and there was even talk that the President and First Lady would be making an appearance, which never materialized.

Virtually every business, at least in the southeastern United States, with a marquee or another means of advertisement paid their respects, mostly with sayings such as "Pray for our town" or "Lake Barrow Strong" or something of that nature.

School was canceled for the remainder of the week, which of course meant that our next game was canceled also.

Dixie and I got in the car that Wednesday and decided to spend three days in Savannah, where we had spent our honeymoon. We got as far as Jacksonville, before deciding to turn around and head back. As nice as a change of scenery sounded, it just didn't feel right leaving. Besides, I had gotten word that morning, right as we were leaving, that Soul's funeral was to be held in Detroit the following Monday. Planning for that trip became a priority.

"I wish I could go with you," Dixie said, as we skirted Gainesville and made our way home.

"Me too," I said, kissing her hand.

She leaned over and laid her head on my shoulder. Neither of us said anything for several moments. Neither of us needed to.

"You boys all riding together?" she asked.

I grinned, as I pictured all of us piling into the minivan that now belonged exclusively to Woody. Max had bought his own compact car a few months earlier. "Yeah," I answered. "Ahmad included."

We drove on.

"I still can't believe it," Dixie said.

"I know."

More silence as residential areas turned into farmland. Lake Barrow was getting closer once more.

"Deke called me," I said. "He wants to talk about donating money; helping out the town; maybe something for the football team down the road."

Dixie smiled. "He's an amazing guy."

"And an even more amazing brother," I replied. "Came home and has been watching over Mikayla like a hawk since this happened."

"Soul would have wanted it that way," Dixie said. She grasped my hand once more and squeezed. "Have you talked to your mom today?"

"This morning," I answered.

"And?"

"She still has her job," I stated. "At least for now."

Dixie said nothing. An uncomfortable silence fell over the car.

"What are you thinking about?" I pressed.

"About when I found out that there'd been a shooting," she said, looking at me with a pained expression. "About not being able to breathe until I saw you standing in Rick's parking lot after I flew up there. About how it often takes something like this to destroy our illusions about what's important and what's not. Last week we were worried about being unemployed and having your unemployed, disabled mother to care for."

I stared ahead as I drove.

"Tragedy's biggest accomplishment is that it destroys pettiness."

I held her hand as we crossed the county line.

# The following Monday

The bitter mid-autumn wind blew multi-colored leaves across the cracked sidewalk in the small, predominantly black Muslim community as we found a spot in a parking garage nearby.

We had checked out of our cheap motel that morning and had spent the majority of the day with Soul's family. His parents had always been two of the most gracious people I had ever met and probably always would be. The same was true for his brother, Salaam, and his sister, Aisha.

None of us said anything as we exited the garage and walked in the direction of the mosque.

"My kind of weather," Woody said with a smile.

"Not me," Max countered, pulling his thick coat tighter around his large frame. "Guess I've become a Florida boy after all."

Ahmad just chuckled. "I'm just glad that clunker van of y'alls got us here."

"Of course," Woody said. "Had that bad boy since college."

"That's what worries me," Ahmad said.

I grinned as I listened to them. Humor had sustained us during the whole trip so far. We'd driven through Yearwood the day before, visiting the coaches and some of the players, and the memories with Soul had washed over us like flood-waters. Whenever things became too real, Woody would say something off-the-wall or start an argument with Max, which would trigger raucous laughter. And that's how it went; that's what kept us from falling apart.

"It was great to see the folks in Yearwood," Max said, as we rounded a corner.

I nodded. "Nice of the Pearlmuters to put us up for a night; helped us cut our trip in half."

"Not to mention, leave with us the next day," Woody added.

"Are they here yet?" Ahmad asked.

"I haven't seen them," I said.

There were people milling about outside as we drew clos-er. Soul's father, Hasan, was the first to greet us.

"A'Salaam Alaikum," he said in a thick Middle Eastern accent, greeting us with a hug and a handshake.

"W'Alaikum Salaam," I returned, certain that my accent alone had butchered the greeting.

"W'Alaikum Salaam," said Max. Ahmad followed suit.

"Alkaline Salami," said Woody, drawing laughter from Hasan, as well as a few other relatives and friends, who greet-ed us.

Max slapped his brother on the back of the head. "You're an idiot."

"Shut up."

I kept it together until I saw Mama Freddy. She was wear-ing a black dress and had her hair and make-up done up like I had never seen before. In her hand was a tissue, which she clutched and sporadically dabbed her eyes.

Both of us broke down when we embraced each other inside the small prayer room in the mosque, where Soul's life was to be commemorated and celebrated. The same was true for the Twin Tanks, both of whom hugged Mama Freddy at the same time. Bud, dressed in a black suit, shook hands with Ahmad. There we were; a small group of non-Muslim individuals, united by friendship and football, in a semi-private room, mourning the loss of our friend.

As we made our way to the cramped inner room where the ceremony was to take place, Bud walked next to me and directed our group to a spot way in the back. Soul's closed casket was at the front.

"You may not remember this," he told me as we stood. "But we came up here with Soul right after you boys' freshman season when his uncle passed. He didn't have the money to get home, so we drove him."

"I remember."

Bud nodded. "Freddy and I learned a lot," he went on, "mostly about funeral customs. I can walk you through what's happening if you'd like. I'll just have to whisper."

"I'd love that," I said, looking at him with red-rimmed eyes.

The ceremony began, and several rows of people leading toward Soul's casket began to form. "Funeral prayers," Bud explained. "Each member of the Muslim community prays. It's called 'Salat al-Janazah.'"

I nodded.

"By the way," Bud went on, "you can pray too."

I smiled. "Thanks."

We lined up, each one of us coaches taking a line, with the Pearlmuters lining up directly behind me. We moved forward slowly, but steadily, as each member of the Rasheeds' community offered prayers that I couldn't decipher, but which I had no doubt were heartfelt. I glanced over and noted that each of us were shoulder to shoulder and would likely have our turn around the same times.

I nudged Max. "Let's make sure we go up together when it's our time," I whispered.

Max nodded.

"Let Woody and Ahmad know."

Max passed the message.

One by one, the mourners offered their prayers before turning and giving the next person their turn. Finally, we were at the front. I glanced at my coaches and, together, we approached Soul's casket. Standing there, side-by-side, we admired the ornate mahogany and decorative artisanship that had gone into the design, but were careful not to touch it, per Islamic tradition. I began weeping once more as I reflected on the life of my friend; my teammate; my assistant coach; and the one guy who had taught me more about life, and perseverance, and loyal friendship and integrity than probably anybody else ever would.

I would miss Soul Rasheed.

Through tears, I looked at Max, Woody, and Ahmad, all three of whom were also wiping their eyes.

"Tested and tried," Ahmad said.

"Spartan Pride!" we all said quietly but with vigor. One by one, my friends walked away, leaving me standing there in front of the casket.

"See you, Soul," I whispered.

Two nights later, Woody dropped me off in my driveway.

The first thing I noticed was a strange car. That's when the front door to our house opened, and Mikayla emerged.

"Hey," I greeted her.

"Hey," she said with a faint smile. "Glad you're back."

"It's good to see you," I said, as I hugged her.

"Had to keep tabs on your lovely Dixie," she said. "What kind of husband leaves his pregnant wife to go hundreds of miles away?"

"The crazy kind, I guess."

"That's for sure," she continued with a playful frown. "Of course, that doesn't piss me off nearly as much as not being able to go to Soul's funeral."

"You could have ridden with us," I said sincerely.

"I could have," she agreed. "But this place needed me. Starr especially needed my help getting this memorial ceremony planned."

"Starr," I said quietly to myself. Dixie's words about tragedy being the destroyer of pettiness came back to haunt me. Just over a week ago, Soul was practically an afterthought to Andrew Starr. Now he was a legend.

"Besides," Mikayla went on, "riding in an old van with a bunch of smelly men doesn't really appeal to me; even if it is ultimately for the man I loved."

I smiled. "Think you'll go up there soon?"

Mikayla nodded. "I'll probably visit during spring break. I can't wait to meet his family."

"They'd love that," I told her. "And they'll love you."

"I hope so."

"How's the planning going?" I asked.

"Good," she answered. "Are you going to speak?"

I hesitated.

"That really wasn't a question, Jayce," Mikayla asserted. "How can you not speak?"

"I'm thinking of not going," I said.

"What?"

"You heard me."

"Jayce…" Mikayla was indignant.

"It's just…"

"Just what? 'Too much'?"

"I can't explain it."

"You don't have to explain anything," Mikayla's eyes cut into me. "He was your friend, and it hurts. But we all need that closure. And we need you to help us get it. This town needs you, Jayce."

"This town needs more than what I can provide," I said. "The last several months have proven that."

"Bull shit," Mikayla protested. "Do you have any idea how many people you'd be letting down by not showing up? Hell, the football team already thinks you let them down by not getting a funding effort together so that they could all attend his funeral in Detroit."

"I know."

"Then step up, Jayce," Mikayla chided. "One more time. Do it for Soul, if not for Lake Barrow."

I glanced at her, and then managed a slight grin. "You're definitely Deke Hudson's sister."

"Both of us inherited our momma's attitude."

I chuckled.

"Tell me you're coming," she persisted.

"I'll try."

"You've got to give me something besides that," she needled. "This town needs healing, and they need their coach."

I said nothing, but reached into my pocket, and pulled out the prayer beads that Jordan had been given by Soul; the same beads that had been at the center of the controversy that would have gotten us fired.

"These are for you," I said, extending them out to Mikayla.

She looked at them for a long moment, and then back at me with tears in her eyes. "I can't."

"Jordan said someone else might be needing them more than he did," I said. "At first I thought he was wrong, but… he had a point."

Mikayla began crying softly, and we embraced once more. "I loved him," she whispered. "And I love you."

❧

Dixie rose from the sofa, where she had been reading a parenting magazine, and hugged me as I entered the house. Mikayla had left moments earlier.

Both of us sat down.

"I'd ask how the trip went," she began, "but..."

"Yeah," I finished for her, as I kissed her on the lips.

"How was Yearwood?" she asked.

I paused for a moment, wondering if now was the time to break the news that I had been keeping a secret from everyone.

"I got offered a job," I finally answered her.

Dixie's jaw dropped.

"Jeff Swicegood," I said. "Same guy that recruited me out of high school just got the head coaching job there. Wants me to be quarterbacks coach. Says if I stay on long enough, I could become offensive coordinator one day."

"Jayce..." Dixie was in shock.

"I didn't accept anything yet," I clarified.

Dixie studied me. "Are you going to accept?"

"I don't know," I said. "Need to think about it, and can't even do that right now."

A smile crept across Dixie's face, and she leaned in and kissed me. "I'm proud of you."

I nodded. "Thanks," I said, taking her hand.

"Who knows?" she said. "Maybe it's time to move on."

"Maybe," I agreed.

"I always thought that I'd spend the rest of my life in Lake Barrow," she said, "especially after we got together and you got hired here."

I smiled at her.

"But," she continued, "the more I think about it, the more I kind of like the idea of a crazy, nomadic life where we never settle anywhere."

"Might get your wish," I chuckled.

"I kind of like the idea of calling a new place home."

I rose from the sofa and walked over to the living room window which overlooked our front yard. It was a clear night, with stars and a full harvest moon illuminating the night sky. Lake Barrow was awash in the silver ambiance that radiated from above.

"Home," I said to myself as I took in the view.

# Epilogue

## STUDENT BODY PAYS TRIBUTE TO FALLEN COACH

*By Biff Kilgore*
*Barrow Times Staff Writer*
*Saturday, October 25, 2003*
LAKE BARROW

Friday marked a bitter occasion as students, faculty, and staff from Sims County High School gathered in the school gymnasium to pay their final respects to Soulemain Rasheed, a beloved football coach, and teacher, who was killed during the violent attack on the school back on October 13. Though "Coach Soul," as he was known, had taught and coached at the school for less than a year, his influence and impact could be felt as football players and colleagues alike stood to honor him with words and public readings during the hour-long event this past Friday.

Among the participants in the ceremony were Andrico Handler, the football team's quarterback, along with Woody and Max Tankersley, two assistant football coaches who had joined the coaching staff along with Rasheed the previous winter. Mikayla Hudson, another first-year teacher at SCHS, recited an original poem and gave a heartfelt tribute.

However, the highlight of the afternoon seemed to come from first-year head football coach, Jayce Leonard, who stood and regaled the crowd with tales of his days playing alongside Rasheed in college at Yearwood State University. Many tears were shed as Leonard shared from his experience, and few dry eyes could be seen when he concluded with the following line. "He was a man of peace, rightly guided…just as his name is translated."

Later that night, the Sims County Spartans won their game against Torrance County, 55-3.

## SPARTANS END SEASON ON A POSITIVE NOTE

*By Biff Kilgore*
*Barrow Times Staff Writer*
*Saturday, November 9, 2003*
LAKE BARROW

The Sims County Spartans closed out their season last night against South Grunwald High, by defeating the Buccaneers, 44-14 at Jim Gill Stadium. It was the final game of the season for the Spartans, due to a penalty they incurred prior to a match-up with San Mateo Catholic. The Spartans chose to forfeit that game following a public protest staged by the players prior to the game.

"I'm proud of these boys," said first-year coach, Jayce Leonard. "They've endured so much, stuck together through so much, sacrificed so much. To see them end it the way they did tonight; come together as a team…it's special."

On offense, senior quarterback Andrico Handler led the way, throwing for 240 yards on 15 of 22 passing attempts. Running back, Tre Bell, also chipped in with his third consecutive 100-yard game, rushing for 110 yards on 18 carries.

Defensively, middle linebacker Isaiah Waters led with 10

tackles, 3 tackles for loss, and 1 sack. Kyle Messina had 2 interceptions and 6 tackles.

Skyler Hemphill had a solid game with three field goals, and five extra points.

## GRETA'S CORNER

*By Greta Kilgore*
*Saturday, December 6, 2003*

Jim Gill Automotive held its annual Employee Honors Banquet at Lake Barrow City Hall this past Friday, and presented two of its full-time employees with accolades for superior performance rendered over the past year.

Cheryl Leonard, an executive assistant to Mr. Jim Gill, was honored by her boss as Employee of the Year. Mr. Gill described Ms. Leonard as having "demonstrated impeccable administrative skills, which have proven to be invaluable as Gill Automotive seeks to ever expand its operations and service to customers far and wide. Cheryl is an integral part of our team, and will continue to be so for the foreseeable future."

Donald Hill was designated Employee of the Month. Hill, a maintenance worker, was lauded by Jim Gill as having "proven himself as an integral and seasoned member of the maintenance staff, and ensuring top quality service to customers and valuable training and mentorship to co-workers."

## LEONARD MAKES DECISION ABOUT COACHING FUTURE

*By Biff Kilgore*
*Barrow Times Staff Writer*
*Saturday, January 3, 2004*
LAKE BARROW

After much speculation and rumors that have swirled in the aftermath of Sims County High School's eventful 2003 football season, Coach Jayce Leonard has announced via school administrators that he has decided to stay at Sims County for the 2004 season next year.

Sources have confirmed that Leonard will remain at the school after it was unofficially revealed that the twenty-five-year-old first-year head coach had received an offer from his alma mater, Yearwood State University, to return as an assistant coach.

"Coach Leonard will be here next season," said principal and athletic director, Andrew Starr. "We have discussed his future, and while there have been some minor issues that needed to be addressed regarding his time here as head football coach, we feel confident in his ability to continue leading this program."

Leonard was not available for comment.

## HUDSON TO INVEST IN SPARTAN PROGRAM

*By Biff Kilgore*
*Barrow Times Staff Writer*
*Saturday, February 7, 2004*
LAKE BARROW

Tampa Bay Buccaneers running back and Sims County High alum, Deke Hudson, announced Friday his intentions to fund construction of a new field house, as well as purchase a sign for the newly-named football field at Sims County High School.

"It's an honor to give back," Hudson said at a dinner hosted by the Lake Barrow Rotary Club. "And it's an honor to pay tribute to a real hometown hero."

The field, formerly known simply as "Jim Gill Stadium," will now be known as "Jim Gill Stadium at Soul Rasheed

Field." The change occurred after members of the school board voted for the change in a decision that took few by surprise. After the measure passed at last month's school board assembly, discussion about funding began to take place in earnest, and culminated in the commitment by Hudson to provide funding for a new sign to be constructed and placed just under the east end zone scoreboard.

Jim Gill III, owner of Gill Automotive, and son of the stadium's namesake, could not be reached for comment.

## GRETA'S CORNER

*By Greta Kilgore*
*Saturday, May 16, 2004*

Congratulations to Jayce and Dixie Leonard on the birth of their new baby boy, James Soulemain Leonard. "Baby Jamie" was born on Thursday, May 14, 2004, at 1:38AM at 9 pounds, 11 ounces. Mother and baby are doing well.

**August 2004**

"That's all I've got," I said to my coaching staff, as we got up from the chairs in my office. "Go home, get some rest."

"Don't have to tell me twice," Max affirmed, walking out the door.

"Or me," Woody clarified.

"See you tomorrow," Ahmad said.

"Looking forward to it," I told him. "Boys have been wanting to hit someone, even if it is in an intrasquad scrimmage."

"Beezer gonna have the field ready?" Max asked.

"When does he not have it ready?" I chuckled.

"Speaking of," Ahmad said. "Here he comes now."

*Great*, I thought.

Ahmad chuckled and said, "See you later."

Everyone left as Frank Beezer entered wearing his trademark coveralls, green jacket, and red baseball cap. "Coach," he announced. "Got the lines refreshed, end zone painted, and someone's working on getting the sign spruced up."

"A bit of overkill, isn't it, Frank?" I said.

"Anything for the field," he said. "And the program."

I smiled at him.

"Coach," Beezer said. I noticed his hands begin to tremble. "You forgive me, right?"

"What did I tell you the last dozen times you asked that question, Beezer?"

He grinned. "That you'd forgive me for what I did to Soul as long as I forgave you for almost taking my head off with that football."

"Couldn't have said it better."

"Thanks, Coach Jayce," he looked at me gratefully.

"Anytime," I returned. "Say, Beez?"

"What is it?" he asked, turning.

"You said someone's out there getting the sign spruced up. Who is it?"

"Go out there and see," he responded with a grin.

With that, he walked away before I could say anything.

I gathered my things and prepared to leave. Dixie had called earlier and had given me a shopping list of items to pick up for Jamie before heading home.

As I made my way to the car, I glanced out at the field. Sure enough, a metal ladder was propped up against the steel beam, and a large, familiar figure was buffing the metal sign that bore the words, "Soul Rasheed Field."

I smiled, not fully believing what I was seeing, as I ambled down the concrete steps toward the field.

I reached the grass just as Jim Gill climbed off of the ladder, and both of us stopped within ten yards of each other.

"Since when do you do manual labor?" I asked him.

Jim wiped his brow with a cloth he was holding. He was dressed in a dirty t-shirt and grungy shorts; a look I had never seen on him. "Hard work keeps you humble," he said.

I studied him, still in disbelief. We had not spoken since my visit to their house the day after the shooting; when Jordan had told me the truth about how Soul had saved his life. Since then, Jim had kept a low profile, and had not had any involvement with the program whatsoever.

Until today.

"Lord knows, I need all the help with humility that I can get," he continued, arms akimbo as he looked at me with a weary expression.

I nodded and kept my eyes on him, feeling the friction of months past begin to cool. "How's Jordan?" I asked. "He enjoying Gainesville?"

Jim nodded. "Dropped him off last week. First semester's a killer; academically and financially."

"It's good that you're paying his way," I affirmed.

"Yeah," Jim answered.

I smiled and nodded upward. "Sign looks good," I said.

Jim turned and glanced up at the large placard bearing Soul's name. "It's a nice one," he told me. "Marty Danforth even said so."

I was surprised. "Marty?"

Jim nodded. "Met him for coffee the other day," he said. At that moment, I noticed his eyes. There was a contrite look in them that I had never seen before. "Believe it or not, I've actually met with him several times over the past few weeks. Had some good conversations."

I smiled. Neither of us said anything for a moment.

"My Jamie would have liked that sign," Jim said to me,

turning his gaze back upwards. He wiped his face again, and I thought I saw him brush away a tear.

"I know," I answered. "Someday, my Jamie will, too."

Jim turned and smiled at me. "Guess I better be getting home," he said.

"Same here," I said.

Slowly, Jim began to walk toward me, extending his hand as he approached.

I accepted it, and we shook.

"Spartan pride," he said to me.

"Spartan pride," I responded.

"Thanks, Jayce."